Dedications:

To my Grandma Eunice, for editing all my grammar mistakes, which were far too many to count.

To Grandpa Jim, for telling me I could be anything I wanted.

To my Mom, for telling me when this story was getting really long and boring and when I accidentally wrote something that sounded good.

To a host of wonderful friends and family who told me to just keep writing. To make a few of them happy, I'll list some of their names: Austin Schleusner, Jacob Mattys, and Annika Kueng. To everyone else, I'm sorry there wasn't enough room but I appreciated the encouragement.

To Coach Boevers, for giving me a love of baseball and teaching me to never ever quit.

And equally important, to everyone that said I could never be a writer or make anything of myself, here it is.

You can't sit on a lead
and run a few

plays and just kill the
clock. You've got

to throw over that goddamn
plate and give

the other man his chance.
That's why

baseball is the greatest
sport of them all.

-Earl Weaver

Chapter 1:

It was springtime across the country and with the return of the flora and fauna of the expansive wilderness came the familiar sights and sounds of another approaching March: Birds singing songs sweeter than the honey poured out by the millions of bees busily pollinating the even greater number of plants, the sound of water as babbling brooks began to push the water reintroduced to them by the melting of snow, and the strange sound of children exiting their abodes and once again becoming a mainstay of the outdoors scenery. Yes, spring was a glorious time celebrating the many beauteous wonders of the natural world, but somehow the inner workings of God's green Earth played second place to the most important event of the year for Daniel Westboro and the rest of LeHigh County. Today was the first day of baseball practice for Daniel Westboro's last year in high school.

Today was going to be the first day back after a disappointing loss to the El Paso Mustangs, a second chance to redeem the disappointment he and the rest of the LeHigh County Rangers had given to the town last year. Today was when the Rangers were all going to show up at the baseball diamonds behind the high school and begin for the last time the greatest four months of every year. Perhaps all the other events proved secondary to Dan because today was the day that life restarted for him too. Like the melting of the snow from the previous winter, the confinement of the 6'4" heat-slinging right hander to a life without baseball was also going away as his 1985 Yugo pulled into a place he deemed appropriately off the road and more importantly, non-intrusive to the practice of baseball.

"You still drive that piece of shit?" asked Ben Crawford, being the only man on Earth that would arrive 40 minutes early to a baseball practice just to be ready for his pitcher who was coming in 10 minutes after himself.

"Well, Ben figured you would like it. I mean all the women you drag around in that little bean can of yours seem to be competing to look as ugly!"

The two then chuckled as they realized two things were true in this life: Ben Crawford would forever be Daniel Westboro's best friend and West would never sell that "piece of shit" for it was his car and no bank, girlfriend, teacher, principal, or police officer could take it from him. Sure, some may have looked at the actions of Westboro like wearing the same pair of shoes since the seventh grade, walking everywhere unless he knew that ambulation would not allow him to arrive in a punctual manner, and refusing to back down on his own opinions as odd behaviors explained by an innate stubbornness which made mules appear reasonable animals, but above all Daniel Westboro was determined to prove to everyone, and most importantly to himself, that he was his own man.

"So Ben, you still know how to use that glove or have you just become a full-time bullshitter?" asked Westboro.

"Well, we should be asking about your eyes, West." said Crawford.

"Why is that?"

"Well see, I put down two fingers and that means changeup, but you decided to throw that bender into the dirt last year," said Crawford in reference to the last game of the previous year; the one where the boys of LeHigh fell to a tie on the following pitch, a belt high fastball that Westboro still sees flying over the left-field fence. He watched relief pitcher Joe Krieger meet the same fate with the first pitch of his appearance. That ball left the park along with the hope of being the first LeHigh baseball team to make it to the state quarterfinals since the Rangers made it that far ten years ago.

"Well Ben, I've got a new signal for you!"

"Why don't you show me you blind ol' man?"

Prompted by the comment from his comrade adorning the tools of ignorance, Westboro removed his glove, and after rapid gesticulations of his surprisingly dexterous hands, produced one solitary middle finger for Crawford.

Crawford said, "That's the one that people give you when they drive around that pack mule of yours though! I don't want your dumb ass self to get confused up there either!"

While these two continued their light-hearted bullpen session, Coach Carlson pulled into the recesses of the outfield alongside the two other vehicles and looked out to that little ninety-foot square in the middle of what used to be some guy named Dorsey's farm yard. He had a hard time fathoming the amount of baseball talent he was given to coach. He also understood that this came with great responsibility. He had coached this little ball club in the middle of nowhere for most of his life, and now he had the caliber of athletes to effectively coach a state title for the townships in the LeHigh County area, a county so sparsely populated that none of the towns within it were big enough to claim true ownership of the school or the baseball team that was formed by them.

Behind the plate was Ben Crawford, a man who had the fight of Carlton Fisk, the arm of Johnny Bench, and everybody knew the stupidity of Yogi Berra. Ben Crawford wasn't your typical kind of stupid though, he was as Ms. George said to his mother during his middle school conferences, "a special flavor of stupid." It wasn't that he was exactly dumb; he just wasn't interested in the finer intricacies of objects. He believed all that mattered in the end was that the heart of the matter was expressed and understood. How it arrived to the individual receiving was entirely unimportant. The catcher seemed to only have an undying pursuit of punctiliousness and perfection when he was behind the plate for the arms of the Rangers and after having "observed a lot by watching" the senior backstop had established a reputation as one of the best game callers in the state and arguably the country. Like some poker players read the countenance of their opponents and determine from the slightest uptick of the jowel whether a bluff was present or not, Ben Crawford could read batters better than he could read books. A stride towards his plate was an invitation for the up and in fastball, an outward stride a plea for a curveball down and away. A little error in swing mechanics undetectable by the hitting coaches that spent many dedicated hours of their lives watching for these imperfections would be an obvious hint as to what Crawford would ask for next, and for sure, Crawford mixed game-calling strategies better than most computers spat out random digits. He was so utterly in tune to the slight leans, the spitting in gloves, and nervous expressions of baserunning stress that he had been accused more than one time of stealing the bench signals of his opposition as no one could understand how this 2.3 GPA catcher with a reputation for being unfocused could suddenly be knowledgeable of what the runner was to do before he even considered doing it. Obviously, baseball was the thing which Benjamin Crawford dedicated his entire attention and heart to. In this regard, he was similar to Daniel Westboro.

  The other members of the cult began arriving perfectly on pace with Carlson time, which as the previous three to four years of baseball had taught them meant that they were to arrive fifteen minutes early.

Jerry Tiner, the Rangers second baseman, walked on to the field.

"Gonna grow anytime soon, Tiny?" said Crawford

"Well, I was hoping one day I would stop being a little boy, but you sons of bitches keep dragging me back down to your level," remarked Tiner, half in humor and half in indictment.

Tiner was one of those unfortunate individuals that in life was not only poisoned by receiving the bad side of genetics for anyone with athletic dreams, but a last name which seemed to be endowed upon him by God for the sole purpose of developing his character through many trials. No one doubted that he put all 5'6" of that smallish frame to work on the baseball field, but the speedy second baseman with a high batting average would be overlooked by many programs simply due to the fact he could not see over most dugout fences without standing on a batting helmet. Despite this, Tiner had come to accept his stature at a young age. He wasn't a quitter; you don't get to your senior year of high school with opportunities to go to Stanford or Harvard or Yale by being one. If there was one thing anyone couldn't take from Tiner, it was his determination.

"You guys know if Hart is coming or did he dedicate himself to the practice of pizza consumption?" said Tiner

"I dunno, Einstein. You seen our second baseman? He was jus' here and then this damned English professor showed up..." said Crawford in reference to Tiner's tendency to speak more like he was writing another essay than talking to his teammates.

Before Tiner had a chance to respond to the remark, the topic of conversation arrived. All 6'5" 260 pounds of him. Luke Hart was a big boy, corn fed and reared by a mother whose cooking showed on him; it could be said Luke Hart stood as a man among boys. He was that difficult sort of rotund where one couldn't describe him as fat for he was too productive with his weight. For example, he was rumored to have shaken a reporter's hand so hard that he broke three of the four fingers and was known to have carried entire halves of cattle out of his truck by hand and into the packing plant. All in all, no one had ever seen Luke Hart get in a fight he didn't finish.

The disparity in size between Tiner and Hart made it extremely amusing when "Hart Attack" came up and pseudo-tackled his best friend. The two had been through everything together, from burying Hart's sister to ditching school early to go fishing, and every year of baseball they ever played Hart would be standing on first waiting for Tiny to fling him the ball in the ridiculously quick snapping of his right wrist. Although no one would suggest it, for it was unmanly and the streets of Holt, LeHigh County, and the rest of the United States of America despised any indication of less than utter masculinity out of their athletes, it was hard not to see Tiner and Hart were the embodiment of Platonic love. Sure, they arose biologically from different parents, but it was of their disposition internally, and those that observed them, that friends were the family you chose for yourself.

After Hart, the collective three affectionately called "The Zachs" showed up. Zachary Brown, Zachary Stevens, and John Zachary, who was made an honorary Zach by Zach Stevens after the Junior was called up the year prior and caught a foul ball that ended a contest against Glencoe that was crucial in setting up the Rangers lengthy playoff run. It was amusing to watch them in the outfield. The desolate wasteland that is the outfield seemed to have vitality when they stepped on it. The collective Zachs over the years had honed into a well-oiled machine, the textbook communicators that every coach desires in an outfield. With Westboro on the mound the three didn't have much work to do most games, but when destiny or the voice of Coach Carlson called upon them yelling "Zach", they would work admirably.

The last of the starting lineup had arrived once the lanky Randy Bowman, or "Bones", showed and "The German", Christian Vier, arrived.

"We've got a long season ahead," said Coach Carlson as the team snapped their attention towards him.

"We've got something to prove. Everyone through their entire life has something to prove. Today, boys, is the day you decide whether you want to be remembered as winners or as could've-beens. You have the privilege of being allowed by God to play the greatest game on Earth, and I know how talented he made all of you. For many of you," Carlson looked at his seniors, "this is the last year of your life you get to put on these pinstripes and fight for your hometown, the last time you have to get nervous the day before we play any team dumb enough to step on our field, and most of all, your last chance to play the game the little kid in you fell deeply in love with. Let's have a hell of a good time."

The huddle broke as the players ran to their respective positions on the field, now ready to fight for that little kid inside themselves.

Today was the start of spring. Today, life had bloomed once again.

Chapter 2:

After four weeks of strenuous practice, the Rangers' first game had approached on the calendars spread across the diners, teacher's desks, and auto repair shops of LeHigh County. It was April 14th, a date of almost religious standing that was circled on every single one of those calendars in that little part of Northwest Texas lost somewhere between Hereford and Amarillo. To the team and the town as a whole, it was the end of the hibernation, the primal stirrings of the approaching season being shaken and the feeling of life without baseball soon being forgotten in Callihan Park. With the first shout of "Play Ball!" erupting from the man who all would once again learn to love to hate, another year of baseball would commence. The base pads would be in perfect condition, the foul line laid out in perfectly linear fashion stretching towards the fences 320 feet away from home, and those sodium lights would burn their way back into the soul of the community. At that moment of elation, and only that moment, Coach Carlson would send the full-grown boys to take the field as if it were their last chance.

These images raced through the mind of Daniel Westboro as passing between classes for the right-hander served no purpose but to fill the eligibility requirements of the Texas High School Baseball League for one who wished to play in a varsity baseball game that night. Trigonometric identities adorned a white board at some point in the day, and some lecture about the works of Shakespeare had come forth from Ms. Davis in her

English classroom, but Westboro could only think about one thing and that for sure was the one thing the rest of LeHigh County thought of, baseball.

For the next four months the sole topic of conversation would be the Rangers. The signature blue of the Rangers would come to be so prevalent it would seem that every other hue on the chromatic wheel had dissolved like the business a diner in Holt would have gotten had it not been an away game. The sign in front of the Southern Free Baptist Church ministered by Pastor Thomas would say "Go Rangers!", the mayor would be at every single game ready to shake hands for the cameras with whomever the star of that particular night happened to be, and it would be deemed sacrilegious for the gas stations to not offer some sort of discount as reward for the hard-fought victory attained by their favorite men in blue. True, being a desolate place with rough land and even rougher people, the only thing that inspired any vague semblance of enjoyment in life for the streets of Holt, Fox, and Pine City was the rise and fall of the roller coaster ride that was cheering on a high school sports team. All of this was the occupation of the mind of West.

Just then, Benjamin Crawford, in his characteristically lackadaisical approach to school, meandered through the hallways and managed to intersect paths with Westboro, a feat only he was capable of performing on game day.

"You scared enough, West?" asked Crawford

"I ain't scared!" responded Daniel in that sort of rapid fashion where whatever was being refuted was instantaneously confirmed.

"Dude, last time I seen you this scared was when you fell off Old Man Rogers chicken coop, broke your ass, and swore you was gonna die!" said Crawford, trying to the best of his capabilities to coax a smile from his friend.

Benjamin Crawford's effort to use humor to draw out some sort of happy countenance failed on his friend West. It was not that Westboro didn't like the musings of his boisterous friend, but it was game day and for Westboro game day was a sacred ritual, and this morning like all others began the same way.

He arose from the little crawlspace and entered the upstairs by way of the rickety case which extended to the cellar where he slumbered. Once he had made his way upstairs from the dusty basement, he began preparing breakfast for his brother, David, and himself. Daniel then set about lifting the piles of trash that adorned the floor along with the empty bottles of liquor his father left upon the same locale. An overwhelming amount of sloth and inebriation lead to Daniels's father, Robert, to lie on the worn old sofa stained with coffee, time, and cigarette burns.

In many ways, that couch was a symbol for Daniel's father, as both had been beaten by the world; not in a way unexpected, but in a way that was withering them to nothingness. The ugliness within themselves was casually working its way out of the rips, and the flowery cover was still trying with all its might to maintain an outward appearance of contentedness, but anyone who had examined either from afar or with politeness would swear wholesomeness persisted in both. Although for many years both had been very capable of portraying this facade of some dominant and persistent happiness, it was quickly clear that the death of Daniel's mother had concluded the maintenance of such outward expressions. With that, was also the evaporation of these illusions of correctness. Many in the town who came to the Westboro house and saw the state of disrepair could only imagine the depth of sorrow amongst the Westboros since Daniel's mother died three years ago in a car accident somewhere near Abilene. In a way, it was fitting that the couch and Robert slept together for each entity was the embodiment of the other, a befitting quality in matrimony. Nonetheless, Daniel continued cleaning around his drunken father, for if he didn't do it, he understood like many things in life they would never get done.

Then David came down the stairs in his Batman pajamas and yawned in that curiously adorable manner that is common to those whom are the ripe old age of eight. David was a young boy with the full exuberance of youth and delightful ignorance to most of the issues of the world.

To David, the pressing matter of the day was debating with his friends whether Josh Hamilton or Vladimir Guerrero would go down in history as the better batsman or perhaps the absolute hot button issue of whether Cliff Lee or C.J. Wilson deserved to be the first man in the Texas rotation. Like his older brother, David had a strong will in his determinations and it was hard to distinguish whether this trait was explained by genetic outcomes, or if it was just David once again trying to be like the older brother he so idolized.

At church David was told that God doesn't approve of worshipping false idols, but to the eyes of an eight-year-old boy it was hard not to worship at the altar of baseball, and Daniel was David's personal connection to the game running so deep in his blood. David had the sole privilege of calling himself Daniel's younger brother. David told the story of the time Daniel peeled open a letter containing the announcement he had been drafted by the New York Mets to practically everyone he could find, an offer which Daniel rejected to go to college. It was David who got to call LeHigh County baseball his older brother.

"Are you goin' to win today?" asked David

"Gonna try," responded Daniel who was preparing eggs at the stove.

"Why are you always so nervous?" asked David beaming with his large innocent eyes.

At this, Daniel stopped and thought about why he was nervous. He was one of the best arms in the country and he truly had no reason to fear the batting order of those Strathcona Gators, but he had the mentality of a champion and he played every game like it was the World Series. Maybe it wasn't the thought of failing himself that frightened him. He had learned through the years that failure was one of the truest forms of success. No, it was the thought of letting his team and his city down that frightened him. He was terrified. Not many things happened on these rolling plains, and if he were to fail, it would be the primary discussion of LeHigh County for painful days on end before he once again got to climb that mountain mistakenly thought of as a pitcher's mound. Unlike most of his teammates, Westboro had a certain level of expectation placed on him by the community, nothing anyone else could begin to sympathize with. He knew all too well that every single play of the ball could be traced back to his releasing of it, and that however the play evolved, he would be assessed as the primordial ancestor. Speaking in the terms of Darwin, he was the common ancestor to the two main species of the baseball diamond, success and failure.

Success was built on that little pronation of the wrist that he practiced for hours on end towards a peach crate. That was truly the ticket out of this dead end town for Daniel, for it was the only thing that was going to give West the capability to afford a secondary education. He thought of how much it would've meant to his mother to see him put on a uniform for the Texas Rangers, so he could have the same uniform that he wore for Halloween as a little kid saying "Westboro" rather than "Ryan" on the back. Baseball would be Daniel Westboro's freedom from this town and be the start of his new life when all came to fruition. Failure was anything else.

Nevertheless, talking of college and freedom and the pressures of the community was not going to be a message resounding of any value with an eight year old. So a smile spread warmly across the face of Daniel shortly before David said, "I want my eggs over hard, Dan."

"Okay, buddy!" said Daniel.

And with the welcome change from the topic at hand, Daniel ate breakfast with David before driving them both to school.

Chapter 3:

After yet another school day, Callahan Park welcomed its beloved residents as Coach Carlson swung open the front door, otherwise known as the gate in the left field fence. It would be a couple hours before the house guests arrived, but right now there was some housekeeping to take care of.

"Bowman!" shouted Carlson, taking roll call for the off chance someone had not arrived yet.

"Here!"

"Brown"

"Here!"

"Hart!"

"Here!

The intermittent calling of names was not heard by Westboro since too much was on his mind as usual. It was quite routine for Westboro to entirely miss announcing his presence during Carlson's ritual. Everyone knew it wasn't due to some belief that he was better than everyone else that precluded him from hearing the announcement of "West", and some have argued it was in fact some sort of inferiority complex that was persisting in West during this calm before the storm, but in all reality the complete lack of any thought of anything was the primary concern of the gunslinger. Regardless of the reasoning, it was a moot point to call Westboro's name during roll call and finally in his senior year, Coach Carlson had learned not to waste time waiting for the answer of "present" from Daniel.

The pre-game stirs were different for everyone. Some listened to music, some pondered life while rolling the bat between their hands waiting to take some practice swings, and others really didn't show any sort of contemplation.

A good example of that would be Daniel's best friend.

"Hey, Bowman," said Crawford.

"Yeah?" replied Randy Bowman.

"Why does it take longer to get from second base to third base than first to second?"

"I don't know . . ." Bowman looked strangely at the man behind the plate with this statement.

"Because there's a shortstop between second and third. Well, at least with your girlfriend there is."

"Oh" responded Bowman.

Bowman was new to this entire feeling of being a starter for LeHigh County. This combined with a strong shyness made Bones rather unaffected by Crawford's crude humor, but Crawford was not about to deprive himself of the ability to laugh at his own joke, and he heartily chuckled, pleased with his wit.

Meanwhile, Bones possessed a look reminiscent of a deer in the headlights during the infield practice, and it worried Coach Carlson as he watched his team prepare from the dugout. He wished more would be like Crawford and the delightfully ignorant Zach's, for he knew as well as anyone that baseball was a game won and lost in the mind. As Sun Tzu said of his men thousands of years before in the catacombs of history, "Victorious warriors win first and then go to war; while defeated

warriors go to war first and then seek to win."
Wanting the mental state of victory so clearly
bubbling from Crawford to permeate to the rest of
the team and at the same time to disarm the
possibility of terrible consequence from the victory-
seeking mentality of Bowman, Coach Carlson
shouted, "Bones!"

"Yes sir!" shyly responded Bones.

"Come over here."

Randy Bowman approached the bench
cautiously unaware of what was going on and
obviously fearful as any player is of a coach that has
just called for them from pregame exercises.

"What are you thinking about right now? Just
say it," said Carlson.

"What?" asked Bowman.

"I want you to tell me what all is spinning in
that head of yours right now," said Carlson.

"I'm scared," said Bowman.

Carlson poked his tongue at the wad of
bubblegum implanted in his cheek and due to a
lifelong career of tobacco spitting, instinctively drew
an amount of saliva to discharge what would've been
another wad of Copenhagen had he not decided once
again this year to try to stop chewing to set a better
example for his players. Carlson was a man like that,
taking his coaching job not as an opportunity to boss
around players and make them run meaningless laps
or to snitch on the shenanigans any high schooler
would partake in, but to develop them into men he
never could have been. The truth was Carlson was a
flawed man. The vice of addiction had gotten to him.
He was a bad father to his children and an even
worse husband resulting in divorce. Truth be told, he
had the same exact problem racing through his head
as Bones, fear. Bones had no reason to doubt
himself for he had turned into a good third baseman,
but after getting this far along in life and truly having
no tangible success, it was hard for the lanky third

baseman to stop thinking ceaselessly of the oncoming war with Strathcona. In this way, Carlson could understand Bowman entirely. Regardless of what numbers say, the baseball diamond routinely has a different story to tell once the dust settles and the last batter is retired. In spite of this, Carlson would not allow anyone to know what he was thinking for the sake of advancing his team.

So he said to Bones, "Randy, there are times in a man's life when he has to prove himself. There are going to be times you get up, look a problem in the face and say "I'm scared" and you're going to try and fight that fear by running away from it rather than towards what you actually want. Sure, the world may look at you and see you "taking action" against the problem, and congratulate you for trying to "solve it", but you really aren't. You'd be like every other "normal" person out there who chooses to do just enough to bullshit the people around them into believing they are solving problems when in reality, they're just running scared like my boy did from the dark. But you're not an ordinary man, and you will not hold to the same standard as everyone else when it comes to playing today. You are a LeHigh County Ranger; you truly are the best third baseman this team has. Win or lose, you won't play scared and try to run from your fear of failing. Today, you're going to run towards victory, and you and I can laugh our asses off after this one in the end looking at that lopsided scoreboard. Alright?"

Bowman responded with a smile, "Yes, Coach!"

So with hands in his pockets he left the dugout shortly behind Bowman to have the typical pre-game conference between coaches and umpires.

The only thing Carlson wished for now was finding belief in what he just said.

Chapter 4:

"Our Lord who art in Heaven, hallowed be thy name.
(Which is Rangers Baseball...)
Thy Kingdom come thy will be done on Earth as it is in Heaven.
(For the sinners will be wrecked with this fucking curveball here too...)
Give us this day our daily bread and forgive us our trespasses as we forgive those who trespass against us.
(Bullshit, they were dumb enough to come today...)
Please lead us not into temptation, but deliver us from evil,
(If anyone ever could...)
for thine is the Kingdom, the power, and the Glory,
(Let's go)
Forever and Ever. Amen."

After reciting a familiar prayer, the team was now set to wait two minutes on the battlefield. With hats over their hearts, a love song called the "Star Spangled Banner" poured through the ears of every man, woman, and child who was lucky enough to stand in Callahan Park for the home opener of the LeHigh County Rangers.

The Rangers ran out to their positions with the fans holding signs to address them by the various monikers and nicknames an infatuated populace had come to call their heroes by, while cheers echoed through the canyon walls of Callahan Park for the "Men In Blue". The familiar sight of sodium lights was once again in the peripheral vision of the Zachs, and the signs adorned with glitter saying "Bomb it Ben" and "Time for another Hart Attack!" adorned the sea upon the bleachers. With one utterance of "Play Ball!" from the umpire, the renaissance of baseball began. One call from the bottom of the valley ended the brief moment of unity as those who were so recently tied together by the love of their country under God became enemies to one another once again. It was fitting that George Reagan was the first batter for Strathcona.

A self-described hick with rage issues, the center fielder wore the number one and every part of his egotistical identity was identifiable not only by his own actions, but by that same yellow figure on his back acting as an arrow and pointing towards the name he actually played for. Reagan walked into the on deck circle and began twirling the bat behind him like it was some sort of enticement for a raging bull. Unfortunately for Reagan, he was not a matador nor was his opponent bovine.

Instead the soul which he enticed was the soul of a fighter, The soul of a champion. George Reagan had faced Daniel Westboro many times in his life, and although history indicated Westboro would get the best of him, both had yet to prove themselves this year on that beautiful gem, the baseball diamond.

"This son of a bitch thinks he's gonna beat me?" thought Westboro on the mound.

"What a fucking poser. We'll put that cocky bastard back in his place."

With these thoughts, Westboro watched Reagan walk into his batter's box. Nothing annoyed Westboro more at that moment than to see this redneck from the middle of Strathcona standing on his plate. He made mental note of the left toe that was clearly touching it.

Coaches always tell their players that playing in fury is not the way to go about business, for emotions confuse the true mission of the game and ultimately cause failure as the selfish action of trying to exert your internal rage was something that would only lead to failing the team and doing the unthinkable, losing.

However, Daniel Westboro wasn't your typical player.

He was extremely talented and although he wouldn't outwardly proclaim his accomplishments, internally he knew the same thing the rest of LeHigh County and the entire Palmata Baseball conference knew: he was the best pitcher that not only the Rangers and this conference could offer, but the best thing the state of Texas had in the field of high school pitching. There were plenty of college scouts in the stands from Arizona, USC, The University of Texas, and Louisiana State University who could tell you everything they saw in Westboro that merited flying all the way to this God-forsaken town in the middle of nowhere. If you knew him, they probably would ask if you could try to convince him to talk to them. Obviously, they would make it worth your time. They may not know as they stared at this product of Holt who was standing a good seven feet tall from his elevated position on the loneliest island on Earth, but the motivation for that extra bit of heat came from having a spite of something. He wouldn't let it get the best of him; he kept his cool, but this rage was crucial in giving this game a meaning that wouldn't stress him out like thinking of what the fans may think, what his team may think, or what all these people with suits and ten thousand words on why they were the best choice for his future were thinking. The motivation at the moment, and for the rest of the night, was to know the sweet satisfaction of watching George Reagan and his Gators lose.

It was this confidence that lead the right-hander to stand on the mound while gently tossing the ball up and down. It was as if he were trying to hypnotize the batter with the gentle rise and fall of a free body in gravity, and many of the Little Leaguers in Northwest Texas would repeat the same motion as if it were some sort of magical incantation that made possible the defeat of batsmen. While pawing the ball, he would look to the right hand of Ben Crawford dangling between his legs and the two would have a conversation without words to decide what to have the next victim face. Ben extended one finger to the ground and quickly pointed towards the batter. He was calling for an inside fastball.

Westboro then nodded his head, and revealed his trademark grin.

After one more pump of the ball, his hands came even with his hips, the ball tucked beneath his glove to conceal the grip taken ensuring his assault would be unpredictable. After getting set, the counting began.

"1"

The knee of his front leg rose as high as his head, looking as if he were trying to rifle his knee into his jaw. With this motion of his lower body, his hands remained adjoined and formed a rearward swing behind his head, a move which concealed the bared teeth of an overzealous smile for the moment his left bicep covered his lips. Once he got to the summit of this maneuver, the havoc began to unfold in its perfect biomechanical chaos.

"2"

Westboro's body began rushing toward the plate, his right foot pushing off the front of the rubber to protrude his long leg ever closer to Ben Crawford's glove, reaching for what seemed like an eternity for a distance that seemed to encompass forever. The left foot eventually returned to Earth and his index finger which stuck outside the back of his glove pointed toward the center of Crawford's oversized mitt, all while his chest puffed out as if he were showing to the crowd the fullness of his pride.

"3"

His right arm came rushing with an extremely quick contortion of his upper body, his leading right elbow shortly followed by his hand gripping the ball as one would grip an egg, just as Coach Davis taught him in his first year of baseball when he was seven years old. The hand became a blur by the once again successful and efficient shifting of his weight, where all muscular forces were successfully exerted in a perfect utilization of leverage to deliver that little ball at 90 miles an hour over the longest sixty and a half feet on Earth.

It was during this eon, this .4 seconds, that Daniel Westboro felt the world slow down and almost stop. That little planet was turning rapidly and moving towards his best friend's glove with an immense amount of backspin generated naturally by the 108 stitches of the world ripping across his fingertips. The crowd couldn't see it, but Daniel Westboro felt as if he could see every single rotation as the ball progressed towards destiny. After letting go, it was no longer his decision what would happen to that little piece of leather and string. As much as he told himself that, he couldn't help but feel it was his fault if that sphere returned to him by force of the pendulum of time, that is, the bat. Westboro watched as a flash of red painted aluminum flew towards the ball, moving faster, faster, faster....

"Strike One!"

Just then Atlas lifted the world from his shoulders. Daniel Westboro was at peace, for one more bullet struck true into the palm of Ben Crawford. Daniel would do it eight more times that inning, hoisting up the world, and just as quickly knowing peace once again.

"Westboro's on tonight!" said Jack Crawford in the stands to Bob Tiner.
Jack Crawford often doted on Westboro. "Seriously, when's the last time you saw three K's in an inning?"

He seemed to have turned into a sort of extra son over the years due to the immense amount of time his son spent with him, and because he was as prevalent as any other member of the Crawford family, he found it as necessary to heed Daniel's actions as he would his own son's. Some may have accused Crawford of being desperate to know Daniel, for in this town Westboro was the unilateral monarch of the baseball hierarchy, and therefore respected as the royalty he was, but Jack had a sort of connection with Daniel that wasn't based on this "superstardom". It was that special sort of feeling that occurs when a man looks at his son's friend and sees no difference between his own children and the ones they associate with. Maybe it was some act of God, maybe it was some cosmic occurrence bound to happen because of something in the stars, or maybe it was some sort of illusion because of the strange tendency of the people one spends time around to become integral units of the nuclear components of the social soul. However it happened, Jack acted as if he were the father of Daniel.

"Yeah, that was impressive, but we are playing Strathcona," said Bob to Jack.

"Come on Bob! The kid is chucking 90! Do you know how hard that is for a high school kid?" said Jack.

"It is hard, but what makes him different from any other kid who throws 90 out there? This night doesn't prove anything. He's gotta pitch against a real team," said Bob.

The dialogue concluded as Bob looked towards the diamond to see number 5 walk into the left-handed batters box.

Jerry "Tiny" Tiner was always fully aware of the situation at hand and took to the box understanding his role as the table setter. What genetics lacked giving him in horsepower, it made up for in top end. His job was simple.

"Get on base. Just get on base," thought Jerry.

While that thought went through his head, a Strathcona pitch had been caught by the Gators catcher in front of the eyes of Tiny.

"Strike One!" called the umpire.

"Dammit," Jerry thought to himself.

It was yet another time when Jerry had been caught thinking in the box.

"No matter, I got two more," added Tiner to the catalogue of his thoughts.

Another pitch approached, this time a changeup. Waiting, waiting, and then Tiner had swung and missed. He was deceived by the change in velocity.

"Strike 2!"

"Goddammit!" thought Jerry.

Again! He had let this backwoods Neanderthal release a ball over the only seventeen inches he had to protect.

The third pitch came.

"Strike-"

The umpire watched the ball spin out of the catcher's mitt into the backstop, and the dropped third strike played exactly into the mind of Tiner which was fixated on perfection and awareness. Having performed the maneuver several times when he was younger, Tiner instinctively began running towards first. The wheels were turning with ever more acceleration, one stride in front of the other as the short pistons drove hard into the infield dirt between home and first. The mind, body, and soul of Tiner were driving the dirt at that point, more pushing the world away from him rather than moving him forward. Four point one seconds of hard work and determination later, Tiner's foot came in contact with first base where he ran past it turning to the right to indicate the end of his attempted advancement.

"Safe!" shouted the umpire.

Perhaps no exclamation had ever been more unnecessary. Strathcona's Billy Brown knew that his mishandling of the pitch had caused his pitcher to lose a strikeout and Tiner's sheer quickness had just beaten any chance of reversing his mistake. No matter how Tiner had achieved his presence on the base pads Coach Carlson, Bob Tiner, and the rest of LeHigh County congratulated the first Ranger of the year to reach with a round of applause. Then Ben Crawford came to the plate.

Number 17 was an oddity being a catcher that could hit, but nobody could contest that the senior deserved to be batting the two-hole. One couldn't help but think of Joe Mauer when Ben was in the batter's box. His feet would be miles apart, the bat held high over his shoulder slanted to a 45 degree angle, and the look of determination would burn into the soul of the pitcher. He wasn't flashy when he walked up, he didn't have some certain swagger or conduct that would arrive at the plate with him. Instead, Crawford had a reputation that preceded him. When he came to the box, that immature kid with all the dirty jokes became a man. A man that had a .700 batting average from the previous year; a statistic that made everyone think twice about even giving him a chance to swing. Benjamin wasn't going to be intimidated by any man. Like was often the case, he was too busy waiting for a chance to advance his second baseman.

The first pitch arrived.

Ben Crawford watched the ball flutter into the dirt and skid across the floor of LeHigh County's baseball cathedral. Billy Brown swept his glove and body in front of the ball as it skipped into his chest protector. He quickly transferred the ball to his throwing hand and looked at second, hoping for Jerry Tiner to get cocky and attempt to outrun an easy throw down. But, Brown was disappointed as Tiner had kept his feet planted firmly on the first base bag, knowing it was the correct decision for his team. Brown returned the ball to his pitcher.

Thirty seconds later the ball was delivered and once again bounced off home plate, and Brown would engage in the same maneuvers again to tame the wild pitch.

"Goddammit Coit," thought Brown.

Five pitches into the game and he was already failing at the fundamental component of his job, giving his defense something to field.

"Time," said Brown to the umpire.

The catcher trotted to the mound to try to console his pitcher.

"Come on man; let's just play your game okay? Pretend that we're throwing against anyone else and just let me catch a goddamn ball. Alright?" asked Brown.

"Dude, do you know how fucking hard it is up here realizing there is a seventy percent chance that I let y'all down? I thought we were pitching around this guy? Maybe we should just walk him," said Coit.

"Pitch around?!?!?!?! You miss by much more and I'll be digging that ball out of the Rio Grande."

"Shut up, Billy. Maybe you're just too shitty of a catcher to see what I'm doing."

"Alright, time's up," called the umpire.

So Billy Brown ran behind the plate taking with him all the hatred he had for his pitcher at this moment in time.

The next pitch was a hanging curveball, belt high and as obvious to Crawford as to the rest of the crowd what was happening next to the pitch that just didn't break. With flat fast hands, the ball was pummeled into submission and flew straight towards centerfield where George Reagan was running in futility to attempt to catch it. Four-hundred feet of flight later the ball came back to Earth outside of Callahan Park as Tiner and Crawford celebrated the departure of the ball from their home. Two batsmen later the same ritual would occur as Hart delivered on his promise of the first pitch of the year to him being a home run.

Coach Carlson had looked over towards the Strathcona bullpen and noticed the shaking of arms and stretching of legs as the relief pitchers for the Gators were preparing to come and salvage the contest, but to him and the rest of the Rangers who noticed, such a thing was the clear indication of a team lacking confidence in their opening day starter. It was an admission that their best pitcher was not better than LeHigh's lineup, at least for today, and Carlson and the Rangers couldn't help but conclude the ball that jettisoned out the back of Callahan Park was the final nail in the Strathcona coffin, even if it was the first inning. Strathcona had lost on that pitch for they had surrendered and decided that it was no longer a fight they could win.

Eight innings later, Randy Bowman and Coach Carlson were laughing their asses off staring at the lopsided scoreboard together.

Chapter 5:

Daniel Westboro was elated. He and his brothers in arms had conquered the Strathcona Gators, and he could not help but feel an immense amount of pride in being able to say, "We won". Westboro had won before, and he had beaten this team worse at points along his career, but he was especially pleased with this one for it would be the last time he would have the privilege to pitch in Callahan Park against the Gators.

"We fucking did it, West!" said Crawford, who then rifled his right hand between the shoulders of Daniel to give him a congratulatory pat on the back, which ended up being more resembling of atomic warfare.

"One down, 29 to go! We aren't losing this year! Goddammit, Daniel, you keep throwing that sexy ass curveball like you did tonight and you might make every girl in the stands wish you would make them pregnant! Way to go you mother fucker!" continued Crawford in his typical post-game invective charged with the adrenaline of victory.

Westboro did have a good night, he had pitched nine innings and allowed one hit that could've easily been assessed as an error by the shocked Randy Bowman who saw the first ball come into play in the top of the seventh. It was an immense amount of athleticism out of the 6'6" 165 pound third baseman to throw that large twiggish figure far enough to knock down the infield chop, but number 23 for Strathcona was just too fast for Bones to be able to recover and send the ball to Hart before Strathcona had gotten a runner on. Nonetheless, Westboro would not even care about what the stat book had to say about 17 strikeouts, 0 walks, 0 runs allowed, and one hit. He couldn't care less that his chance to get a no-hitter was lost by a sophomore caught up in the surreal feeling of watching a pitcher dominate a team so badly that not a single ball could be touched. In this, Westboro's senior year, he didn't look for praise in starting the season with yet another complete game shutout. Instead, he would praise the efforts of his teammates in amassing a score of 20-0. To Westboro, the only number that mattered was the first one in the Win-Loss column and he was proud to have the opportunity to collect his 55th career victory. That number meant to Westboro that he had given his team 55 chances to win that they had fully capitalized on, something which only one other man in the history of Texas is able to proclaim. Even crazier was the fact that Westboro had yet to know what losing a baseball game as a LeHigh County Ranger felt like, a painful couple of no-decisions in playoff games his sophomore and junior year, but still no loss attributable to his pitching. The scouts, radio stations, and everybody in town found it remarkable how the senior was preparing to not only be the first high school pitcher in Texas to ever win fifty-six games, but could potentially leave this little blot on the map without having ever lost.

That is, at least on the mound.

"You did good Danny," said June Winters to Westboro, wearing her old softball jersey with a 22 stitched on the back. The second two was covered with a duct tape one, partially in humor, but mostly for support of her favorite pitcher.

She was outside the LeHigh dugout awaiting her knight in shining armor to return from the recesses of the barracks.

"You did well-"

"Nice fucking job, Dan!" exclaimed Christian Vier, who produced his fist for Westboro to strike with his own. Westboro then tried again to speak to his girl.

"You did well too, June. Only thing prettier than your voice was you out there tonight," Westboro produced his hand which was wrapped by hers as they began moving towards the parking lot and to Daniel's vehicle.

"I find it pretty damn funny," said Daniel.

"What's funny?" asked June

"I find it funny God gave me both things I love on this Friday night," said Westboro.

"Well, I find something funny too, Dan," replied June.

"What's that?"

"I find it funny that God gave you so many words to try to get in my pants. Sadly, you're gonna bc a loser on that front tonight. But nice try," said June with a chuckle.

Daniel also chuckled.

June truly was something Daniel loved. She was a Brunette girl with those brown eyes that he was sure were the topic of Van Morrison when he was rattling off some poem about "transistor radios" and "skippin' and a jumpin'" in that song he couldn't remember the title to at that moment in time. June was a very well put together girl that enticed half the boys at school to discuss their aspirations with her. It was true, West was prone to discussing the perfect attenuation of her curves and how the hourglass shape of her torso enticed him so when he was around his friends too, but unlike the others he looked past the superficial qualities of attractiveness. June was good to him. She didn't have to say anything to the heat-slinging right hander beyond the volumes that were spoken through her pouring eyes and radiant smile to console him. When her hand was intertwined with his, it seemed natural and perfect like some aspect of nature that wasn't meant to be reversed. Her long bony fingers felt comfortable deposited in the recesses of Westboro's pawish hands that were scarred and stained as was bound to happen from the difficult life he was born into. It may have been the only object on Earth that wasn't a baseball that looked as if it belonged in those hands.

"Can I at least buy Ms. Winters some ice cream?" asked Westboro.

June revealed the sparkling smile, the smile that was the object of Daniel's dreams and made him forget all the trouble he'd seen. That smile was like life to Daniel, in its presence nothing could bother him.

"Of course, that is, if you can stop the gentleman act and bring back Daniel for me," said June.

"Sorry, Mr. Westboro is busy right now. I guess you'll just have to deal with me," said Daniel.

"Can you take a message for him?" asked June.

"Yes, I can," replied Daniel.

June Winters then got on her toes to extend her face towards the giant of a man called Daniel. Daniel made it easier for her by bending down and their lips interlocked in a way that for sure made some angels up in heaven smile, all in the gravel lot of Callahan Park on what seemed to about 7 billion other people to just be another Friday night.

That ballpark and June made it fully known to Daniel that home wasn't where he was parking that Yugo and sleeping tonight, but it was right here in the backyard of his ballpark, in the gravel parking lot, with the girl of his dreams holding him.

Chapter 6:

Daniel had dropped June off at her door and was making the three mile journey back towards the graying building with the ripped wallpaper where he slept. He looked at the clock and knew it was now midnight, but he needn't worry where David was for Jack Crawford had already taken him home after the end of the ballgame. He had no desire to wake his young brother, so he shut the headlights off as he pulled into the front yard and turned the engine off. Riding the high of victory all the way to his front door, he deposited the key into the front lock. He snuck through the front door into the living room, an absolute abyss. Daniel was proceeding towards the staircase to the basement where he slept, but before he could swing open the worn-out door with a busted hinge, a lamp turned on in the recesses of the living room. It was his father adorning a look of hatred, the obvious signs of intoxication poisoning his scornful stare to possess an even more disapproving demeanor.

"Where the fuck were you?" asked Robert.

"I was just out getting some ice cream with June," said Daniel.

"What the fuck were you doing?" asked Robert, his speech slurred from the effects of alcohol.

"I went to Bill's and got some ice cream with June," said Daniel with more agitation.

"Boy, you tell me the fucking truth or I swear to God I will kick your ass like you couldn't fucking believe!"

"Jesus Christ, I went and got some ice cream!" shouted Daniel.

"No, I was your age once, you little son of a bitch. You were out fucking that girl because you are an ungodly, ungrateful, skinny, little-peckered son of a bitch that," Robert rose from the felt chair in the corner of the room, "Can't do a fucking thing and should've been goddamn slaughtered by your mother," said Robert.

"Your entire life is due to the fact that I told your ma that I'd find a way to afford your little ass because killing unborn children is wrong. Fuck that, I should've let her cram a coat hanger into your fucking skull."

Robert was approaching with his words growing in ferocity and hatred as he stumbled over his own drunk self, his breath smelling strongly of Jack Daniel's No. 7 whisky and his words smelling of lies and condescension. Daniel was enraged by the deceit of Robert and responded to Robert's invective

"When the fuck were you there for me! Did you even know I still play baseball? Get your drunk ass back in your chair, old man. I can get along just fine without you," said Daniel.

Robert was enraged. In his frequent drunkenness and repeated dishonesty, Robert had finally convinced himself that he was purely a man of God and righteous in all ways of the word. Even though this tangent about everything wrong with

Daniel was the first time he had talked to his son since Christmas, he was entirely convinced he was the father of the year for he thought whipping this boy into line is what made him behave.

"You ungrateful son of a bitch!" shouted Robert.

Robert ran headlong towards his eighteen year old son and attempted to tackle him into the kitchen table still set with the supper he was too drunk to eat. Daniel stepped to the side, and due to the loss of coordination, Robert fell into the pile of cold stroganoff, breaking his nose in the process.

"Get over here, you bastard, and fight like a man!" Robert shouted, producing a steak knife that had been on the table.

Terrified, Daniel quickly sprinted towards the front door and didn't even bother turning the handle as the thing simply fell down when hit with ample force. Robert continued the chase brandishing the knife ready to stab him, shaking the cutlery the entire way as he moved his overweight body towards the Division 1 bound athlete. Daniel fumbled the keys as he tried to put them in the lock of the pickup. He turned the key once it was in the receptacle and tried to pull the handle.

"Fuck!"

He had forgotten he had left the doors unlocked. Turning the key he had managed to lock himself out of the car as Robert was getting ever closer to Daniel.

"I'm coming for you, pussboy!" yelled Robert, laughing merrily as he was getting closer to assault his son the way some fathers laugh when they play catch with their son for the first time, an act which Robert would never know, for he never did, and at this point Daniel never would.

Daniel was looking for an escape. He had no desire to fight his father, it wasn't right in the eyes of the Lord to hate one's father and somehow Daniel managed to maintain some sort of connection to this principle in the Ten Commandments, despite this situation.

Running out of options as Robert got closer, Daniel punched out the window with his Rangers ball cap over his fist to keep it unmangled by the glass and jumped through the recently opened portal into his car. Robert was three steps behind when Daniel turned the key bringing the engine to life. He slammed the transmission into reverse and stomped the gas pedal trying with all his might to feed the beast under the hood and satiate the requirements of all four cylinders to quickly assist in his departure. Robert was then by the window and thrust his arm towards Daniel's throat as the spinning tires rolled over his foot and the front pillar adjoining the roof to the body of the car rammed into his extended forearm leading to the dropping of the steak knife onto Daniel's lap as his Yugo moved into reverse towards Highway 5, the artery of this section of Texas that would take him anywhere but here.

"FUUUUCKKK!" shouted Robert staring at his broken foot and bruised forearm. His voice cackled into the night tearing through the air, like a wolf howling for his pack, but in this case no one would come. Instead, the exclamation would dissipate into the surrounding night and be consumed by the circling air between the grasses and the trees as the Berlander Ash and the squirrels were the only things in this world that heard Robert as he shouted. In the cool dry air of a lonely Friday night in the Texas panhandle, Robert's voice died like the dreams of yesterday as Daniel Westboro began driving South towards Pine City.

The entire time, David was upstairs in his bedroom sobbing softly into his pillow wishing that his mama could be there to hold him.

Chapter 7:

That Saturday morning, Daniel peeled open his eyes and saw the rising of the sun over the plains of Texas. The landscape he stared at out of the backseat of his Yugo appeared to be what Lee Greenwood was talking about when he wrote about God blessing the USA in 1985. No plants were tall over these sprawling farm fields, for the crops still had yet to germinate in some cases, but even without the stalks of corn reaching for the lower extremities of Heaven in the fields, it was still quite a sight to see. It was one of those things in life that no matter how long an artist might spend trying to paint it, how high the resolution of a camera may be, or how many words an author used to try to describe the pulchritudinous quality of this perfectly tranquil moment, no one could understand unless they were Daniel himself, in that Yugo, looking at that field. Daniel almost forgot about what had occurred between him and his father last night until he looked into the front portion of his car and saw the shattered glass in the front seat.

"What the hell am I going to do?" thought Daniel.

He wasn't unfamiliar with this location. Being displaced from his homes in various states of disrepair had made him quite experienced in how to attack life as a homeless child. Still, this thought is pervasive in this dog eat dog world, and like anyone else, he had to ask himself questions. Once again he had to ponder where he would live, where he would eat, who he would tell, and most pressingly, what to do about David.

The truth was Daniel was well-conditioned to the unfair treatment of a rough world, and it was the many occasions like this that put pain in his eyes. The pain that those who cared about him could see beneath the bright green turned towards a waiting world, wanting nothing out of him but his excellent pitching mechanics and victories. June could see it in his eyes. Benjamin could see it in his eyes. Even Jack and Coach Carlson, could see the pain. His eyes were stained with having observed the years when his mother was alive, beaten by his drunken father for trying to stop him from doing the same thing to Daniel or David. The pain was the recollection of having to shoot his dog between the eyes for it had "pissed on the carpet." He had to perform this task while his father threatened to shoot him if he didn't shoot his dog while Robert yelled, "No son of mine is going to be a pussy!" With tears, he had pulled the trigger of his Remington Model 700 and ended the life of his best friend Rusty. It was because of this that Daniel had grown desensitized to any transgressions unto his person. It was a version of mental strength training to live the life Daniel had, and at eighteen years old he probably had seen more trouble than men who live to eighty.

Still, he knew of the innocence of David. David was the good in his life. When he looked at that little brother of his he felt a welling of pride because David wasn't at all like him and that was perfect. David may have tried to emulate the baseball career of his older brother and perhaps sometimes tried to have his character reflect what Daniel would do, but Daniel knew that little boy with a peanut butter and jelly infatuation wasn't like him. David behaved in school, and when Daniel took him to conferences, his teachers told how good he was in class, and how his grades reflected a strong work ethic that they all agreed must've come from his older brother. But Daniel knew that he wasn't a good student like David. He spent most of his time in grade school trying to tie June Winters hair to her desk and had perfected the art of applying tacks to teacher's chairs with his partner in crime Ben Crawford. David was the embodiment of respectful. No adult had ever been contradicted by the boy. Daniel, not so much. Daniel was one of those rare individuals that had a greater concern for the people around him than with himself, and because of that, and the fact he viewed David as a greater version of himself, of all his questions the ones pertaining to the condition of the youngest Westboro were of his primary concern.

So, after working his way back to the front seat of the Yugo, Daniel began driving past Leonard McCutchen's field and arrived at the front door of the Hart household. The door was decorated with a woodcut heart made 25 years ago when Kyle Hart and Ruth Dexter got married. The occasion was at the same Baptist church they were still members of. The heart was worn from the years of dealing with the fluctuation in weather in Pine City, but Kyle would always look at that sign when he got home and remember the woman he fell in love with at the LeHigh County Fair 27 years ago. It was approximately four inches under this sign that Daniel's knuckles contacted the door.

"Hey man, what's up?" asked Luke Hart who happened to have answered the door.

"Not much, just rolling through town and wondering how the big man is doing," said Westboro.

Luke Hart was not a fool. He looked at the knuckles of Daniel Westboro and noticed the visible agitation from swinging into the window of which the glass was still clearly blown out. Hart also knew how fiercely Westboro would deny that he left his home because his father had gone through yet another bout of drunken ferocity, so he pretended as if he didn't know the obvious.

"Well shit, you're lucky, came just in time for some eggs!" said Hart with a warm grin.

It wasn't essential to ask if Daniel could come in, for Luke knew that Mama Hart thought well of

Daniel and the Hart household was ready at all times to feed unexpected guests. Ruth heard the exchange and the overweight mother of Luke cracked four more eggs into the skillet she was preparing and another two potatoes, for there would never be a time anyone would be allowed to leave the Hart household hungry. It was also true that Ruth was strong in her Christian belief and swearing was one function of the English language she simply did not allow in her home.

"What did you say, Luke?" scolded Ruth.

Luke looked at his feet and Westboro found it sort of funny that the strong man of LeHigh County would be like everyone else and come to be a blushing mess whenever his mother scolded him.

"Nothing Mama," said Luke.

Ruth Hart was a very kind person, but the art of observation eluded her, and it was a marvel how many things went unnoticed under her nose. It wasn't that Ruth didn't care about people. She was known throughout her church as one of the most generous people the congregation had ever seen, but it was very easy for obvious hints towards an extraneous circumstance to go unnoticed by her, perhaps attributable to an undying belief in people that led her to be appropriately labeled as a gullible person.

"What brings you here this mornin', Daniel?" asked Ruth.

"Not much. I was just driving through the area and I wanted to say hi," said Daniel.

"Well, where were you headed to?" asked Mama Hart.

At this moment, Daniel was lost. Westboro was a hideously poor liar and since Ruth believed him this far, he would have to come to some other reason as to why he was at the Hart household on this Saturday, for Ms. Hart was also the inquisitive type and would not let up until she had gotten all the information she had wanted.

"Well, see. I was.... uh.... I..."

Luke then cut Daniel off laughing at how much difficulty the boy had in being slightly dishonest.

"He was jus' joinin' me and Tiny to go fishin', Ma. Musta been out too late with that June Winters since he forgot why he was here," said Luke with a chuckle at the end to make the white lie believable.

"Well, shoot, didn't have to dawdle along on that, Daniel! You know I don't mind you spending time with my boy. Now about this June girl-"

Luke again interrupted his mother.

"Now mama you let him alone on that girl. You know he ain't doin' nothin' wrong in the eyes of the Lord."

"Yes but I-"

"Mama, please just let Daniel have his girlfriend without you gettin' all curious and gossipin' about it."

"Luke!" said Ruth. "You're being rather disrespectful to your mother this mornin'. You're lucky I ain't groundin' you. If it weren't for Daniel bein' here I'd crack you with the spoon."

"Sorry, Mama," said Luke, again with the same look of embarrassment that again made Daniel laugh internally.

Daniel was thankful that Luke stood up for him and kept him from actually telling the details of what brought him to the Hart's home on this beautiful Saturday morning. Some may have found it strange that neither Daniel nor Luke told the police about the situation, except for the fact that Robert was the sheriff of LeHigh County. Any attempted legal action against him would be turned around on the one who stepped forward, for it was his office that would handle his indictment.

Daniel knew of only two people who had ever
seen the extent of his father's abuse, and both of
them were high school baseball players who would
easily be dismissed as kids just trying to get their
buddy off the hook. That meant ultimately that
Daniel had come to accept drifting from one empty
couch to the next to find somewhere safe, because
the only thing that complaining to the police would
do is bring a department looking out for their own to
find "insufficient evidence" and result in whoever
spoke up for him receiving extra harassment from
the LeHigh County authorities. The worst part was
that during the scattered occasions in Westboro's life
when he or someone around him spoke up, he would
arrive at that same little house next to a sparsely
traveled section of highway 5 and find Robert in a
greater fury than normal. As for what happened to
him, Westboro was well-versed in fistfighting and
receiving punches to the face, and because of that
experience, he didn't fear being beaten. The true fear
for him was what would happen to David.

"Hey, Mama Hart," said Daniel.

"Yes, Daniel?" asked Ms. Hart who was now
moving the eggs from the skillet to the large plates
with enough food for two grown men on each.

"Could I crash here with David?" asked
Daniel.

"Well sure, Daniel, I have no problem with
that. May I ask why?" said Ruth

"No reason mama, he just wants to f--," Luke
caught himself right before letting go of an
effenheimer.

"Mess 'round with Jerry and me. Besides, I
think David would want to go and visit Joey." said
Hart, alluding to the younger version of Jerry Tiner.

"Alright, but if y'all think you're stayin' up and
missin' church tomorrow mornin', you are entirely
mistaken," said Ms. Hart, trying with all her might to
avoid showing how happy she was that her boy had

such great friends while trying to remind them how important the Sabbath truly was.

"Wouldn't dream of it," said Daniel.

"Okay, you boys have fun and be home by supper," concluded Ms. Hart as she now thrust the mounding piles of skillet towards Daniel and Luke.

"Thank you, Mama," said Luke.

Chapter 8:

"Holy shit, what happened man?" asked Hart as they were standing around the Yugo, examining the damage to the driver's side window.

"Locked the fuckin' car on myself and had to get in the son of a bitch," said Daniel.

"Jesus Christ, there is such a thing as using your fob, Dan," said Luke, knowing that he was beyond the range of Ms. Hart to hear the vulgarity he was speaking to West with.

Daniel then pulled out his keys and looked retrospectively at the events of the previous night. Both were laughing with much gusto as they realized the depth of idiocy in punching out the window when one simple push of button would've sufficed.

"That really was a stupid fucking thing to do," said Luke.

Daniel began racing through his mind to find any way he could merit his actions, for although he could laugh at his actions being judged, he would not concede he was wrong.

"Well, I..." Daniel was stammering searching for any reason whatsoever, but couldn't find one.

"Yeah, that was pretty damn stupid," Daniel finally said.

"Still haven't told me what happened, dude," said Luke.

"Pops and I got ourselves in a little row."

"That's pretty goddamn obvious. How'd you blow out the window?"

"Hit the fucker."

"Why?"

"Cause he was coming at me with a knife. In fact it was that one right there."

Daniel then lifted the piece of cutlery from the floor which was hiding between the floor mat and the well-worn floor of the car.

"Shit, that's damn scary," said Luke.

"How do you stay in that shit hole man?" asked Luke, still contemplating the horror of what a truly life-or-death situation Daniel had been in last night.

As for how to answer that question, Daniel didn't know where to start. Maybe it was to make David feel as if all was alright, and not to make the child have one of those childhoods you hear on TV where they bounce between homes and grow up lost for they never truly find home. Perhaps it was because he had promised to be there for David when his mother had died, and the house was the only place Daniel could accomplish that without the education or years to raise a child on his own. Maybe it was due to the undying optimism that Daniel dreamed of one day having a normal relationship with his father where they wouldn't fight, and he saw a chance of giving David a normal and comfortable upbringing by staying in that shit hole and trying to reconcile with his father. But it was impossible for him to put that all into words, and no one could expect someone to explain why individuals choose to willingly stay in abusive climates. If circumstances were different and he could freely flee or he could conjure up some master plan to liberate David and himself he would, but the few attempts that Daniel made at escaping were met with being captured by the deputies of Robert Westboro and being sent back as "runaway children."

The problem with justice is that it saw no difference between Daniel trying to take his brother to Oklahoma to save him from his own father and a random teenager who was looking to escape authority. To the court, they were one and the same and damned if the police department would ever turn on one of their own or answer the dials of 911 from the Westboro household asking them to come and take care of a domestic violence situation dealing with the sheriff of LeHigh County. Besides, if he were to flee he would be ineligible to play baseball his senior year, and the only way he was getting out of Holt and far from Robert Westboro would be by showing some guy from Austin, Los Angeles, or Baton Rouge the curveball that all the scouts eagerly discussed in the smoke filled rooms they encountered each other in. But regardless of all the thoughts going through Daniel's head, he had to come up with some semblance of a coherent thought for his first baseman.

"What else could I do man?" asked Westboro.

At this Hart pondered momentarily. As much as he didn't like to believe this vagabond lifestyle was the only method by which Westboro could eventually reach paradise, he also was well aware of the mitigating circumstances. When he asked the question he may have known all the reasons Daniel had and was simply asking for confirmation of his suppositions, but one can never know for sure what one truly knows and doesn't. Truly, it didn't matter how well-aware Hart was of the thoughts going through Westboro's mind, all that mattered was he was one of the few people that mattered because at this moment, like many others, he could see the pain in those eyes. As much as it hurt Hart, who would do anything for one of his brothers, he knew he could do nothing due to his station in life. But Hart also had to summarize all these thoughts in his head and like Daniel come up with some semblance of a coherent thought for his pitcher.

"I don't know, man. You know you're welcome here anytime," said Hart.

"Seriously, you can come and live downstairs, mama can plump you up a bit." Luke Hart poked Westboro's rather small gut.

"And it would be nice having two brothers at home again," said Luke Hart as he thought of his older brother who had moved to North Dakota to get in on the oil boom.

Daniel and Luke paused in the fashion behest to the inhabitants of the rural community, then discontinued communication and began staring at the beauty of April in Pine City. They stared with thumbs in pockets standing side-by-side gazing at what seemed to be the never-ending grasslands of these high plains of Texas, with nary a word exchanged between them. It truly was the mark of how intimate friendships were in these sparsely populated areas. Even two hundred years ago when cowboys were rounding up the free-ranging cattle on these plains, they were prone to falling to this same position, thumbs hooked in pockets and eyes towards what seemed like opportunity.

Standing around and being romantic about nature wasn't going to get anything done so Luke said, "Come on, we'll take my truck. Tiny is probably having a temper tantrum 'bout now."

"And don't you think you're payin' for gas, Daniel," added Luke.

The ten minute drive to the Tiner household was filled with a familiar Johnny Cash tune playing on the radio. The voice of Johnny Cash was something familiar to Daniel. When he was a younger boy, his grandfather would often sing the works of the Man in Black. To Daniel it was one of the few memories he had of that big man with a hooked nose and a love of the game of baseball that must've been passed through some working of genetics. Still, like the fading memories of youth with a grandfather who taught him the Texas two-step, the radio died when Luke Hart's truck pulled in front of the blue farmhouse of Jerry Tiner. Hart cracked the horn loud twice as was befitting of his boisterous nature and Tiner produced himself from the household.

"You could come and knock you know," said Tiner.

"Yeah, but why fix somethin' that ain't broke?" asked Hart.

This was a typical Saturday, Luke Hart's rusting Silverado pulling in front of the Tiner household and calling for him by way of horn, shortly followed by Tiner saying he could just knock, and Hart saying he wasn't going to try and fix the unbroken system. None of them had any clue what they were going to do with this day of reprieve, but it was also true that they never did, and their enterprising minds would eventually come up with some sort of mischief to partake in.

"How's Ditch 95 look?" asked Tiner.

"Haven't had a chance to check yet. Gotta stop at West's place," said Luke.

"Alright," said Tiner.

So with that the three continued meandering towards Holt.

Chapter 9:

Robert walked towards the sheriff's office which was right off Main Street in Holt, a residency for LeHigh's law enforcement which sat squarely between the bakery and pharmacy of the small town. Robert usually parked behind the bakery, before proceeding into the small aging establishment where Lois sat behind the glass counter, already pouring his coffee and picking out his customary two chocolate old-fashioned donuts.

"How you doin' Robert?" asked Lois, the old woman who owned the establishment.

Robert produced a grin beneath his broken nose while hiding his stiff limp.

"Alright Lois, just had a late night run in at Jack's bar. I swear Crawford needs to start handling them drunks, I'm getting' too damn old for this."

Lois was like the rest of Holt in the fact she stuck true to the conservative principle of respecting authority. Besides who couldn't like Robert Westboro? His son was the starting pitcher of the first thing that was happening in LeHigh since the Worlitz brothers moved off and made their millions, the person who protected them from all criminal atrocities, and beloved as the father of Daniel, for like many communities across America, parents are given some sort of respect for having produced such fine specimen like Daniel. The community also credited Robert for being the influence which made Daniel into the man he was.

Robert did not deny these claims, instead he embraced them and years of this had Robert Westboro believing he was as perfect as the Sheriff Westboro that LeHigh County had created. It was a symbiotic relationship in a way. Robert gave LeHigh County a man to love as the embodiment of a perfect father and man of the law, and Robert received the attention he had desired his entire life from a community infatuated with him.

"You know Mr. Crawford oughta start taking care of them hoodlums, Robert. It's nice we have you 'round to take care of it all, though," said Lois.

"Thanks, Lois. Just doin' my job," replied Robert.

"You know what; you get your donuts free today, Sheriff. It's nice havin' someone 'round here that cares 'bout everyone so much," said Lois, who was now removing the charge from the register.

Robert was native to this territory, getting paid in donuts, oil changes, and groceries for his service to Holt. The salary of the LeHigh County Sheriff was one of the few things that the town paid taxes for and didn't find a problem with. Like most rural communities, not much happened and there were some days people wondered what the value of having a sheriff was, but on the rare occasions when fights broke out or some teenagers were gathering together and smoking, Robert's value was once again clarified.

Robert thanked Lois for the donuts and exited out the red door on the front of the whitewashed building and heard the familiar clang of the dinner bell that had been on the top of that door for the past forty years, announcing all who came and went from the bakery with a small jangle of interest and then nothingness once again as it waited for the next person to arrive and happily cheer for. For Robert it happily jangled once again as the familiar face passed through on his way to his office. Robert knew full well that he had done nothing for these donuts, and that the details of the previous night if discovered by the town would probably be met with a city which was scornful of the actions and philosophy of an inebriated Robert. But perhaps the fundamental and solitary talent of the shiftless man was being able to articulate or manufacture anything to sound as if he were the hero, and convince himself eternally that he did no wrong, as he was doing now. Maybe the only other thing he had learned was to be able to so effectively hide his alcohol consumption patterns from the community at large to the point that many had no clue that he had even drank. At this point, Robert had gotten to his familiar locale and being the last one to arrive to work he swung open the door and found Deputy Samuel LaGrange waiting on the phone lines.

"What happened Rob?" asked the young Deputy.

"Nothin'. Little scuffle with some guys at Crawford's place," said Robert.

Deputy LaGrange looked up to Robert. He was a twenty-something year old kid from Austin unsure of how he found himself here. It surely wasn't as exciting as the young boy in him had envisioned, with his day filled with finding bad guys and cuffing them on the hood of his car while camera shutters flashed and caught an officer in action, but he had come to accept this time as a time to learn from Robert, and in a way, Robert was his idol. The sheriff seemed to have won over the entire community and was one of those policemen the kids looked up to and fathers were proud to have watching over their sons. He was amazed by how when Robert pulled people over for speeding they accepted the fact they were endangering others by driving too fast and would willingly take the ticket knowing their best interest was his primary directive. He was a servant of the public to the point that once a child dialed 911 because he didn't understand his math homework and sure enough the sheriff was the first on scene to teach arithmetic. He was so beloved, such an embodiment of what everyone wants out of their police officer that no one had bothered to run for the job against him in the past 22 years because no one could envision LeHigh County law being trusted in any other pair of hands.

"Should we file this, Sheriff?" asked LaGrange who was finding the appropriate paperwork to document an on-the-job altercation.

"No, Sammy, it's just a couple cuts," said Westboro looking rather annoyed.

"But sir," started LaGrange.

"Look, Sammy, when you've been in this job as long as I have, you learn everything they tell you when they're giving you that little badge and gun is not truly that important. If we file this, I'm going to have to try and find that drunk bastard, press charges, lose a day at work to be heard in court, and do this all for something my insurance for working this job will do anyways. We settled the case. Why do anything else when we can just count us all as even," said Robert, still pursuing the same false story.

LaGrange saw his point, but it challenged someone so young to be told not to do what the books and previous 12 to 16 years of education had taught him. School had been a majority of his life not actual practical work. Sammy accepted this moment as one of those points of being adjusted to a new world where productivity was not the hours spent studying some lines of a Shakespeare play to repeat what the teacher wants to hear, but rather actually considering the implications of actions and realizing that sometimes what the book says to do is wrong. Even though the prescribed cookie cutter process of documenting every little occurrence inside a police station was what these schools taught, in the real world it was unnecessary and more trouble than it was worth. Besides, Sammy thought, this was Robert Westboro, the man to whom he was an understudy that told him this is how you handle things, and having been taught by school and the profession he was in to always submit to the demands of authority, that is just what he did.

"Anything come off the scanner?" asked Sheriff Westboro.

"No sir, we are as quiet as my mute Aunt Sandy today," said LaGrange.

Both looked to the floor realizing the drudgeries of police life. This line of work lead to long hours existing in the doldrums before being needed to fire rapidly on the drop of a hat to whatever they were called to do. This ranged from catching shoplifters at the grocery store, to getting cats out of trees, to going and settling domestic violence cases.

In the profession, one wants peace and tranquility in the community, but in one like LeHigh County, it took the most of one's character to be a police officer and not pray for some sort of transgression because one felt worthless and unproductive in the jobs that Westboro and LaGrange were in when law was being followed accordingly. Westboro had grown quite accustomed to the life of being idle at most hours of the day and settled into the old leather chair with the impression of his buttocks upon the cushion, the stain of coffee on the arms.

"Hey, Sammy."

"Yeah, sir?"

"You got a girl?"

"No."

"Huh, guess you should go looking for one, my orders."

Deputy LaGrange smiled. "Thank you, Sir."

And with that Westboro watched his young deputy go off as he kicked his feet up on his desk, beginning his typical Saturday watching over LeHigh.

On the other side of town, Daniel, Luke, and Jerry were busy in their boisterous nature as they proceeded down Highway 5 at a rate which would get them a ticket in the off-chance Sheriff Westboro was actually patrolling today. AC/DC's Back In Black album was blaring noisily as the fields passed by them on their approach to the Westboro home to pick up David. Perhaps it is the fundamental failing of young men that they are so fascinated by loud music and rapid locomotion, but in this regard the unusual individuals in that Silverado shared a commonality with the rest of the populace in their demographic; they seemed to be infatuated with things which brought them to the border of life and death. It is not entirely clear why when we are young we tend to do stupid things that should've resulted in the termination of our lives, but it may just be God's way of giving us things to laugh about when we are old and then fully understand death as it approaches, having observed many of our friends and family with this same infatuation with the border between life and death succumbing to the unthinkable outcome of actually crossing that line, never to return. However, the trio was not pondering the possible implications of their choices in velocity and volume on their future as it was Saturday's like this one that would be remembered by them for the rest of their lives long after high school. It was the fullest expression of American freedom and damned if they were going to falter in their patriotism.

"How many ponies does this thing have?" asked Westboro.

"340," responded Jerry as if the car were his own.

Westboro was like any boy at his age. He was caught between the worlds of boyhood and manhood and in order to prove his ascension to the next realm he would cling to objects which expressed it like this truck of Luke Hart. This truck was something which was the utter expression of masculinity and the amount of envy amongst all the boys at school for this truck was similar to the amount of desire for the sirens of the Odyssey. The revving of the engine to life was like giving birth to all that is good in life as the sweet smell of Diesel rushed to the brain of those who stared at this beautiful rusting entity in awe. This truck was a beautiful work of music as the pistons sang with every compression and decompression making in perfect time the notes of the sweet symphony that was the hymn of Detroit. It was hard not to be proud of such a beautiful thing and it was perhaps Luke Hart's most prized possession.

"You live in this place right West" said Hart as he depressed the brake pedal so that he could maybe be slow enough to take the turn at an appropriate speed.

"Yup, most tired lookin' house in all of Holt" said Daniel as he saw in this daylight how decrepit the abode was appearing.

Daniel Westboro exited the vehicle with the engine still running for gasoline was as usual not a cheap commodity and starting and restarting the massive block would've consumed more than was necessary for the job at hand and even more importantly, the steady rumble appealed to the testosterone-laden sections of the three teenaged souls. He walked up to the unlocked door and turned the knob leading him to the same living room he was in last night, cold stroganoff still on the floor with the random array of liquor bottles staying as they were the prior night for without Daniel being here this morning to put these things away, they stayed as they were, perfectly arranged to show the depth of the chaos from the previous night. Daniel walked over the tipped over chairs and went up the beaten up staircase to David's bedroom. Inside, Daniel saw the wall decorated with the baseball cards David had collected over the years and the posters of the great Rangers like Ryan, Hough, Bell, and both Rodriguez's that adorned the otherwise stale and boring whitewashed walls. The high-traffic carpet of this household at one point was white, but over the years turned into exactly as Daniel described, the most tired carpet in the most tired looking household in all of Holt. David was in his bed still and hiding his face under the SpongeBob blankets that June had bought David last winter after hearing from Daniel the state of disrepair of David's previous bedsheets, and Daniel approached softly understanding how scared his brother was from the previous night.

"Hey buddy," said Daniel trying to get David to produce his face.

"Is dad home?" asked David.

Daniel understood why he asked, it was typically a mystery as to whether or not Robert actually went to work, but on this day both brothers were lucky in the fact that Robert had in fact left.

"No, I came home to pick you up. We're gonna have a sleepover at Luke's. Joey has been waiting to see you! Come on, let's go!" said Daniel trying to excite the young boy with the thought of a fun-filled afternoon as a thin guise for his true goal of evacuating the child from being in the same residence as Robert.

David however was saddened. He didn't understand why Daniel and his father couldn't get along, and he was getting to the age where he knew a sleepover was just a way to get him away from home because "Daddy was acting goofy."

So he asked just that, "Why can't you and Daddy get along?"

Daniel was searching for some kind of older brother advice that would resonate with the eight year old, but he just couldn't find any words. Besides, even if he did have the words Daniel was determined to remove David from this house temporarily, regardless of whatever conditions made it impossible for the elder Westboro to like his son.

"Come on, you'll have fun."

Daniel said this as he tickled the young boy and excited laughter from him. He kept telling him he wouldn't stop until he came outside and let Luke give him a big bear hug. Eventually, as was predictable, the stubborn yet playful Daniel won out in his initiative and David produced himself from his covers to throw some clothing in his backpack along with a couple baseballs for the inevitable game that would occur. David walked out to the car and Luke did give him that big bear hug, and Jerry scruffled his hair calling him "Little West" just like usual.

No boy in the world had a better set of older brothers.

Chapter 10:

The boys would've invited Ben Crawford to come along and engage in their shenanigans, but after all the belly aching he made at practice, church, and in town about having to work "hours longer and harder than an excited elephant" everyone was well-aware that he would be working at his father's tavern that night as a waiter, and due to his infectious personality raise several dollars in tips; dollars that would be spent poorly in the Ben Crawford manner. That is, buying implements for raising havoc on the populace, but a populace that had come to appreciate the joking presence of Ben.

So, instead, like every enterprising group of teenagers that finds themselves in a rare moment where all are amply monied and available they settled that they would visit Ben Crawford at the tavern later that evening.

At this moment however, they found themselves fishing the Cundiff River, passing along the jar of moonshine that Jerry Tiner had concocted.

It may have been seen as a waste of time for such a brilliant individual to waste his time engaging in the activity of making alcohol, but it was one of the favorite pastimes of the unchanging community and every teenager in the county had made at least a little "shine" in their lifetime. It just so happened Jerry Tiner was good at chemistry and had found a line of work that would help pay for living wherever his ample amount of academic scholarship money took him.

"That's some damn good apple pie Jerry," said Hart as he took another gulp, thankful for his large frame that would disperse the effects of the intoxicating spirit throughout his body.

"Thank you Luke. It was important during the fermentation process to pick the right kind of yeast and then-"

"You know what Jerry?" said Luke, cutting off Tiner.

"What?" asked Jerry.

"Sometimes it's better to not explain why something is great and just accept that it is," said Luke.

With that comment the fishing trio looked over the muddy bend of the river and did just that. All of them knew that Jerry could probably name the glacier that carved this little river out of the landscape and tell the year that carbon dating determined that the forces of nature had finally whittled this little section out of Texas and allowed it to fill with the water that gently loped along, forever in the same direction, but it truly didn't matter. One would be obligated to live out what Luke said at that crook in the river as the sun set over the little bend where they were hoping to take some of God's bounty of the sea, and even from the third person it is hard to imagine that it wasn't destiny, that these three would end up in this exact location, at this exact time, sipping just the right whisky, and knowing that none of it could be put into words past beautiful.

Eventually, the sun got too low as the horizon turned a burnt orange. Daniel looked towards his brothers upon the diamond and with a simple nod of the head all knew it was time to go and see Ben Crawford.

Chapter 11:

Ben Crawford was busy shooting the bull with the Saturday crowd that infested the halls of "The Crawford Ranch." It was one of the few locales that succeeded in Holt for it was the sole source of entertainment in the city and functioned also as a forum. It was in the corners of this restaurant that political aspirations began, bands were formed, and the local gossip, true or untrue, was exchanged between the ears of the bar patrons. Ben Crawford would complain about losing his Saturday nights to work in his father's restaurant, but he couldn't complain about the tips, and he became wickedly in tune to the pulse of the community by being able to traipse between the several discussions of all things related to Holt, Pine City, and Fox. He would hear of this farm that was foreclosing, or some divorce with monied implications, or maybe of some adventure he had yet to pursue.

Perhaps the only time it was disheartening was upon the rare losses of the Rangers, whereupon he would have to listen to a multitude of individuals' issues with Coach Carlson, Randy Bowman, the bullpen, or whomever may be having less than perfect performances. It was even more painful due to the law of "The Customer is Always Right, "the 11th commandment for him and the rest of the waiters in the world. He would have to swallow his pride and accept the fact that no one in the stands could truly ever understand what was happening between those outfield fences, for their life was to observe and not to perform. It wasn't that such talks were limited to this bar, it just so happened that the information would be concentrated in this epicenter, increasing the exposure and resulting diaspora of the new jokes, tales, and happenings of the town. Ben Crawford was no student of anything besides the game of baseball, but he was thoroughly educated in the happenings of LeHigh and was paid for his time spent discovering the intricacies of the community. At this moment he approached the good pastor and began bantering.

"Hey, Pastor Thomas!" Ben said eagerly.

"Hello, Master Crawford!" responded Pastor Thomas, who knew what followed next from Benjamin.

"Have you ever heard the joke about the three nuns?" asked Ben.

"No..." said Pastor Thomas, looking with peaked curiosity towards the young man who would be in his congregation the next morning.

"Well, see, three nuns go on up to Heaven and God says, 'To enter these Pearly Gates and live a life everlastin', you must answer a question. Don't worry, sisters. You are well prepared.' God then turned to the first nun and asked 'Who built the ark for all the critters of the earth when I flooded it?' The nun said 'That's easy. It was Noah.' Then the music played and the first nun walked into Heaven. The second nun walks up and is asked 'What was the name of my one and only son?' the nun responds 'Ha! That's too easy, that would be Jesus.' So once again the music played an' the gates opened for her to go into Heaven. The third nun comes up to God an' He asks 'What was the first thing Eve said to Adam?' The third nun was lookin' 'round tryin' to think 'bout what it was and finally she says 'Well shoot, that's a hard one.' and the music played and she got into Heaven."

Pastor Thomas for a moment tried to preserve the ministerial look of disapproval of such a jest, but like many teachers, parents, and coaches, he gave in to the infectious humor of Ben Crawford and broke into a deep belly laugh, a sort of laugh that with its volume left little room for anything else in a room.

Pastor Thomas was a man of the town and he had been the minister of the Southern Free Baptist Church since he was in his twenties forty years ago. Every man, woman, and child in the area in that time had been married, buried, or baptized by his hands ever since. Ben Crawford was no exception. Pastor Thomas a good fifteen years prior may have tried to explain the sinful tendencies of such humor, but after trying so hard to make the kid that whittled his pews for so long listen and change his ways, the good minister had decided that just tolerating his off-color humor would form a more meaningful and productive relationship with God for the both of them. Yes, it was at this age that Pastor Thomas had started to realize that the truest members of his congregation were the ones that didn't make it to every Sunday congregation and told dirty jokes in hushed breath while he was around them. At his church, like many, one could find that he who sang loudest on Sunday was generally the one that sinned most on the prior six days. Besides, he wasn't into pretending he was above anyone, for Pastor Thomas was like any man and that was just flesh and bone, mind and soul, and forever searching for purpose. In his eyes, he wasn't around to serve as a connection to God, but to help the members of his congregation find God with him.

Ben Crawford continued meandering around the crowd of bar patrons bussing their dishes and keeping true to promises of not letting their drinks go empty. Just then he saw the trio of LeHigh baseball players approach him, announced before being spotted by the riotous uproar that took place upon entrance of the heroes. Like a group of soldiers returning from war, it was commonplace to have frequent encounters with members of the community who would approach and want handshakes, autographs, or perhaps the opportunity to take a photograph with their heroes. Some like Crawford

were quite adept at accepting praise and it seemed
sometimes as if he sought out those who idolized
him. Others, like Luke Hart, as monstrous as they
may be in stature and popularity, took the attention
gratefully and with a shy smile. Those like him would
have their face turn beet red and eyes begin to scan
the floor, on a journey to discover something that
wasn't the eyes of a peer, teacher, or anyone else he
may or may not know lauding him in praise, for he
would much rather see his team get the credit for
victories rather than his upper cut swing.

"Well shoot guys, we don't serve outlaws
around here," said Ben Crawford with his boyish grin
teeming with mischief.

"We wouldn't trust you to serve us anyways,
you piece of shit," said Luke, chuckling with the boys
of LeHigh.

They all exchanged jeers for the better part of
ten minutes as Jack Crawford allowed the massive
interruption of Ben's shift. That was, until an
impatient customer called for him to refill his stein
with that oh-so-fine nepenthe of America, beer.

It was the lifeblood of this town, and was
attributable to many great stories and tragedies
alike. The fine drink of grain washed down the gullet
and passed as easily as the years seem to in these
dead ends of the world, one swig at a time to try and
drown the pain or perhaps invigorate the spirit of
youth from those many years separated from it. Each
glass turned empty like life seemed to when one
found themselves exactly where they started. Alas,
this Friday was like several the older patrons had
experienced since high school, sitting around this
bar talking about how this world screwed them over
and discussing the same stories that were aging
faster than they were. The same friends were still
sitting around, but none of them ever really did
anything anymore but listen to this halfway decent
country band play sad songs while watching each

other get drunk, and that made life rather
unfulfilling in God's country. Alcohol, the favorite
poison of a great many essentially lead them here,
sitting around looking at these 18 year old men with
their whole life ahead of them. A group of young men
that they would vicariously live through on any night
those Sodium lights lit up in Callahan Park, and
basically the only thing left for them to talk about
that ever changed.

As Ben Crawford meandered between tables to
serve these people, those who glorified every action of
his as great, and those who resented him because he
had a chance to be something, he looked around and
was hit at that moment that this was the last place
he wanted to be twenty years from now. While
pulling another pint, Crawford looked over at his
friends and wondered which, if any of them, would
be exactly where Pastor Thomas was this evening.

But for now, Ben Crawford put up with the
three ordering the most difficult items on the menu
to carry to watch him struggle most for the smallest
tip he would see all night long. After all, that is what
best friends are for.

Chapter 12:

Luke woke up for church bright and early.
Being a born and bred farmer he was used to
watching the sun rise after he did. On this day,
Sunday morning, he would rise early to engage in the
proper hygiene to go to church. Luke would go to the
bathroom and after showering shave the way his dad
taught him two years ago when follicles began
sprouting forth from the non-whiskered face of a boy
and these days the grizzled one of a man. The razor
would gingerly lope on by the roundish structures of
his face removing his facial hair, making sure to cut
in the direction in which his hair grew. After shaving

he would go downstairs and start making breakfast.
Luke knew his mother would complain that he
started doing "her job", but Luke was that kind of a
kid. His love belonged to his mother first in all
regards. He didn't care if he was called a Mama's
boy, he didn't care that the going tides of teenagers
in his country he loved so dearly was to disrespect
their parents. All he cared about was being the best
man he could for her and doing all he could. In this
case, it was his job, at least in his mind, to cook for
his mother at least once a week. He removed the
fatty bacon from its brown-paper wrapping in the
refrigerator and produced a cast-iron skillet from the
recesses of a cupboard. Shortly after, the gas burner
spat forth heat the bacon began to crackle in that
sweet melody of boiling grease.

"Mornin' sleepin' beauty," said Luke to a
Daniel recently awakened by the spackling.

"Mornin' sweetheart," said Daniel in return.

"Y'all better not go Adam and Steve on me.
Especially on this, the day of the Sabbath,"
responded Jerry finishing his sentence with what he
deemed the voice of a Preacher.

"So what's for breakfast, hun?" asked David,
having quite a bit of fun with the running theme of
the morning which seemed to be inappropriately
labeling Luke with sexist assumptions and
stereotypes about the role of a housewife.

"Who knew a man would receive so much grief
for trying to feed his family?" asked Luke Hart, who
was too busy working on chopping potatoes to make
a better retort.

"Hey, you just keep that sweet ass of yours in
that there kitchen and we'll worry about making the
jokes," said Ben Crawford.

Mama Hart meanwhile was coming down the
stairs to tell Luke he shouldn't be cooking because
there was going to be a brunch after the service
today, but instead she chose to let it slide for he was

having way too much fun making a mess. It was true, little boys never do grow up.

"Y'all better be ready for church in an hour," said Mama Hart, who had already put on her Sunday best.

"We will Mama, I just need to feed our dogs," said Luke.

"Hey!" responded David.

"Sorry, a couple puppies, too," retorted Hart quickly, knowing the only thing that would wear on David and Joey more than being called a dog was being called young.

Benjamin knew what he wanted to say, but he knew Mama Hart, too. Instead of angering her, he just quietly uttered the joke about intercourse between dogs he was going to say in the deeper recesses of his often uncensored and unrestrained mind.

Daniel liked how this felt, being part of a family. He was enthralled with the sensation of belonging and not having to be the adult in the room when he was a guest of the Hart household. To him, the value of this moment was being able to sit in that kitchen chair passed down with the dinner table from Luke's grandparents, and enjoy the company of people who appreciated his existence. After consuming a breakfast they unanimously agreed would've been better made by Miss Hart, they got dressed in their church clothing quickly and proceeded to the assemblage of vehicles in the front yard of the Harts. From there, they would go to church.

Chapter 13:

Church was something one simply did not miss. The only reasonable excuses were either illness or visiting family elsewhere or the off-chance

someone actually found some time and money to be
far away from the little church in the middle of Pine
City. It was the weekly meeting of the community
that seemed to travel together and served for some to
be a place where one felt closer to God and to others
the location where they could most explicitly display
their piousness. In recent years, the congregations
were getting smaller and the minority of "Christmas
and Easter" church families was on the rise, but for
the most part Pastor Thomas had a congregation
very similar to the one he had when he started.

"The Bible says we are to love one another,"
began the good pastor. "In the world we have today
we don't use that word enough, and more
importantly, we really don't know what it means. I
look around at all of you and I hear you say, 'I love
that' and 'I love this' and 'I love you.' For some
people, they pretend their entire lives to know what
those phrases mean."

Daniel was looking over at June Winters and
observing how beautiful she was on this Sunday. She
was dressed in all white and all of her attention was
directed towards Pastor Thomas, as he now realized
he probably should too.

"I think love is a greater priority than being
something we can feign in existence. In the book of
John, Jesus says, 'if you love me you will follow my
commandments.' Later on in that book Jesus also
tells us 'I give you a new commandment: love one
another; just as I have loved you, you must also love
one another.' Paul says, 'Love does no wrong to a
neighbor. Love, therefore, is the fulfillment of the
law.' I know I seem like an old man who doesn't
know how to do his job anymore, drawling on, but
the logic of Paul that love fulfills the law is simple. If
one loves thy neighbor, he will not commit adultery
with his neighbor's spouse. Lying to his friend will be
impossible if he loves him."

Daniel looked at his friends, realizing how laughable it was to even think any of them would do that to him.

"And if he loves his enemy, he will not slander him."

Daniel looked at his father, who was predictably sleeping in the corner of a back row pew.

"Love fulfills the law, because if we truly love every person because they are a person, we will not desire to hurt him or her, so we won't break the law. Love is the law of God. When we demonstrate Christian love, it distinguishes us from everyone else. Another good quote was when Jesus tells us 'By this love all people will know that you are My disciples, if you have love for one another.' Notice Jesus did not say if you wear Christian T-shirts or a WWJD bracelet or have a fish decal on your car, but rather if you love one another. The world will be won over not when our values are promoted but when they are incarnated, when we show them all what love is. Jesus has given the entire world the right to judge whether or not one is His follower simply by observing their love for fellow human beings. Christians are distinguished by love. Let's not confuse Christian love with its modern counterfeits - lust, sentimentality, and gratification. Love is a wonderful, warm feeling, but it is not only a feeling. According to the Bible, love is primarily an active interest in the well-being of another person, that is, love acts for the benefit of others. In the end, the goal of the Christian life is love. The measure of who we really are is our love for God and our love for others. If we fail in our love, we have missed what it means to be a Christian. So with that I leave you all a question, can we love each other?"

Pastor Thomas walked down from the lectern.

Chapter 14:

"Jesus Key-reist! That was one long-ass service," said Ben Crawford, now comfortably outside the critical distance where the pastor or Luke's mother could hear.

"I don't know. Pastor Thomas seemed to keep it pretty short," said Luke.

"Yeah, I'd agree with Luke on this one Crawdaddy, in comparison to his usual ordeal, this sermon was almost as short as the time you last in bed," said Daniel.

"Whatever you say one-pump chump," responded Ben.

"The thing I think needs to be answered right now, is what we are goin' to do with the rest of this day," added Ben.

"We gotta go home first, Mama will be waiting," Luke said.

With that the boys climbed into Luke's Silverado and proceeded down the highway. The drive was like any drive that would happen on a Sunday, the rolling fields forming the beautiful face of mother Earth as she was kissed ever-so lovingly by the warmth of the radiant Texas sun. That was until a peculiarity was spotted on the road by Luke Hart.

The big man observed the oddity in the distance next to a vehicle that looked to be parked in the middle of this road in the middle of nowhere.

"*That's weird*," noted Luke in the back of his mind.

As they approached, Luke noticed there was something even more strange as a stroke of orange caught his eye.

"Goddamn, you seein' this shit?" asked Ben.

His foot applied a slight increase in pressure to the accelerator pedal. Luke didn't know what was going on, but he was going to find out. So, as he drove by he looked in the front seat and saw the figure of a person. Luke's mind began to race, he saw the danger at hand, but he also saw another human life at stake. Luke slammed the car into park and quickly threw the door open.

"You better not even think about it, you crazy son of a bitch," said Jerry.

Luke heard nothing but the stomping of his feet on asphalt as he made progress towards the burning vehicle. He removed his dress shirt and threw it as he approached.

"Goddammit Luke, you get away from that fucking car!" yelled Jerry, this time with more worry clearly present in his voice.

Luke still didn't listen.

"This is one of God's children; I have to be there for him. If I was him I would want the same done unto me," all part of a laundry list of thoughts going through the mind of Hart Attack.

Luke got to the door and began pulling hard.

"Goddammit, fucking open!" yelled Luke

All 260 pounds of the big man were put into employment as the first baseman tried with all his might to access the driver's side door. Sweat raced down his brow with the addition of each tug and the sinister tongue of a building flame upon his face. Struggle, the one word that could describe the scene these words failed to.

"LUKE!" yelled Jerry now running towards him.

The door opened, a moment of satisfaction as Luke Hart reached inside the smoke-filled chamber of the Toyota Camry and tore at the seat belt freeing the body from the chair. He began to put the man over his shoulders to carry him to his vehicle. Just then the distinctive hiss of the fuel line leaking gasoline was audible to Luke, and Jerry stopped running as he saw the terror in his eyes. One solitary finger of the flames stroked the fluid and the rapid expansion of gasses propelled Luke and the man several feet from the vehicle.

Jerry was in awe. The shortstop began sprinting towards the heap of flesh that was sitting there on the middle of county road six, and found a dead man and one fighting for his life.

"Luke, you son of a bitch," said Tiner.

"Jerry," gasped Luke.

"I never told you this enough, but I love you man-" Luke winced.

"Tell my mom," Luke stopped and began choking on tears.

"You're not going to die Luke. Fuck that," said Jerry.

"Jerry," said Luke, "Don't worry man, I'm going home."

And it was there in the middle of a country road that Luke Hart died.

Chapter 15:

The service was held the next Sunday at high noon. It is uncommon for a high school student to die, let alone one in the middle of LeHigh County where the graduating class had to try for all its might to get into the range of triple digits. It is in communities like this that the funeral of a young man feels so sincere and real. Everyone remembered the time Charlie Retch died serving in Vietnam, or William Bernard dying in a car accident when a drunk driver hit him in Dallas. Everyone who went to those funerals knew how much it hurt to watch a father bury his son. So, with a heavy heart and tearful eyes the whole of LeHigh arrived at the Southern Free Baptist Church. Some to remember. Some to cry. Some just to say goodbye one last time. Jerry Tiner was at the podium.

"Luke was a good man," he began. "My memories of him begin when I was knee-high, and we played baseball together for the entirety of our careers. I remember how much bigger he was than I and how everybody loved to laugh and jeer that the smallest kid in school and the biggest were best friends. Little did people know they were talking about his heart," Jerry paused a moment to stop tears. Jerry promised himself he wouldn't cry because it was for Luke, not for himself.

"I was bullied when I was little and Luke would stand up for me. When people called me a nerd, he made them pay for it. To everyone that doubted I could even swing my bat, he would brag to about me louder than I could ever dream of doing. Luke also helped me build a shed. He helped harvest with my father. He was always dirt poor because even when he made hardly anything, he gave 10% of it all to God. I guess it's fitting he gave all of himself to Him in death." Jerry paused, thinking of what to say next.

"I don't know what more I could ask of him. He gave me more than I could've asked. He treated me like a brother. There might be some folks at the courthouse that would say I'm an only child, but I don't think so," Jerry was fumbling the words as speaking in front of such a large congregation was proving stressful.

"I'm not going to stop thinking about him today, and I just want to thank God for the time I had with him. I know he wouldn't ask for a big funeral like this or me to speak so highly of him, but I still hope that there's a diamond up in the sky with perfect baselines and a nice little mound just for him. I know he deserves it." Jerry stopped and stepped down from the podium.

He worked his way back into the pews and sat with the men in blue, all in their Sunday best with their ball caps on and a lonely number fourteen laying on the right endcap of the pew, exactly where he would sit if this was a night in Callahan Park. Mama Hart was carrying his bat, and had put together bouquets of white and red roses to adorn the front of the church, arranged in a pattern that made each individual collection of flowers appear as a baseball. The pallbearers were called to the front of the church and carried out the casket, slipping it into the back of a hearse as the church band played a somber Amazing Grace. From there, the casket was brought to the side of a grave dug for the Pine City Product. Pastor Thomas gave a short sermon on the meaning of Luke to the community and how God would accept him with loving arms in Heaven above. Coach Carlson draped Luke's jersey over the top of his casket, and the team with a nod from Pastor Thomas began letting the ropes lower the coffin into the ground. When it had reached the bottom, a little bit of every heart in LeHigh County sunk realizing the finality of the action. The men in blue gathered above the casket and called for one final chant with the too soon departed first baseman.

"One, two, three! Go Blue!" they called.

So with that, Kyle Hart took a shovelful of dirt and put it atop his son's casket as Ruth held tightly to his arm, sobbing into his shoulder as tears streamed down an over-worked face that still managed to appear stoic.

Chapter 16:

Daniel Westboro was standing there staring at the grave, still in the suit he borrowed from Mama Hart. He had known like all boys do that someday he would start seeing the names of those he loved appear on pieces of marble much like this one, although he didn't expect to see the dates a mere seventeen years apart. No one did. Daniel was used to dealing with adversity as the hard road was the only one the boy had ever known, but Daniel couldn't help but think this funeral felt like the one they held for his mother when he was twelve years old. He remembered the roses he put on her grave and how he tried to talk about how much he loved her, but he couldn't find the words. He figured no one did. Authors had been trying to talk about it throughout history, but even their creations had no real description for love, only a bunch of bullshit metaphors that really served no purpose but to invoke memories in people. He felt the pull in his chest. Yeah, he felt exactly like this at his mother's funeral.

"How are you Daniel?" asked June Winters.

June knew it wasn't a very good question, but it was the only one she could think of. June knew Daniel like no other person on earth, and she knew the hell he'd been through even more. Even with all the context and intuition into the nature of Daniel, June knew nothing except the fact that she loved the man they called West and she would do anything for him, especially right now.

"I'm fine," said Daniel.

Westboro was determined to maintain his composure. He refused to cry, especially not in front of June. He couldn't do that, no, he would not show weakness.

"Can I take you home Mr. Westboro?" asked June as she unveiled a smile to Daniel.

"I'd love that June," Daniel said.

So with that, Daniel and June got into her car. Dan rode in the passenger seat as June rolled down the winding roads of Fox as Daniel watched rows of corn lazily float by while the car progressed towards somewhere else that wasn't here.

"Daniel," said June.

"Yes June?" said Daniel.

"It is okay to miss him. He meant a lot to you," said June.

Daniel was angry. He was insulted June could even suggest such a thing.

"June, I said I'm fine already!" said Daniel.

June was visibly disturbed. She couldn't understand him sometimes. He didn't react like a normal person. He was never sad; he didn't get overly happy; he seemed to just get this sort of expression lost somewhere between content and angry, and the only thing he felt he could show anyone was his rage.

"Daniel, you're not," June calmly said.

"You don't tell me what the hell I am," yelled Daniel.

June pulled the car to the side of the road.

"Yup Daniel, you're the biggest motherfuckin' man I know! Look at you all big and tall and yelling at little ol' me. What is wrong with you? All I've ever done is try to be here for you and all you do is try and make it hard to love you. I don't want you only at your best. I want you when you're at your worst, when you're sad, when this world chews you up and spits you back out again, whenever you are you!" June was tearing up as she yelled at Daniel.

"What do I have to do to prove I love you, Daniel? You don't have to cry Dan, but you don't have to yell at me for trying to be there for you."

Daniel was still in the passenger seat looking at June Winters shocked that June swore. It was the first time in his life he ever remembered June dropping the f-bomb. The thing that surprised Daniel even more was the movement he could feel in his brain, and all parts essential for him to speak sprang up, ready to respond, and ready to attack. But for the first time looking at that face he loved, Daniel could see a reflection of himself. He could see what the things he did did to June. Upon that afternoon, for the first time ever, Daniel listened to understand rather than to respond. Daniel looked at her heaving chest as she sobbed, and he knew he hurt her.

"I'm sorry," said Daniel. "I don't know what's wrong with me. I have no clue what to do anymore."

June was still crying as she undid her seatbelt to wrap her arms around Westboro. Westboro put his long arms around her.

Daniel cried.

Chapter 17:

At practice that Wednesday, Coach Carlson looked at his team now short one man. While watching the lineup going through a routine to open the shoulder capsule to prevent injury during a light day-before-game practice from his old car with a cheek plumb full of bubblegum, he wondered what to tell these boys.

What many don't understand is there really isn't a book on how to tell kids why their friend died. Nothing prepares a coach for changing the depth chart by removing a name and knowing that boy would never play baseball again. The only thing Coach Carlson was aware of was that the hole Luke Hart left behind was bigger than the 6'5" 260 pound form. He could see it in their faces, the eyes of Jerry Tiner most evidently affected as a purple hue that stretched underneath each eye made it incredibly obvious that he did finally shed tears for his friend, a fact that Jerry would lie about. The problem with the world is that these boys weren't allowed to grieve. For some reason it is deemed good and right that a man have no emotion, and for a similar reason all men since anyone can remember have followed a creed of keeping what hurts to themselves. Carlson knew that he had to say something, but he didn't know what, and in no way would he be more ready than when he finally stepped on the field and the players all ran to the mound to listen to him speak.

"I don't need to tell any of you what happened," Carlson began. "But what I do need to tell you is that I knew that boy since he was born. I knew that boy's father, and in him, I saw all the qualities of his father but stronger. I know we may start to believe the season is over and this is the time for grieving, but we don't have that option. Luke wouldn't want us to have that option," Carlson said, hoping his speaking wasn't becoming overly callous.

"The thing is we have a game tomorrow night. I know some of you may hate the thought, but tomorrow we don't stop being champions. We can't stop being successful. I think I speak on behalf of our recently departed friend that we should play every inning like it is our last, because clearly he didn't know when that was. I can tell you he did not ever show me he knew how to quit," Carlson continued. "Boys, I want us to go out there tomorrow and prove for number fourteen that we are the best team in this state. Win or lose, he will watch us play like he wanted us to."

Chapter 18:

The lights in Callahan Park illuminated an outfield strewn with the animated bodies of orange and black uniformed men. Tonight the Abilene Arrows were in town; a bunch of big city boys with their big city ways which included a coin toss for batting order among other things. LeHigh County lost this game of chance and would thus bat first at home, but the Rangers weren't worried with Daniel on the mound. Rap music blared from the beaten up school bus the team came in and obnoxious was the first word that came to mind when they walked out for batting practice. They walked out with a certain swagger typical of those who have achieved nothing but place themselves above another. Unlike the farm-raised stock of LeHigh they had clean-pressed jerseys, alternate uniforms, multiple bats, and a stench of pretension and angst. Of all the teams that came through Callahan Park not many were so blatant to not only not sign autographs for the small aspiring athletes but to steer them to the sides with their hands as if they were some sort of cattle. Because of this, the Rangers loved this game every year.

Daniel Westboro meanwhile was pacing through his mind the names of each batter.

"Jose Barrett... Hunter Rodgers... Alejandro Rodriguez..."

West was into the science of it all. He took pleasure in tearing apart batters by using their own strengths against them. Blowing heat past a power hitter on the outside edge, testing the weak and unproven to hit inside, and most of all undermine whatever game plan they thought they could implement against him. By changing speeds, eye level, and halves of the plate Daniel Westboro was the rare combination of power and finesse.

Fellow strike-king and senior Robert Goulding had similar visions in the other bullpen. A laser arm from the middle of the inner-city, Robert grew up on the rough side of the block. He was sent home frequently from school for the numerous fights he got himself into as evidenced by the scar on his left cheek sustained during a rather violent attack with a razor blade as he and a classmate fought over a $1 bill. Goulding would never take no for an answer, and he would fight to the end to get it, on and off the field.

And so, the stage was set as the two most stubborn men in baseball would square off for nine innings in a contest everyone knew would come down to pitching.

After an uneventful first half inning, Jerry Tiner, like he had done his entire career, would bat first. When Jerry walked from the dugout to the plate the entire crowd began applauding, Abilene and LeHigh alike. As Jerry scanned the outfield, he could see Arrows on the wide open range tipping their hat towards him, and the same could be said of each of the men on the bags. Robert Goulding was noticeably unmoved. He spat on the mound and went into his windup.

Goulding raised the beaten leather glove to his face and was covering his mouth with the webbing yet still somehow displaying the ridgeline on his face that evidenced his prior altercation. Goulding didn't need the scar to look intimidating, his tanned arms bulged with rippling muscle and his legs indicated a man who never broke from a position ready to pounce. A short choppy biomechanically hazardous motion later would send strike one flying over the plate down the middle.

"Strike!"

The lone call heard down in the valley as Jerry Tiner desperately tried to collect himself like he had done a game prior.

"Strike!"

It seemed as fast as the ball touched the hands of the beast from Abilene that another bullet would come sailing in, and the cracking of leather would be heard again to confirm it. Jerry desperately needed to do something with the third pitch when-

"Strike Three! You're out!"

Jerry went back to the dugout a defeated man. He had done it, he approached the plate with thoughts in his mind that weren't about baseball, and cost his team one twenty-seventh of their chances.

"Fuck me," Jerry said in hushed breath as he returned to the dugout.

In a battle of deception and pitching, the game would go back and forth in a seesaw fashion for the next 8 innings. The only notable things in the box score were a single by Randy Bowman, a double by Jose Barrett of Abilene off of a changeup left too high, and Christian Vier reaching on error. By all accounts the game was nothing spectacular, while at the same time, each pitch carried with it the hope of getting a victory for LeHigh County, and even more importantly, for Luke Hart. For Abilene, they needed to prove that they truly were the real champions of the Palmata baseball conference, and beat "that cocky pitcher" from Holt. In a long battle of trading bats, the two found themselves locked in a dead heat tie of 0-0 in the top of the ninth.

Daniel Westboro was looking amazing. The Abilene Arrows had come to Callahan Park knowing that all they really needed was to pound the ball into the field and they would have a fair chance of victory. Abilene had decided early on that the only way to beat the men in blue was to remove Daniel as a factor.

"We don't need home runs," Coach Terry said to his Arrows.

"We need singles. We need to steal. We will play small ball because we will make them try and field on us."

And to this point Westboro did have a clean bill. Other than one hit in the box score surrendered to Jose Barrett there were no mistakes that Westboro made, as Ben Crawford kept calling the right pitch and Daniel kept executing.

At this moment, it was that romantic time in baseball whereupon what sometimes seems a long drawn out staring contest with funny looking gloves became a thriller like no other. The pitches mattered more and more, for the loss of outs were like the loss of years in life. In both regards, the chances for redemption were slowly ebbing away. Daniel lived for moments like these.

Chapter 19:

"You feeling good?" asked Coach Carlson.

Carlson was looking down at the scoresheet the team manager presented him and realized Daniel was nearing 110 pitches by this inning. He wasn't a man much for pitch counts as he believed personally that a pitcher wasn't put together to have the time spent on his masterpieces determined by a timesheet. A pitcher wasn't like a secretary. No, a pitcher, especially one like Daniel, was an artist.

"Yeah," muttered Daniel who was in the process of stretching out his arm, something he did following every inning of work.

Coach Carlson knew Daniel. He knew he wouldn't say no. Daniel was too stubborn for that. West might've gone out there and thrown without his left arm or a pair of cleats if it was necessary for his Rangers. Because of that, Carlson felt conflicted. He realized the undue risk that was inherent in sending him back out to the mound as the risk of damage to his arm was always prevalent, and the last thing any college wanted was a damaged product, especially one that was put back together following Tommy John's surgery.

Meanwhile, he also thought of what this moment meant to Daniel. He was playing for his friend, this game meant more than anything in the world to the boys that got sent out under the lights tonight and there was no way you could expect a competitor like Daniel to leave a contest like that. But he was a coach and lived in the matter of today, and he told himself in the back of his mind the right thing to do was to give his team the best chance to win.

"Daniel, you're gassed. I'm putting in Krieger," said Carlson.

Daniel looked up slowly from his shoulder stretching routine and looked in the direction of Coach Carlson as if what was just uttered was abhorrent enough to merit the unleashing of the wrath of God. When the phrase finally hit him entirely, he rose quickly with fury in his eyes and his posture indicative of a man fit to kill.

"You are not pulling me out of this fucking game!" shouted Daniel.

"Daniel, I have to do this for the team," said Carlson.

"Bullshit, I am going back out there and finishing what I started! This is mine! Coach, please just let me do this. Let me do it for Luke," said Daniel the emotion in his voice coming through on the last words of his statement.

"Please Coach. I gotta go and win this," said Daniel, looking ready to cry.

Coach Carlson was busy watching the field. Randy Bowman had just stolen second and was fit to come home. Christian Vier was at the plate.

The young ballplayer had his heart racing in his chest as even as inexperienced as he was he knew every bit of the meaning to his at-bat. Goulding delivered a nasty sinker and he-- he hit it! Christian Vier began using his long legs and in a deer-like stride raced to first. It was hit square into the gap, and he was bold enough to go to second. Ever faster, faster, Bowman was crossing home as the throw came from the outfield and landed in the grass before even reaching the diamond.

"I did it!" Christian thought as he smiled while Callahan Park shouted in approval.

"Mama's gonna be so proud," he thought. Christian saw the pitcher return to the mound and began setting up his lead-off.

That turned out to be a poor decision. The second baseman had hidden the ball in his glove and Vier was embarrassed in front of all of LeHigh County when a nonchalant tag was made upon his shoulder, a tag which recorded the third out of the top of the ninth inning.

"I'm going," said Daniel who defiantly grabbed his glove and began his march to the pitching rubber.

Coach Carlson, still leaning against the dugout fence, had a coach's smile spread across his face knowing he'd made the right decision.

The scoreboard in right field read 1-0, a site of artificial illumination Daniel's eyes were not very familiar with. He began the first inning with a fastball down the middle that was hit towards third and quickly swallowed up by Bones. One light bulb lit up in the line which indicated the outs recorded by the visitors. With a confidence ever-growing, Daniel continued to burn holes through the back of Ben Crawford's mitt with a stare that could cut through silence itself. Another fastball was thrown, this time it was pounded hard by Alejandro Rodriguez who by all accounts should have reached first had it not been for a spectacular catch by Zachary Stevens. The crowd's cheering intensified as the end of the game approached and the Rangers were on the winning side of the scoreboard. Even Daniel could feel a slight uptick in his heart rate with the gravity of the situation.

"Settle in, settle in," Daniel thought.

On four consecutive pitches Daniel had missed Ben Crawford's directive, not by an amount to warrant attention from a coach and have himself pulled, but definitely a sufficient amount to merit the umpire allowing the runner to walk. Jose Barrett was in the box with the tying run on first.

"Time!" called Ben. Ben ran to the mound to talk to his pitcher.

"Hey man, what's up?" said Ben.

"Nothing. Just nerves," responded Daniel.

"Look, Daniel, I got your back. I do now and I always will, alright?" said Ben as he grabbed the well-worked shoulder of West.

"Of course, brothers right?" Daniel said.

"Always."

With that Ben went back into his crouch behind the plate and signaled for a curveball on the outside edge with the pointing of two fingers to the dirt. Daniel agreed with the proposition.

The curveball is a beautiful pitch. A round stitched ball whirling at a rate only God knows to take advantage of the laws of physics and send a batter chasing, or as Daniel was hoping for, grounding out towards the right side of the infield as the ball hopefully scuffs the end of the bat sending a roller to second and ending the game.

He let go and the ball began pirouetting towards home and much like life, things began to change from what was expected. The ball danced in the air for a brief moment, but it never broke. It flew by belt high and the eyes of Barrett lit up as the slugger took advantage of the hanging curve and pounded it over the left field fence. The Arrows celebrated at home plate with their own hero, as Daniel Westboro buckled at the knees still staring where his pitch left the park.

Yes, it is true. Sometimes the curveball perfectly describes life, and this moment was one of them.

Chapter 20:

Daniel was devastated. He would not get to set the record for wins by a high school pitcher on this evening and even more disappointing to him was not winning for Hart. As much as Daniel would tell everyone who rushed to talk to him after the victories that the wins were on the shoulders of all the men in blue, he would just as easily claim this loss and refuse to assign the blame to anyone but himself. The final scoresheet showed 115 pitches thrown by West and it would be impossible for Daniel to forget the one he would want to pull back. Of all the statistics from that Wednesday night none of them were more painful than seeing the score.

"Hey, you did good, you son of a bitch," said Ben Crawford.

"We lost," responded Daniel who was staring at the floor.

"Look man, no one is perfect. It's jus' one game," said Ben.

"I don't want to talk about it," said Daniel.

"We should've won, but I left a bender high. Game over," he added.

"Look, West, you go on thinkin' whatchoo want but at the en' of the day, it was us, too. I shoulda got on base at least once for you," said Ben.

"Crawdaddy, it ain't that simple."

"Well fuck if it ain't. You know, you ain't the only goddamn person on this team. Fuck, if we're gonna win witchoo let us lose witchoo, too," said Ben irritated by the hard-headedness of his friend.

"Ben, jus' let me alone for a bit," said Westboro.

"Fine. You got somewhere to sleep tonight?" asked Ben.

"Yes," said Dan.

"Alright," said Ben.

Ben began ambulating in the general direction of his vehicle navigating through the moonlit parking lot. He got to his car and drove off towards home from the diamond.

David approached a hunched over Daniel and put his hand on his shoulder. Daniel had driven him to the game, and had it not been for the gesture by David he may have forgotten his sibling was even here.

"How you doin', little man?" asked Daniel.

"I'm okay. Can we go home?" asked David.

Daniel was planning on not leaving this park ever. In his mind, it was perfectly rational to expect he could wait forever right here in the home dugout of Callahan Park. Eventually he had to go somewhere. He had been absent from the Westboro residence for a week, so Daniel proceeded home to his father's house thinking the week of desertion was enough.

Daniel truly wanted things to work with his father. He was never quite certain why he couldn't seem to forge a meaningful relationship with his father, and it troubled him. He thought about how at one point his mother must have thought well of him, how he still had the woodcarving on the wall that said "Maggie and Bob" on it that was carved by an old friend, how it seemed that every person that Daniel had ever met seemed to gravitate to Robert; he loved people and people loved him. Still, the more pressing matter to him was finding somewhere for his little brother to sleep tonight, and he didn't believe the backseat of his Yugo was enough. So he pulled up to the most tired house in all of LeHigh county and opened the front door.

"This isn't a fucking rental you know," said Robert with the strong scent of whiskey on his breath.

"The least you can goddamn do is appreciate what you're given," he continued.

Daniel bit his tongue. This was not the moment to make a scene; instead he started up the stairs with David to bring his blankets and clothes upstairs to his bedroom.

"Are you going to fucking talk to me or not?" asked Robert standing from his chair.

Daniel maintained his silence as he was now bringing in David's bag of baseball belongings and ushering him to his room.

"Daniel, the least you can do is apologize to me for leaving," Robert said.

Daniel still would not break the seal of his lips as he was moving his bags upstairs.

"DANIEL!" screamed Robert.

"If there's one thing I won't accept in this house, it is you being disrespectful! Who the fuck do you think you are?" asked Robert with his face inches from Daniel's, a cigarette limply held between two fingers of his right hand.

"Fine, be like that," Robert said. He raised his hand and applied the ember of the burning stub to the right side of Daniel's neck. Daniel felt the burn begin tearing at the epidermal tissues and recoiled instinctively from the excitation of nerve endings. Robert took his other hand and used it to sandwich Daniel's neck between both of the appendages so as to make him feel the full excruciating force of his wrath.

"You gonna talk now boy?" asked Robert.

Daniel screeched in pain as he sent the crook of his elbow firmly into the diaphragm of Robert who violently expelled a grunt from the blunt force agitation. Daniel went out to his car and started it as Robert lay on the kitchen floor trying to regain his breath.

Daniel swore this would be the last time he would ever see Robert Westboro.

Chapter 21:

Following school the next day, the team took to the field to practice after their loss to Abilene. As was typical, Daniel and Ben were there early playing catch.

"Hey Danny boy, what's the difference between bein' hungry and bein' horny?"

Daniel pondered momentarily and then said, "I have no clue Ben, what?"

"Where you put the cucumber."

Daniel chuckled at the joke. The rest of the boys arrived on the field at some point in the next thirty minutes followed shortly thereafter by the arrival of Coach Carlson, who parked in the same little spot he always did to go back to work with his kids. He knew he didn't have to tell any of them they lost, for being a former high school ballplayer himself, and a good one at that, he was well aware of the harsh reality of defeat to the high school ballplayer. As much as this town tried to pretend it was their problem, by ostracizing the defeated and debating whether Carlson himself was fit for the job anymore finding a way to lose one of "the games that mattered," and as poorly as Carlson felt watching normally smiling faces essentially pretend he didn't exist, he knew above all else that it would hit the boys in blue the worst of all. Carlson was not the kind of selfish coach that was going to make his players listen to him spout off about how "they didn't try hard enough" or that it was "their fault" they lost, because he wasn't a liar and he knew saying the latter wouldn't help anyone. The one thing he knew was the best thing for him and the rest of the LeHigh County Rangers was to focus on their most important game. The next one.

With that in mind, Carlson blew the whistle and the team assembled on the mound to listen to what Carlson had to say as every practice began.

"Alright, y'all, we lost but that doesn't change a damn thing. I want you to run around the fence line once and come back here. We're gonna take batting practice," said Carlson.

"West, you stay here I got some stuff I want you to do," he added.

Daniel was wondering what the problem was. He wasn't much of a fan of being interrupted while in a baseball frame of mind, but he also knew that what coach had to say mattered more than any objection to breaking out of "the zone."

"What is it coach?" asked Daniel.

"What happened to you last night, Dan?" asked Carlson.

"What do you mean?" asked Daniel in response.

"Don't you bullshit with me, Dan. I can see that shit on your neck. Now, what happened?" asked Carlson, still maintaining a low volume in the conversation to avoid the overhearing of any eavesdropping ears.

"Nothin'," said West.

"You can either tell me the truth now or I can run your ass until you do," said Carlson, this time growing in the sternness of his voice, as he pointed at his own neck in the same place he saw the burn marks on Danny's throat to try and incite a response in the off chance Daniel was unaware of what he was trying to reference.

Daniel looked at the ground and was kicking the clay, the back of both hands on his hips as he knew that Coach wasn't lying. At this point, he was deciding how long he could try and put off telling him, for Daniel was never very eager to talk about defeat, and even more so his personal life.

"It was my pa," said Daniel finally. "We got in a little row."

Coach Carlson was shocked. Over all these years he thought the strange bruises were just a series of Daniel's clumsiness and misfortune, but now, it made sense. He felt terrible about his inability to observe such a thing and conclude what the epiphany in his mind had right now; Robert Westboro had beaten Daniel for years. But Carlson didn't want to believe it; he didn't want to think that was true of a man he and the rest of the county held in the highest regard.

"No. He's bullshitting me and I'm falling for it," Carlson thought. "You ain't lying to me are you West?" he asked. He paused then added, "I won't ask anything from you except the truth."

Daniel began choking up and suppressing tears. He hadn't told anyone for years because he was so hell-bent on being his own man, and it was killing him that this false façade was collapsing. He no longer had any outlet except finally admitting the truth. Daniel was much happier letting people believe it was his fault he had so many black eyes, burnt hands, and sore ribs. This was the first time in Daniel's life he confided in one of his elders ever since his mother died.

"Yes, Coach, it was him," said Daniel.

"Has he done this before?" asked Carlson.

"Yes," said Daniel as the years of stress and suppression began to flow ever so slowly out the corner of his eyes. Daniel found himself hating everything about him not only crying, but letting tears go in front of his Coach, a man he had taken to be a dad to him because his father never was. Daniel turned and started walking away to stop breaking the many promises he made to himself of being the stoic man he normally was. Coach Carlson thought to bring him back to finish practice, but he knew that Daniel needed some time to himself. Regardless,

the team was beginning their turn back towards
home, so Carlson provided reasoning as to why
Daniel was leaving early.

"Go and get your arm looked at, I'll see you
tomorrow," said Carlson.

"Of course, Coach," said Daniel, thankful his
coach helped him find a way to leave when he was
clearly emotionally compromised.

The rest of practice functioned in the normal
way with members of the team periodically asking
Coach what he thought was wrong with his ace.

"Just a sore shoulder, he'll be back
tomorrow," he told them all.

At the end of practice, Coach Carlson climbed
into his car and thought more about the situation.
He believed Daniel as much as he didn't want to
because he knew that Daniel couldn't lie. It was one
of those moments in his life where he knew his job
was more than coaching the bases, but standing up
for his players. Carlson knew what he had to do for
West and because of it; he didn't take his normal
left-hand turn on the road past the high school, but
flipped the burning out turn signal to the right and
proceeded to the Westboro residence one country
mile at a time. When he got to the Westboro
residence, he rapped the door with his knuckles, and
out from the house came Sheriff Westboro.

"How are you, Coach?" said Westboro in a
pleasant tone.

"I'm doin' just fine, Bob," said Carlson.

"You have somethin' to tell me about Daniel?"
asked Carlson.

"Why no, I don't know where the boy is. He
went runnin' off somewhere, I'm sure," said Robert
who chuckled heartily as if doting upon the way him
and Carlson would run around the whole state after
a ballgame in their playing years.

"Don't bullshit me, Bob," said Carlson.

"I don't know where he is, I swear, "said Robert.

"Besides, I'm the sheriff. Aren't I supposed to be asking you where your children are?" said Bob, still acting in a jovial and dismissive manner.

"Look Bob, I know what you did to Daniel. I'm here to figure out why," said Carlson.

Robert paused and adjusted his belt, still in his uniform having recently left his shift.

"Now you listen here, John. I ain't gotta explain to you how I raise my kids, so why don't you stay the fuck out of it?" said Robert, knowing Carlson knew what had happened.

"Bob, you ain't gonna lay another finger on that boy. If you touch my pitcher again, I'm gonna come back here with the boys from Dallas, and they can take care of your ass," said Carlson, meaning every word he said.

Robert was enraged.

"How dare anyone question what I do with my kids?" thought Robert.

Westboro swung at Carlson and hit him square in the jaw in his blind fury, for he was not going to listen to some baseball coach tell him how to live his life, or threaten him with the law. He knew he was the law.

Carlson recovered from the blow and struck Robert in the nose with his right hand. After a slight daze, Westboro regained his footing and ran back at him, this time trying to tackle him like the linebacker he was as a younger man. Carlson sidestepped him and drove his elbow into the spine of the sheriff, causing Westboro to scream in pain. Westboro grabbed violently at Carlson's legs and pulled him down sending them both on the ground in a wrestling match of flailing limbs in all directions that sent them out the front door and into the yard. Robert in the struggle bit Carlson's arm as Coach wrapped the sheriff's throat into a half-nelson.

Westboro was losing air, and his face was turning purple as his windpipe was being constricted by Carlson. Robert grabbed for his gun with his free arm as his hand shook. He began to raise it at the same time he sent his entire body backwards to agitate the testicular region of Carlson and cause him to let go. Fortunately for Carlson, the gun was stuck in the holster and it wasn't until Carlson ran up that the gun was finally free from the holster and in Robert's left hand. In a swift abrupt motion, the gun was struck from Robert's hand and onto the gravel driveway with the struggle having taken them to the passenger side of Coach Carlson's car. While Robert turned to lunge for his service revolver, Carlson grabbed the back of Robert's neck and pulled it close to his body whereupon he grasped his head with both hands and pummeled the skull repeatedly upon the side of the red Chevrolet pickup, using the full capacity of core strength to pound Roberts head into the metal fender. Robert collapsed with black eyes and blood gushing from his head onto the gravel below. Feverishly, he used what little of his strength was left to still try and grab the gun, until Carlson beat him to the weapon and kicked it into the ditch that ran alongside the gravel driveway. Robert looked up in a dazed and confused state, writhing in all the pain his body was experiencing when Carlson stood over him and leaned close to his face. He spat in his eyes and said softly, "And next time, I'll really kick your ass."

Chapter 22:

Daniel pulled to the side of the road as the radio played, crackling as the local radio station played some old jazz music with an unidentifiable alto singer wailing away indiscernible words. He listened to the melody as the heartbreak came through in waves, the minor chords reaching to the sadder ends of a blue-tinged soul, the song speaking to the place he was at this moment. Daniel was in a place where he didn't know where to go. He was in a place that some people are never familiar with and some unlucky individuals spend their entire life in, sitting on the side of a dark road with a bottle of whiskey in a brown paper bag. Tonight was the first night in the life of Daniel Westboro that he decided to get drunk.

There was a time he wondered why anyone would give in to the intoxicating spirits, and that time had whittled away with the passing of years. Daniel was often optimistic, but he knew he had lost what little semblance of a family he had when he ran away from the Westboro home that night. He knew that was the last time he could ever return. He knew his friend Luke Hart was up in Heaven at this time and that there was nothing he wouldn't give to trade places with him. He knew he couldn't go to Mama Hart and ask her for help because she couldn't possibly be in a state to take care of him and David. Daniel looked up at all those stars up above him and wondered why they had to line up against him. Daniel let the rye slither down his throat to keep down the emotions, to put to bed all the ill-will he had for life and to help kill the pain.

Daniel was sitting on that crossing thinking of where he could go, what he could do, hell, he didn't even know who he was. Daniel thought of the only person he would trust to see him like this and began driving towards the home of June Winters.

Daniel went down the veins that stretch into the ever-expansive plains of North Texas, swerving as the contents of the bottle battled with his focus, while somehow the mission stayed ever-prevalent in his mind. West had been to the Winter's home several times before and felt elation whenever he started down the driveway surrounded by a grove of trees planted by June's grandfather eighty years ago. He knew that the love of his life was there, one of the few good things he could always find in his life, and he would go through anything to be there. The only thing he really wished for in life was that one day he would have the privilege to call her his wife. At the moment though, Daniel needed her to love him.

His Yugo entered the grove and came down the winding driveway while the prices of grain were being read off for the last time before the radio station would sign off for the night. But to the surprise of Daniel, a vehicle that wasn't his was there. Daniel saw the car, and initially thought nothing of it. But then, his mind started again, and he thought of all the things this car could mean. A burglar, an unexpected guest, a...Adulterer.

Daniel felt his blood boil. "How could she betray me like this?" thought the drunken Daniel. "How could this bitch lie to me?"

Daniel in his outrage threw the door open and started stomping towards the door to surprise the two fornicators, and to impose his wrath upon the evil man who tried to take June from him shortly before telling her she no longer meant anything to him for she betrayed him. Daniel was going to get revenge. In a world where he was beaten down so often, and the cards stacked against him, Daniel would not accept fate this time. He would redeem himself. He would do the wrong thing to make himself feel righteous. The heavy oak door flung backwards as he saw the shadow of a man atop June project on the white walls of the house, the contours of the wall concealing what atrocities were taking place from vision beyond the projection on the wall. Daniel now quickened his stride and his breath became more rapid as he rounded the corner, rage flowing forth from him. Daniel decided this time he would get his revenge.

Chapter 23:

Daniel looked at himself and felt the pounding of a hangover in the topmost part of his head, and hurriedly went through the glovebox looking for a bottle of Advil. Daniel was wondering where the hell he was, and why he was covered in blood. He was trying to think about where he had been the night before and had absolutely zero recollection. Daniel pulled down the overhead mirror and looked into the reflection to examine his face. He noticed a black eye and lacerations on the side of his cheek. The horror he experienced while gazing at himself was unimaginable, there was nothing that he could think of as to the valid reasoning as to why he was coated in what he presumed to be his own blood. Daniel then saw the revolver on the floor.

"Dear God!" he exclaimed. "What have I done?"

Daniel in his alarmed state thought of where to go. He knew he was going to go to the police and turn himself in, because he was sure it was a simple misunderstanding; that he was acting in self-defense and had just drifted off to a state of not remembering induced by the alcohol and concussion from the prior night. First though, he was going to go and see Ben Crawford.

"What the hell did you do Daniel?" asked Ben.

"I don't know, man. I'm as lost as you are," he replied.

"Well, look I'll help you out," Ben said.

"Go out back to the barn. I'll go to town and figure out what happened," Ben said. 'You just keep yourself out of sight."

Ben Crawford began heading towards the center of Holt to go to the police station. He walked in and swiped his boots as he entered the door, looking to keep from appearing suspicious.

"How's it going, Ben?" asked Deputy LaGrange.

"Pretty good, sir. Yerself?"

"Alright, what are you doing in here?" asked Deputy LaGrange.

"Jus' wonderin' what happened last night," said Ben.

"Why? Ain't you s'posed to be in school?" asked LaGrange.

"Seniors day off, they assume if people are dumb as I is that I don't need that damned ACT again," said Ben.

LaGrange chuckled and said, "Well, nothing I've heard of yet."

"Have you seen Daniel's pops?" asked Benjamin.

"No, I wonder what he's up to," said LaGrange, as he walked over to the voicemail machine to do as he would every other day, and observe either zero voicemails in the inbox or play a couple of recordings of some noise complaints, or some farmer whine about those "damned cow-tipping teenagers." The voicemail machine had a number 0 blinking, and LaGrange hit play in case the display was wrong as he was pouring a cup of coffee for himself.

Meanwhile on the other side of town Greg Winters returned from his business trip and opened the oak door at the front of his house.

"Damn, that was a long ass trip," he thought as he grabbed a beer from the fridge and proceeded around the awkward corner he'd always hated in his house.

"Should've sold this damn thing by now," he thought, almost stubbing his toe on the edge for the umpteenth time. As he got around the edge, he paused abruptly, and dropped the can to the floor at the sight he saw.

Greg ran to the phone and quickly dialed 911.

"Hello, this is the LeHigh County Sheriff's Department. What is your problem?" asked Deputy LaGrange, expecting just another early morning complaint from an old man with nothing better to do.

"June was murdered," said Greg Winters as he stared at the corpse of his one and only daughter, sobbing with every word.

Chapter 24:

Ben looked at Deputy LaGrange for a brief moment before they both began their journey towards where destiny was supposed to take them. Deputy LaGrange drove to the Sheriff's home as Ben went the other way back to his house. LaGrange ran to his car to go immediately to the Winter's home, but first he needed help in navigation from Robert Westboro. LaGrange was excited, this was his first chance to be a real cop, to lead an investigation and pin the first thing that happened in this wasteland.

"Damn, this is so cool," thought LaGrange as he went to the Westboro's place with images of a Hollywood crime show playing in the back of his mind.

"They're gonna make movies about me someday," LaGrange thought.

LaGrange pulled up the driveway and saw Robert lying on the driveway still bruised, bloody, and beaten from his encounter the day prior.

"Officer Westboro!" he shouted as he ran towards the lump of a man lying on the ground in the pathetic state that he was.

"What happened?" asked LaGrange.

"Nothing, just help me up," Westboro said.

"Are you sure I—"

"I told you to help me up. Just listen to orders for once, Sam," said Robert.

Robert experienced some difficulty breathing from the dried blood accumulated about his nose. Samuel then did as was ordered and helped Robert Westboro get off the ground, as his joints popped and creaked with inflammation in several locations readily apparent to LaGrange while he looked at the Sheriff's injuries.

"Now, why the hell are you here?" asked Robert.

"Mr. Westboro," Samuel paused. "June Winters was murdered last night."

Chapter 25:

Ben Crawford drove back to his house and thought about the message he heard. Befitting the emotion the rest of LeHigh County was going to experience shortly, he felt confused. He pondered the ways June could've died: overdosing on some pills, suicide, maybe his friend killed her? He wondered if the unthinkable was true, as was the case more and more of the time as of late, what should he do about his friend? He wondered what the Christian thing to do would be, to give his friend to the authorities, or protect him from the law, to stand for the law, or to stand for one's friends, to snitch, or to serve as accomplice. He thought of all these things in the laymen's terms that rolled through his head and walked out to the barn to see Daniel.

"Did you learn anything?" asked Daniel who produced himself from the rafters.

"Yes," replied Benjamin.

"What?" asked Daniel.

"June was killed dead last night," said Benjamin. "Stone cold. Ol' man Winters done called the police this mornin' to tell 'em."

Daniel again looked at the blood upon his person and thought of the evil he had done. He thought of what he did to June. There was no room in his imagination to envision a world where the sin committed last night wasn't his.

"I did it," said Daniel.

"I fuckin' killed her," he continued.

Benjamin looked at his friend who had a picture spread across his face, a gristly combination of shame, shock, confusion, hurt, sadness, and rage. A look that said how could I do this, why did I do this, how did I do this, why did this happen to me, how did she die, and why do bad things keep happening to the people around me all at the same time. Daniel was overwhelmed, he not only lost one of his best friends, his perfect record, and the one game he ever felt was necessary to win, he lost his love, his life, his everything. The fact that alcohol addled mind of his didn't reveal to him what exactly happened last night, but Daniel was not going to accept that his bloodiness and her death were coincidental. No, he would be the man he always told everyone he was.

"I have to turn myself in, Ben," said Daniel. "I have to, I'm a goddamn murderer."

Benjamin looked at his friend again and began to ponder the consequences of said action. Although confessing one's sins was the Godly thing to do, it was not readily apparent to Benjamin whether it was the right one. He thought of the years he would wile away, the opportunities he would miss, the years he and Daniel would lose together as the best friends would only ever communicate to each other through Plexiglas on an outdated corded telephone, the world of freedom and condemnation separated by the slim see-through barrier, the glass serving as a window to the life of Daniel that could've been. But then Ben arrived at the same conclusion as Daniel.

"I don't like whatchoo did, Daniel, but I will get you there. I'm with you man. I just want you to know that even if this turns out to be your fault, I'm your friend. It's jus' a mistake," said Ben. "Let's get you on down there"

Chapter 26:

Robert limped slowly behind Samuel LaGrange as they made their way to the Winters residence and observed Greg sitting on the front step with his head in his hands and tears in his eyes.

"Samuel, get your goddamn hand off your gun," said Robert. "I don't think Greg would've called us down here if he was looking for a damn standoff."

LaGrange removed his hand from his hip. He was a young gun with a desire for action; to him this murder meant nothing. He did not know June Winters or Greg or what the two of them meant to the people of LeHigh. To LaGrange, this was little more than a time to finally display his training and be the cop he always watched on the television with his father in his comfortable suburban home. Robert meanwhile was disappointed that his normal state of uninterrupted solitude was interrupted. In that way, this police department was unique in the fact the primary concern was not to administer justice or uphold the law, but to satisfy the sins of pride and sloth. However, it was necessary for them to pretend they were performing their duties, so they proceeded, one looking for action they wouldn't find, and one looking for no evidence of foul play.

"Where is it?" asked Robert, trying to sound as pleasant as possible, but still wanting to cut to the chase and administer the investigation of the crime scene. His question was answered with one protruded index finger that directed the officers toward the odd-angled part of the living room. Robert turned the corner and saw the body at the same time as Samuel.

Samuel ran to the kitchen sink and puked at the sight. He had never before seen the contents of a body and was rather disturbed at the sight of Mary June Winters. It was only at this moment that the young sheriff realized the gravity of the situation, how his matters were that of life and death, how the sterile world of crime solving presented to him before he took this job was wrong.

"Get yourself together, man," said Robert. "Get this crime scene together, call the FBI, and I want Mr. Winters to be removed from the scene as soon as possible. We've got a lot of shit to take care of, and I don't want to be here all day."

Samuel LaGrange wiped his face off with the back of his sleeve and in his investigative report made sure to document the fact he vomited upon observing the crime scene, and following his proper training did not wash out the sink at the risk of further contaminating the evidence that may have been present.

"Yes, sir," said Samuel

Robert was walking around the living room as LaGrange made a phone call to the proper investigative authorities and began tagging certain pieces of physical evidence that he saw on the ground. Robert found a variety of objects, from tissues, to a pair of June's glasses, to a piece of paper with an apparent lipstick stain. All of these things he marked dutifully as the story pieced together in his mind, and Robert picked up something that made him realize all at once what had really happened, much like Daniel and Ben were across town.

"Samuel," called Robert as the young deputy ran to him.

"Put this in evidence," said Robert.

Robert continued his search marking everything and when the representatives of the Federal Bureau of Investigation showed up he presented all the collected evidence to them. They too saw the obvious truth, and began the search for Robert's son. It wouldn't take them long, he was sitting at the Sheriff's office and handed himself over to a pair of cuffs, his father locking the cell he would be held in until his trial.

Chapter 27:

Daniel Westboro appeared before the judge the following Thursday as the city gathered to observe the trial of Daniel Westboro. The trial of the man of the town, the one who would make men smile brightly when their reminiscences somehow brought their mind back to this little town that stood Northeast of Amarillo. The titan on the field had been reduced to nothing but a simple defendant in the tiny courthouse just down the street in Holt where he was preparing to give a guilty plea he arranged with a prosecutor knowing that his bloody baseball cap and bat were all the evidence needed to convict him before all those who elected to watch his public trial, all reporters included.

"All rise, for the honorable Judge Brown," said the bailiff, the voice beckoning from the back of the small courtroom as the moment was finally beginning to feel real to all of LeHigh.

The court rose and watched West walk into the courtroom, wearing a dusty patched up suit and a morose expression of guilt. The former hero walked toward the same spot as all the accused had for the past 50 years. Daniel approached the defendant stand where the judge asked in his professionally cold voice, "How does the defendant plead?"

"Guilty, your honor," responded Daniel.

"Counsel, have you reached a settlement?"

"Yes, Your Honor. The people have agreed to time and probation for Mr. Westboro," answered District Attorney Gerald Waters.

"Mr. Westboro, do you know by pleading guilty you lose the right to a jury trial?"

"Yes."

"Do you understand what giving up that right means?"

"Yes."

"Do you know that you are giving up the right to cross-examine your accusers?"

"Yes."

"Do you know that you are waiving your privilege against self-incrimination?"

"Yes."

"Did anyone force you into accepting this settlement?"

"No."

"Are you pleading guilty because you in fact were the man who shot Mary June Winters?"

Daniel looked at the floor. Anguish spread across his face as he held his hands close to his body, thinking this was the first time in what seemed like an eternity that anyone had called June by her full name in his presence.

"Mr. Westboro, are you pleading guilty because you in fact were the man who shot Mary June Winters?"

Daniel was looking at the decision he was about to make, and he thought momentarily about retreating on the plea deal he made. It was in these last moments of his freedom that he felt the pull towards escaping to freedom. He felt the desire to race out the door and rescind what he said, for he wasn't even sure if he did commit this crime. Nobody in the world could comprehend how much the world weighed on Daniel as he stood there at eighteen years of age preparing to give the prime years of his life to the Texas Correctional system.

"Mr. Westboro."

"Yes, I do your honor."

The writers were already drafting their stories before the gavel struck.

Chapter 28:

They held the sentencing hearing the next day in the same courthouse, with the same members of the gallery. It was strange how in small towns like this how quickly they could assemble to cut a man down. It was peculiar how they would easily celebrate a man and just as quickly vilify him. Even stranger was how the tendency of judgment of these communities often does not befit the doctrine of their Christianity, but instead decides to do God's job of judging for Him. Daniel walked towards the courthouse as spit came forth from the gathering out front, and he became showered in the collective hatred of people examining the guilty. Extra police were brought in from Abilene to insure that the citizens of LeHigh would not try to do anything violent to the guilty man.

Daniel hurt. He was saddened as he looked out to those he had called friends, teammates, and classmates a week ago and saw them gathered about him to condemn him. He remembered reading the book of Luke and trying to fathom the depth of Jesus' disappointment with people and the pain he experienced as he carried his own cross. He wondered when he was younger how someone could want to give themselves to somebody knowing that impending wrath and doom awaited them. On this day, Daniel knew how Jesus felt, and he knew why Jesus wept. Perhaps the thing that wore on Daniel the most was seeing Jerry Tiner out the corner of his eyes march along the edge of the protestors and call him by name, a sound which at one point brought great satisfaction but today revealed the full depth of Jerry's contempt for the one he once called his pitcher. Tiner hated Daniel and made it clear as he was the loudest one petitioning for the escalation of Daniel's penalties, for in killing Mary June Winters, he had killed his cousin. For that offense, Jerry hoped for the most brutal and savage treatment of Daniel. It seemed the whole of LeHigh County hated West except for Benjamin Crawford and Mama Hart, the only two to arrive and wish God's blessing upon West. They hoped for his sentence to be short for they truly believed that he was not as terrible as the media and conglomeration of individuals in and outside of the courthouse tried to make him out to be. Coach Carlson sat in the back row keeping quiet as he watched the sentencing. David sat close to Mama Hart as they prayed that the court wouldn't be harsh with Daniel.

"All rise for the Honorable Judge Brown," said the bailiff.

"Does the state have any prepared closing statements at this time," asked Judge Brown.

"No, we do not your honor, the state rests its case," said Gerald Walters.

"Does the defense have any prepared closing statements," asked Judge Brown.

"Mr. Brown, I ask to speak on behalf of my client Mr. Westboro. I want to address the court and speak of an eighteen year old boy that the court appears ready to imprison for the remainder of his life. I want you to think about what you are taking from him. I want you to think of the marriage he won't have as you decided on this day that some alcohol-induced actions of a teenager happened to cave in to his demographic and become the statistic this world expected him to become. My client is not a violent man. He is active in the church, he volunteers at the school, and as shown by the testimony of many, we, as the defense, may conclude by all accounts he is the man you want your kids to grow up and become. I think that this court when it looks at its actions will find regret as it realizes the scope of their actions twenty years from now realizing that when people speak of Daniel Westboro and the lot that he received, that it will be their name signed upon that register which signifies his punishment. When a question of whether what was given to him was too harsh or not, it will be the court that will have to answer those questions. Your Honor, I ask for you to be lenient to my client and to allow him an opportunity to one day do as this justice system was designed to do and let him pay his debt to society so that one day he may be reintroduced into it. My client has been very honorable in these proceedings, for he confessed to a crime I as his counsel even suggested he shouldn't given the immense lack of evidence beyond his own testimony against himself and a bat that hasn't even been wiped for his fingerprints. Judge Brown, I want you to look at this young boy and realize his life has greater purpose than these iron bars, and that nothing is putting him here beyond his own accord. Your Honor, given the nature of the case and the way in which the defendant, Mr. Westboro, has carried himself throughout it I could find the only appropriate ruling to be one that does not include the penalty of life behind bars per the agreement we have forged with the prosecution for this guilty plea," said Austin Stockton, Daniel's attorney.

"Is that all?" asked Judge Brown.

"Yes, that is all Judge Brown, the defense rests their case," said Daniel's attorney.

"Alright. Mr. Westboro, per the outlines of your plea agreement you will be charged with voluntary manslaughter. On the count of driving under the influence, you will receive a $500 fine, a license suspension of one year following the end of your sentence, and an Alcohol Education Program at least twelve hours long. On the count of second degree manslaughter, you're hereby sentenced to seventeen years imprisonment. You will be remanded into the custody of the LeHigh County Sheriff, who will deliver you to the Texas Department of Corrections. You will serve these sentences consecutively. That concludes this hearing, and you're remanded into the custody of the Sheriff."

Daniel's hands were grabbed firmly by Robert who put the cuffs on his hands tightly, much to the satisfaction of those who attended the court proceedings, wishing far worse upon the man who killed the sweet innocent soul of Mary June Winters.

"I want everyone in this courtroom to remain in the courtroom until the defendant is out of the courtroom and out of the courthouse," said Judge Brown.

With that Daniel walked down the lonely road of the convicted, the aisle that stretched in its infinite fashion from the doors at the front right of the courthouse to the judge who stood high up in his chair. He knew it was hopeless even if he had gone to trial, the prosecutors had shown him all the evidence implicating his guilt and Daniel was not going to try and argue with any of what the legal process had told him. To him, this was the justice he always wished would be served. He had done wrong and was prepared to pay the price.

Mama Hart cried as she realized that this was the second son she had lost in little more than a month, and Kyle held her close to his chest making sure she knew it would all be alright. The ten year-old David Westboro looked blankly ahead, not ready to feel the pain of not having his big brother at home. David didn't know if Daniel did it and he felt daunted looking straight ahead at his own timeline and knowing he was now the man of the house and his protector, his hero, his older brother was going away. It is a shame that the law is carried out in such gargantuan words, phrases, and jargon because to the unlearned, the ones often left hurt most by the outcome of a trial, the law was a mystery and certainty of what really happened was often as ambiguous at the end as it was at the beginning.

David couldn't possibly make sense of the legalese and procedures spoken unto the character of his brother, but he was entirely aware of what guilty meant. Furthermore, he could feel the burn of 721 pairs of eyes that shifted seamlessly from the brother of his that they wished death upon straight to him, as LeHigh was left wondering if he was anything at all like the brother he loved so much.

Meanwhile, Daniel was thrown into the back of Robert's police car as a smug grin spread across Robert's face.

Robert smiled for he was certain God was on his side.

Chapter 29:

Benjamin Crawford was sitting along the Cundiff River with Jerry Tiner that Saturday. He knew the fate of Daniel was beyond his control and Jerry was the final friend left leading Benjamin to try to think of the reason why all this had happened. In the meantime, he had no choice but to try and keep going like this little river that cut the same ground the Comanche sang on. Like that little river, where the fishing was always "piss poor", he would have to move along, short two of his best friends. At least he still had Jerry.

"Hey, Jerry."

"Yeah, Ben."

"You ever heard the one 'bout the blood donor on an elevator?" he asked.

"No."

"Well, see there's this guy and a gal in an elevator and they're talkin' 'bout where they happens to be goin' and she says, 'I's goin' to the blood bank to donate blood. Yerself?' And the guy says, 'Well, see Imma go down to the sperm bank and they said they'd pay me thirty bucks for my jizz.' She says, 'No shit?' and he tells her 'Hell, yeah.' Next day they meet in the elevator and start talkin' 'bout where they was goin' again and she says with her mouth full, 'sperm bank.'"

Jerry chuckled. He was beginning to realize there would be life after Luke and found some hilarity in Ben's jokes once again. He responded

"You know money is tainted?"

"No," said Ben.

"Yeah, 'Taint yours and taint mine,'" Jerry said as he began laughing at his wordplay. A warm grin spread across Ben's face for the joke didn't immediately make sense to him at that moment, but he knew he needed to be there for his friend.

"Well hell, the shit is the root of all evil," said Ben.

"Makes me think 'bout why they keep asking for it at church," he finished.

For the better part of a half hour, Benjamin and Jerry traded jokes on that shoreline, fishing with a box of worms and a couple of beaten up fishing poles. Jerry started to accept that through all of the events that transpired, he would still have a friend in Benjamin Crawford. Jerry was still mourning the death of his cousin and his friend, but at least he saw the hope of becoming happy. Jerry saw hope in Benjamin, and started to cherish each of those moments sharing their limited time together. Jerry was ready to stop letting these memories be impedimenta and rather let them ameliorate his own perspective on life. Yes, after all the things that happened, Jerry was happy to find the tranquil images cast before his eyes on the shores of this river. On that day, on the serene Cundiff River, at the place called Rush Creek even though the water moves so slowly, Jerry was peaceful. For the first time in what felt like forever, LeHigh County was as it should be.

Chapter 30:

Alfred D. Hughes Correctional facility was almost a straight shot south from Fort Worth, a barbed wire encased dot sitting along US Highway 84. It was a high-security prison for those inmates deemed most likely to harm the populace, or the punishment for those who committed the most savage of offenses. This would be the home of Daniel Westboro for the next 17 years. Daniel held his head low as the bus full of soon-to-be inmates transported the men who were preparing to pay their debts to society. The vehicle rolled at the posted speed limit as the outside world scrolled in a melancholy fashion. Many of these men realized these glimpses of the Texas countryside would be the last images of the outside world they would see for a very long time. The repurposed school bus passed by fields, paintings of amber against a blue-hued sky with white fluffy clouds floating dreamily on by. Daniel looked towards the fields and recalled moments in the free-world he would leave forever. His stern outward expression was not befitting the otherwise apple pie features of his young face nor the memories playing in the back of his head. Daniel would show no fear, for in examining the much older and much more seasoned members that lined the rows of the bus, he could see the same false expression of certainty and preparedness upon their faces, too. Some however, were exceptions. Daniel was examining the inhabitants of this vehicle and could see all the evil, the scourge, the scum of the earth, as he would call them. The liars, the beggars, the killers, the thieves, all the delinquents and convicts sentenced the previous week were put into this overcrowded bus and to be shipped to Gatesville. Daniel looked down on these men, believing him above them until he realized once again that he was one of them.

"What the hell did you do?" asked the convict sitting next to him.

"What?"

"Why the hell, are they putting you away? I mean, I robbed a liquor store and shot a guy. What the hell did you do?"

"I don't want to talk about it."

"So you done nothin'?"

"I don't know," said Daniel who rubbed his hands between his legs, the shyness that was pervasive to the core of his soul becoming quite obvious to the amiable burglar.

"You don't have to look so scared man. I mean, don't you know where we're goin'?"

"Why no, I don't," said Daniel.

"We're headed off to Alfred D. Hughes Correctional Facility, the biggest prison full of innocent people in the whole damn state of Texas. I mean, everyone here doesn't know a damn thing about what he did," said the burglar again with a chuckle in his statement.

Simon Juarez smiled revealing his tobacco-stained teeth, the missing incisors from the middle-aged man ever visible to West as he looked at the face of the American-born Mexican.

Simon Juarez was born in Austin, Texas. As a young man, his father left him leaving Simon to fend for his mother and himself. The scars on his cheek were evidence of the times he was left to protect his mom and the slight forward slope of his shoulders the evidence of many years of hard work at construction sites across the state of Texas.

As Simon talked, Daniel learned of the first time Simon had spent time in the Texas prison system. He was twelve years old. He got in a fight with a kid on the playground defending the honor of the Juarez name with a child who accused his mother of being promiscuous. In response to his jeer of his mother, Simon hammered the child's head off the pavement where the basketball courts were and fought through the restraint of two teachers who tried to desperately to keep the boy three years older than him from receiving further bodily harm. Simon used the hatred he possessed from being bullied by the older kids all the time to keep pounding the child's cranium into the unforgiving terrain. When they finally removed him from the sixteen-year-old boy, he was already unconscious and would spend the next month hospitalized from a coma he had sustained. Simon Juarez spent the following year enrolled in the Travis County Juvenile Detention

Center School, where he repeatedly became involved schoolyard fights. It wasn't that Simon was a bad kid; he was just bullied because the older kids were like junkyard dogs, and they were hell bent on proving Juarez was "their bitch". He would spend the next six years bouncing between JDC's from the southernmost reach of Texas towards the panhandle, his mother following him with every transfer. She was the only person who stood by his side. Eventually he escaped the JDC system, and he and his mother moved to North Dakota to live on the Baaken Oil Range to hash out a living where there was plenty of opportunity for a man without a high school education. For several years, Simon avoided the riff-raff and had even found himself a wife. For a while, it looked like Juarez had escaped the binding nature of the American Justice System. Sure, he and his family weren't rich, but they were happy and they loved each other. But like most of Simon's life, things changed.

His mother was diagnosed with cancer and given a year to live. It was her wish to move back to Austin to live out the remainder of her days near all her other family, to die in the arms of the Juarez family and be buried next to her mother. Simon finally saw an opportunity to do something for his mother and uprooted their little family to go back to Texas and work in the oil fields, now being a man well-experienced in running the rigs, a man who would be one of the first people to hire on a rigging crew. So, Simon moved down to Austin and spent a good part of his time fulfilling the last items on his mother's bucket list, and being with the family he hadn't seen for so long. Sadly, watching Mama Juarez near the end of her life, it seemed Simon had finally reached a point of stability in his life. But months dragged by, and Simon could not find any work. They had returned while the peak of oil drilling was fading away, and every owner he went to was much happier to pay illegal immigrants a reduced rate than hire him. The cost of labor dropped considerably hiring a non-US citizen. It wasn't that they hated Simon or the employer didn't hear his stories about needing the job to provide for his family, but they, like all other companies in similar situations, saw the advantage in hiring illegally. The dollar signs for breaking the law lit up their eyes more than the story of Simon lit up their heart.

Simon's mother's cancer was progressing faster than the doctors had originally expected and the medical bills were piling up. Simon needed to find money to prolong his mama's life just a little longer, just long enough for her to see her first grandkid. However, Simon ran out of loans from the bank and had nothing left he could sell. So he did the only thing he could think to do. He grabbed the Colt Revolver his Grandpa had left with his mother before she died and walked down the street. He threw the door open with a scarf around his face and pulled out the gun shouting, "Give me the money!" He threw a duffel bag behind the counter to the young attendant who against his training opened the safe full of cash and began filling it with all the currency that was within. But Simon was unfortunate enough to see a young man running out of the store to call the cops. Out of reflex, he shot the man in the back of the leg causing him to inadvertently cartwheel into the glass door and hit his head. The pain on the man's face was clear. Simon knew what the gunshot had done. He could see the young man was bleeding out and remembered, as a much younger man, watching a friend of his die working the oil rigs because he bled from the same part of the femoral artery. He panicked. Seeing no other options he shot the security cameras out with his revolver and shouted at the worker, "Look at the fucking floor, or I will shoot you, too!"

Simon removed his scarf and tied a tourniquet to the leg of the man he shot, stopping the flow of blood and pouring a bottle of rum on the wound to prevent any infections. He then sprinted to the counter, grabbed the duffel bag, and dashed towards his home. When he got to the door, he threw the bag inside and found his wife waiting in the mudroom where he kissed her, truly thinking that would be the last time he would see her. Simon then ran into the night trying to hide from the police. Not much later, he was caught hiding in a grove at the edge of a playground where he had played soccer with the local kids on his days off. He handed himself over without resistance. Simon paused, and then ended with "And that is how bad luck brought me here. I only hope that my sweet Juanita hid the cash."

Simon looked at the back of the seat having revealed the entirety of his soul to Daniel and Daniel was not sure what to say.

"Eh, don't worry 'bout it, little man. I'm up for parole in ten years." Simon poked Daniel's mid-section, and said, "All this and I still haven't asked your name twig boy, what is it?"

"Daniel Westboro," responded Daniel.

"Daniel, nice to meet you," said Simon.

"Nice to meet you Mr. Juarez," said Daniel.

"Eh, call me Simon, man," said Simon.

The bus finally pulled through the iron gates at the front of the prison and a guard entered the front door.

"Alright, get off your dead asses, you sons of bitches," said the guard. It was the first time Daniel saw Carl Redford, but it wouldn't be the last.

Chapter 31:

David Westboro was sick of courtrooms and today he found himself in a similar predicament, only this time it wasn't to watch the vilification of his older brother, but rather to decide what to do about the kid who was petitioning the state to be emancipated from his father. David had told some of his classmates about the reasons behind the bruises on his chest and buttocks coming from the belt of his father. For this, Robert was going to face the judgment of the community for alleged abuse. David frequently told his teachers, classmates, and adults in the community about his life at home, but they didn't believe him. Who could? He was the son of Robert Westboro, a man of title and reverence. Today, David was taking things into his own hands and asking Judge Brown to emancipate him from the care of Robert Westboro on the grounds of physical abuse and alcoholism.

"All rise," said the bailiff.

"Today the court will hear the case between the parties of David J. Westboro and Robert D. Westboro regarding the emancipation of David from his father," read the bailiff.

"Mr. David Westboro, what do you have to say for yourself," said Judge Brown.

"Your Honor-"

"Mr. Westboro, do you have legal counsel to speak on your behalf?" asked Judge Brown.

"Why no, I don't," said Daniel.

"Okay. I see you filed this suit in your own name, as Texas law allows, but it says here you're 10 years old," said Judge Brown in an almost condescending tone.

"Mr. Brown, I know what the law says 'bout what I must do to be emancipated, but everything else is in order. I just don't want to live with my papa anymore," said David.

"Mr. Westboro do you have a residence in which you will reside upon your emancipation?" asked Judge Brown.

"Why yes, he does," said Mama Hart who came walking towards the stand the slight David was standing behind.

"Mr. Hart and I would love to take full care of David, if'n the court would let us, Larry, I mean, Your Honor," said Ms. Hart.

"The court acknowledges such," said Judge Brown.

"Sir, I cite the physical abuse I have received at home as the reasonin' for me wantin' my emancipation," said David, as he looked down at the paper he had scribbled his reasoning on to.

"Mr. Westboro, you are aware that the law states that I cannot remove the disabilities of a minor from you unless you are sixteen years old and financially capable to support yourself, correct?" asked Judge Brown.

"Yes, I am," said David.

"Mr. Westboro, I cannot enforce this regulation, there is no legal ground,"

"But Sir!"

"Case Dismissed. The minor will be returned to the custody of Robert Westboro and the petition for emancipation will not be enforced," Judge Brown said as he stood from his chair and began making his way to lunch.

"Don't worry, Judge Brown, the kid is spouting off his mouth trying to get me in trouble. You know how children are," said Robert Westboro in a jovial tone, as he went to gather David and take him home.

"Of course I do, Bob," said Judge Brown. "I have full faith and confidence that you provide a caring home for David. Golf next Saturday?"

"Of course," said Robert.

David walked out to the car with Robert
Westboro against the wish of Mama Hart who wanted
to take him home with her. Ruth watched as the car
passed the one stoplight on the Main Street of Holt
and felt saddened knowing where David was going.
Mama Hart could do no good in trying to fight the
matter; instead she prayed for Robert to implicate
himself. Until then, she kept Luke's room neat and
tidy for David when he was finally able to go home
with her.

Robert drove past the most tired house in all
of LeHigh County, and proceeded for about an hour
until he was only but a half hour or so from the
Oklahoma border. He pulled to the side of the road
and ended the silent car ride.

"Get out," said Robert.

"What?" asked David.

"I said get the fuck out," said Robert as he
pushed his youngest son into the ditch on the side of
the interstate.

"If you ain't gonna appreciate me, I'll give you
exactly what you wanted. I wish you good luck, you
little motherfucker. Who knows, maybe they'll let you
go to your piece of shit brother."

Robert Westboro shut the passenger door and
drove away south while David sat on the side of the
interstate with no money, possessions, or pretty
much anything to his name and whispered to himself
as if anyone would hear him anyway.

"Thank God."

Chapter 32:

Daniel Westboro arose at 4:30AM by the sounding of the morning bell. After a solid two months, life in Alfred D. Hughes Correctional Facility had become quite routine for Daniel. He had begun to assimilate to the prison culture, where the respect for one another was determined by nothing more than being the man they said they were. Behind these iron bars, no one cared about the opportunity Daniel had lost because of June Winters, no one cared that Daniel was abused by his father. In the Alf House other things were of interest, such as the punks.

The punks were hated by all and to not hate them was to be as bad as they were. The punks knew who they were, and so did everyone around them. If you were fearful or homosexual, you were weak. The prisoners looked at you like you were some kind of oddity, because in this dog-eat-dog world where strength was the main determinant of your standing in all aspects of life, you were. You were punished for difference, damned for fear, for amongst Darwinian populations, in the animal kingdom and in the jailhouse, the members of your own species and their competition for survival were your main opposition. Daniel saw the persecution of the punk his second week in this new world. It was some guy named Clancy who looked a little too excited during shower time. The next day they found him lying naked with bruising all about his body and socks stuffed with soap lying on the floor.

Even lower than the punk was the snitch. Outside the concrete barriers of the prison, the kids would all joke with the adage snitches get stitches. Within the confines of these walls, it was very true. Daniel had a cellmate named Thomas who after three weeks uncovered a plot by the Hidalgo boys to overthrow the guards and turned them in for a few months shaved off of his sentence. Thomas didn't come back to his bunk that night instead going to the prison hospital for shiv marks to his neck in an attempt that luckily didn't sever the jugular artery, although the barbary was still gruesome.

But, there was one social tier of the undesirables in the prison caste system that was even more untouchable: The rapists, molesters, and child abusers. No respect was thrown to these individuals, none. To the prisoners, they were the lowest of the low, the ones who truly deserved these iron bars and chains. They were the ones who satisfied Satan's voracious appetite for sinners and who all the malefactors in these cold stone walls agreed deserved the wrath of God. To the law, all criminals under the institutionalization of the state deserved the same treatment. To the monsters and scoundrels the outside world spat out, some deserved more. No one shed a tear when the abusers were beaten on a weekly basis, when the prison cooks would blow their nose into the already atrocious gruel, or when they would watch these men ask for administrative segregation to avoid the hellacious wrath of the general population. The hole was the greatest fear for most, but to these individuals, it was the sole salvation.

The hole was the greatest punishment imaginable. An extreme isolation from all social contact for twenty-three hours a day, whereupon the only encounter with a person would be a guard's hand forcefully inserting a meal tray into the cell. A small room sixty feet square where the only noise was the sound of one's own fears ricocheting off the cushioned walls in the small windowless room was the home of the horror of administrative segregation. Texas state law put men in these quarters when they approached death row or perhaps had the misfortune of getting on the wrong side of the warden or his cronies. The idea was to separate and punish the worst of the worst, the biggest rebels in the criminal justice system, and the gangs or as the guards referred to them the "security threat groups". The constitutionality of said treatment of prisoners was brought into question during the trial of Ruiz v. Estelle in 1990 whereupon Judge William Wayne wrote in his opinion, "It is found that inmates in administrative segregation are deprived of even the most basic psychological needs." Administrative segregation was a harsh reality for many prisoners, a necessary evil of the penal code and the administration of the law.

"Hey Daniel, you gonna eat yer cornbread?" asked Crazy James.

Daniel had begun to make friends at the prison, and when he ate breakfast he sat with Simon, Crazy James, and Ole Anderson. Crazy James had gained his moniker honestly due to his obvious mental illnesses. When talking to Crazy James one had a friend, an enemy, a neighbor, a confidant, and a snitch all in one person. Crazy James really didn't have an identity beyond the fact that he didn't have one. Daniel learned early on from Ole Anderson, it was best to stay on the good side of Crazy James. Those who didn't would meet the worst in the guy. Crazy James was the rare exception to the rule of he who isn't who he says he is shall be ostracized based on the fact that everyone knew he was capable of actions bred in the interior of his lunatic mind, and everyone respected that.

Ole Anderson was in this prison for much the same reason as Crazy James. He had killed a man. Ole was unlike James in almost every other regard. Ole Anderson was a man from the Northwest reaches of Minnesota, born in the wilderness near some town called Coldwater. Ole often talked about the lakes of the Canadian shield and beauty of the dairy girls he left behind when he came down here to Texas long ago. He stood around 6'6" and pushed 240 pounds on the scale, a lumberjack in his younger years, a prisoner since he killed the man that slept with his wife thirty years ago. He knew he did it, and he knew his guilty plea was not a lie. The threat of death was enough to make him settle for a life sentence with a possibility of parole on the counsel of his attorney. He would often brag to the others how to settle a score. He "crossed the whole goddamn country" to make sure three ax blows to the chest would release the soul of the man who tried to steal his wife. Ole believed he was entirely right in his actions, and anyone who liked their nose unbroken would agree with him. Beyond his violent temper, though, the old stereotype of "Minnesota nice" was strong in him, and Daniel appreciated his humor.

"Oh James, let the poor kid eat. Jesus, he looks like a bunch of bones," said Ole.

"C'mon pal, I'll be your friend," said James, drool pouring out the corner of his mouth as he eyed up the small piece of prison cornbread.

"Sure. You can have it James," said Daniel for although he would like to have the extra comestible, he knew that maintaining positive relationships within his small circle of friends would serve him well for the duration of his sentence. West was still in his infancy as a prisoner, but the life was rather routine and scheduled.

"You ever heard the one about Sven in Roseau," asked Ole.

"No," said Daniel.

"Well see, Sven was walkin' through the town and lookin' real grumpy, so Ole comes on walkin' up and asks him, 'Ole, what the hell you lookin' all mad about' and Sven says: 'I am a dock builder for ten years, does anyone ever call me 'Sven the Dock builder'? No. Twenty years, twenty years I am the damn banker and do they call me 'Sven the Banker'?

Hell no! But you suck one tiny little cock and everyone says 'Look! There's Sven the cocksucker.'"

The four began laughing in that small corner of the cafeteria before breaking off and heading to their respective work assignments.

Chapter 33:

Daniel was subject to the hierarchy of prison like everyone else. Everything in the Alf House was strictly regulated, and jobs were no exception. One serving a lengthy sentence would be given a job more likely to prepare them for a worthwhile future after their release such as being a plumber, carpenter, welder, farmer, or mechanic for certain operations at the facility. But Daniel had just recently entered, and he would start at the bottom as a dorm janitor. It was Daniel's responsibility to clean the barracks for the approximately fifty individuals who lived in his building. That meant everything from the toilets to the sinks and the plastic mirror in the back of each dormitory's communal bathroom.

Daniel's responsibility was as Carl Redford put it: "To wipe that shit shiny enough that I can see your ass on the back of it."

Daniel worked hard at his job for an emolument of forty cents a day, five days a week, with two days off on a rotating schedule with four guys in the janitorial department. Still though, Lieutenant Redford hated pretty much everything that he did. No sink was clean enough of spittle, no mirror shone as clear a reflection as what was asked by the guard, and Redford made sure Daniel knew how much he did not appreciate his efforts.

"Danny!" shouted Lt. Redford.

"Yes sir!" responded Daniel quickly.

"This may be the most pathetic thing I have ever seen in my life, and boy, I am looking at your queer self. Get your ass in gear, or I'll make it happen for you," said Redford as he pointed at the piece of gum hidden in the deep recesses of the bathroom sink.

"Sir, yes sir!" responded Daniel.

"Daniel, do you know why I am making you do this again?"

"Why yes, I do sir, it is because I am a lazy ass and need to be whipped into line," said Daniel using the rehearsed phrase Redford had pounded into his mind.

"That's right you little maggot, and you do this right or I am taking away your chance at commissary," said Redford.

Westboro bent over and began using the butter knife he was given to scratch hardened gum from the sink, pounding at the grayed wad. West was not looking to make enemies on the inside, but he hated his treatment. In the outside world he was a topic of conversation on all the radio stations, the talk of the town, the champion under the lights of Callahan Park. In here, he was nothing more than another man who had but a semblance of respect among the other inmates. The only thing in his favor was he truly believed in the Good Lord. Prisoners would not attack a man of faith easily for it was the case of those who sinned most to hunt for redemption to the highest degree. The ones they hated were the pious, those of the discipline of "jailhouse religion." When one looked at the others who adorned the orange, nothing was despised more than someone who professed peace, love, and forgiveness and didn't fulfill such ideals. These individuals were quickly dismissed and hated if what they did was not a true representation of what they allegedly believed. At least in the case of Daniel Westboro, one could look at the boy and see someone who truly had a belief in helping his fellow man. He took good care of the barracks and allowed individuals to shower after he had closed them, for Daniel was not one who tried to profit from the other sinners or look down upon them. Instead, Daniel lived his faith, and was rewarded with the respect and praise of his fellow inmates no matter how much Carl Redford tried to demean him.

Daniel broke for lunch at 11AM and after finishing the remainder of his shift at 4:30PM he was left free until about 8:30PM to engage in activities in the auditorium, gym, or recreation yard to exercise his body and mind to avoid being driven insane by the harsh clutches of the jailhouse walls. On Monday nights, Daniel played baseball in the recreation yard with Simon and others. On the nights that others weren't available to play due to visits or their enrollment in programs such as Narcotics Anonymous, Jaycees, or for some the opportunity to finish their high school education, Daniel lifted weights and ran . Westboro was a very committed kid and adhered to his traditions. Even if the state was going to mandate his time of rest, work, meal, and rise, Daniel would still command his physical being. Other prisoners laughed at him as some members of the population were at one point just like him; young, strong, and full of youthful ambition for a career in athletics. Daniel, however, did not care. He convinced himself wholly and uncompromisingly that he would be prepared to take the field even when he walked out of this entrapment 17 years from now.

The hills on the outside of the prison could be seen in the background, the sole reminder there in fact was a world different from this one. It was the only thing that kept the compulsive Daniel sane, for it was the promise of freedom that made him work so hard and put his devotion into maintaining his strong athletic body and his cannon of a right arm. For Westboro, baseball and seeing his brother David again were the only two things left to live for. Daniel would have his redemption. On that day seventeen years from when he entered this institution, the man they called West would find a way to conquer the life that harangued him so. He would be victorious. Westboro was in the middle of his workout when he looked at a calendar on the wall. It was Saturday.

"Oh my God, it is visitation day!" thought Daniel. It would be his first encounter with someone from the outside since his incarceration began, and in the anticipation of the great event, he ran from the gym and straight to the visitation office. Mama Hart had promised to come and see him today to tell him about everything that was happening at home, and she said she would bring David. Daniel was ecstatic, his full optimism devoted to the arrival of his brother and friend's mother. Many people use the phrase "meaning the world to me," but Daniel was honest in using such a phrase. Daniel willfully allowed himself to be frisked by the security detail before proceeding to window number three where he sat down and eagerly awaited Mrs. Hart.

"Hello, Ms. Hart," said Daniel as Ruth picked up the phone on the other side of the partition.

"Hello Daniel," said Mrs. Hart who looked straight back through that infinitely thick piece of glass, the division between freedom and captivity.

"Where's David?" asked Daniel.

Ms. Hart looked to the ground and strung together the answer to this inevitable question. During the four hour drive to the penitentiary she had pieced together all the possible permutations of the words that had to be spoken and none of them truly rang well in her head. So, after a heavy sigh, she proceeded to deliver the dreadful news.

"Daniel, I tried to the best I could to take care of your brother, but the state said I couldn't," said Ms. Hart now weeping with each word.

"I'm sorry, Daniel. The judge, he went and told me that I couldn't take care of him. He said Kyle and I couldn't. I failed you David," said Ms. Hart.

Daniel stared straight on back suppressing the emotions he wanted to express. Daniel wasn't into that storybook bullshit and the life of a prisoner hardened him. Even in his brief exposure, the assimilation to a life as gray as the environment he lived in had begun. Daniel responded,

"So he's at home with Bob still?"

Mama Hart said as if whispering through the telephone, "No, he's been gone for two weeks and no one knows where he has gone. I'm sorry Danny, I didn't want to do this to you," said Ms. Hart who was clearly hurt by the weight of her message while Daniel looked back with a blank and devoid countenance.

"It's alright, Misses Hart. It's all alright," said Daniel.

They looked at each other blankly for some brief moments and then Ruth said, "I have to go Danny."

Daniel nodded before hanging up the phone and proceeding back to the gym. It was unusual for an inmate to have this kind of time following visitation day, and Daniel found himself alone in the weight room of the prison as all the other prisoners still attended to their conversations.

There, he lifted by himself with more ferocity than he ever had before.

Chapter 34:

David was somewhere near the Oklahoma border when he stopped walking. His young feet were tired, his mouth dry from the lack of water and his stomach groaning from the lack of food. He was used to hunger pangs and deprivation of water from his father, but for some reason he felt helpless in this wasteland where the next town was said to be five miles from where he was right now on the side of interstate. David in his exhausted state quit his northward march and instead sat upon a rock with his thumb extended and wrist pronated to the side in his futile attempt to get a ride to the nearest town and start life on his own. In the back of his mind was the thought of maybe trying to march south and return to LeHigh County, but that county line had now become a distinct border between what he was and who he would be.

David had nothing left where he came from, only the ground that his feet trod as his boyish figure trudged towards something new. But for now, David prepared to spend the night alone on the side of the road. He didn't despise the notion, at least it was Texas in May and the temperate climate of the Lone Star State this time of year did not bother him. With that he looked to the star-studded sky and felt his eyes become heavy with the weight of fatigue and stress pulling down his brow. He would've entered slumber on that rock had it not been for the 1996 Chevrolet Cavalier that slowed down as it approached the rock to illuminate David. David stood up and approached the car slowly as the driver remained seated and made no movements towards him. Slowly, deliberately, David walked in the same way one would approach a wild deer to try to stroke the coat of the wild bovine with the back of their hand. Then, when he was about twenty feet away, the latch of the door made a sound as it opened and David saw one well-polished leather cowboy boot as it hit the ground.

The man exited the driver's side door of his car and stood a menacing six foot six inches tall.

Chapter 35:

Benjamin Crawford was in town and walked the streets of Holt. In every corner of the narrow streets of the small towns in LeHigh the voices all spoke highly of "that boy of Jack Crawford's" and "that catcher for the high school." Across the country, people spoke of Benjamin Crawford as the top catching prospect in the country on his way to the Arizona Diamondbacks. The pundits touted him with the potential of being the best catcher the game had seen in years, a true five-tool player. Not to mention, the lovable personality of the country's newest favorite hick in his disheveled and uncensored state had a way of causing cameras to gravitate to his infectious smile, and listen to his off-kilter expressions.

Benjamin Crawford took the country by firestorm being propelled by the story of Mary June Winters. His story of overcoming the loss of two of his best friends and still dominating in the Palmata Baseball conference the remainder of that 2006 baseball season impressed many far beyond the borders of that little North Texas county. Although the efforts of Ben Crawford offensively were not enough to overcome the disadvantages he experienced in catching for an all junior class of pitchers, his highlight reel "balls to the wall" approach to the game was magnetic to the sports writers and scouts.

Ben Crawford provided a patch to the holes in the hearts of the citizens of LeHigh and gave them all something to talk about and watch when Luke and Daniel had their seasons prematurely ended. Fathers looked highly upon him, and Benjamin rewarded their sons with his autographs as his celebrity status had elevated to the point that visiting teams would walk up to the LeHigh backstop and ask their hat, glove, or baseballs to be adorned by his signature.

He did have options to pursue post-secondary education with his baseball talent, but deep down Ben Crawford knew that more school was not going to help him. He would rather accrue four more years of salary in the limited amount of time he could play baseball than waste his time, as he put it, "pretending I's smart". Stories like Ben's make people often wonder if intelligence was really defined by some piece of paper stating the tenure and accomplishments of one's indenture to a university, for if one found a way to be ceaselessly happy with the least amount of effort hadn't they satisfied the fundamental goal of human life? Nevertheless, Ben would argue with his mother from this viewpoint for months before finally swaying Judy to see his side of things and support the foregoing of a college education to realize his dreams of becoming the best baseball player he could be. LeHigh County all the while looked at their hero with reverence. All the praise that at one point was Daniel's had become Ben's and Ben was simply not the kind of man to deny such respect.

Jerry Tiner meanwhile ended his season in a different manner. In all the years of his varsity baseball career he had never posted more errors, strikeouts, or a lower batting average. It was with much pain that Coach Carlson had removed him from the leadoff spot and instead gave a chance to Kris Browning, for Jerry was not doing his job anymore. Carlson knew what was wrong as did all of

LeHigh County. At every game, Jerry took the field serious and saddened, with slouched shoulders, his feet shuffling to the second base position with a glove hanging limply down. He was a mere silhouette of the man he had been. Jerry didn't have the same spring, his wrist didn't snap quite as quickly and the energy pent up in his small athletic body was not as pulsing as it once had been. It was miserable watching Tiny take to the field and is booed so much by the town that once loved him, but as they always say, that is the way she goes.

One day you're the hero and idol of all the inhabitants of your hometown, and the next day you simply disintegrate into an unrecognizable glob of self-pity. The one saving grace was that Tiny spent most of his time brooding by digging deeper into his textbooks and in the process received a full-ride scholarship from Harvard for academics, something which in the world of LeHigh County did not even register on the radar as much as the fact Zach Stevens did get his chance to play college ball at Middle Tennessee State.

So, the story of the 2006 LeHigh County Rangers baseball team could be summarized as a team that went 16-14 in the middle of nowhere containing the most famous men in all of high school baseball. From the funeral pyre of Daniel Westboro rose the Phoenix of Benjamin Crawford, while Jerry Tiner succumbed to the circumstances.

More important to Crawford and Tiner today was the fact that they were departing the dearest of friends. On this day, Benjamin was preparing to go westward to his boyhood fantasy and Tiner eastward to make a name for himself in his own right. So fittingly, the two spent the afternoon before the date of their departure with each other in Jerry's Ram pickup truck, meandering to all the familiar childhood places. They looped past the general store where they got caught stealing gum, went past that lazy bend of the Cundiff River where the fishing was always shit but at least the whisky tasted good, and saw the ends of Fox, that little town they thought even more desolate than their own.

"Hey Ben," said Jerry.

"What Tiny?" asked Crawford.

"You ever wonder what's going to happen man?" asked Tiny.

"What do you mean?" asked Crawford.

"What do you think we'll be like in ten years when we come back to this little spot on the river. I mean, will we even find each other here? I keep thinking all the time anymore about how much each little moment means in life, and I keep thinking I'm fucking up. I keep wondering, you know, if I'm going to lose you, man. You're all that is left anymore," said Jerry as he kept his eyes on the road.

"I don't wanna go anywhere Ben. I really don't. All these people keep telling me I'm so goddamn smart and that the best thing for me to do is go up and learn with those pretty boys in Massachusetts, but I keep wondering if that really is who I am. I look at my dad with his friends and he seems happy having never changed since the day he graduated, and it makes me wonder if he's right and I'm wrong. I keep thinking Crawdaddy, and it hurts," said Jerry with tears welling in his eyes. "Benjamin, are you going to be here for me when I come back, or when I board that plane tomorrow am I giving up this entire little boondock of a town. Because if so, I'm cancelling my plane ticket tonight."

Benjamin wasn't much for consoling people when they needed it. He had a hard time believing in any emotion beyond pure humor or rage. Ben was like most teenage boys; he didn't understand any of it because he didn't want to, and so he did as always and flew by the seat of his pants with his next utterance.

"Look Jerry, I dunno what the hell will happen in ten years. I mean for fuck sake's I could be bangin' Kirstin Bell by that time for all I know. Alls I do know is that I'm your brother, and brothers don't leave each other. I dunno if that will be back on that goddamn river, but I will stand by you. I'm loyal to you, and no matter what, I always will be," said Ben. "Besides, I need some son of a bitch around me to make me look prettier than I am," added Crawford jokingly.

With that, Benjamin Crawford and Jerry Tiner laughed as they rolled down the road and stopped in front of the Crawford home. Jerry unlocked the doors and let Benjamin climb out, who in obligatory fashion complained about his driving skills before trudging off to his little tiny house. Apparently, it was the perfect time for crude humor.

Chapter 36:

Benjamin found himself somewhat lonely sitting at the Crawford residence. He had said goodbye to Jerry earlier in the day, and compared to all the hubbub and publicity he seemed unable to escape from the previous weeks it was silent. A quiet day like today in the Texas Panhandle had turned from the norm to a rarity. Ben Crawford, a social man, wasn't sure he liked that very much. The presence of microphones and reporters was a sight that he gravitated towards.

In one week, he was to report to Yakima and begin playing with the Bears at the Short Season A level. Everyone knew he would progress quickly through this part of the farm system. As low as this team seemed being the absolute floor of professional baseball employment, it was still an essential stepping stone to climbing the minor league ranks in the hope of graduating at each successive level to become a part of the lucrative 25-man roster.

Crawford liked the thought of Yakima, Washington. It was where dreams that were borne in the minds of little boys met the first semblance of reality. To some, this was the first stepping stone to ascending the ranks of the professional baseball world, the first stop on the way to a star-studded career surrounded by fame, money, and most importantly, as much of the game of baseball as one could handle. To others, this was the excruciating misery of watching the toil of a multitude of years prove all for naught as they simply didn't "have it."

Every year approximately 1400 young men get a phone call saying that they got drafted. Of all these, it is expected almost 1300 will go home never having played in a major league contest in their life or ever getting the chance to. It was a sad fate, but a necessary evil to see the best of the best, to have an entire population on the expansive fields in the metropolitan areas of America to wage unruly and unrelenting war against any performance that was less than excellent. When one is competing for the same 270 jobs with literally thousands of others, the pursuit of perfection transforms from desire to necessity as the life on a professional roster lives and dies not with he who has the most heart, but with who performs best. It lies with the guy putting 40 or more balls out of the park on an annual basis, the kid with one error in all the time he spends on the field, the kid that dominates the best of the best as they climb the hierarchy of their respective organization.

In a strict numbers game, mathematics had already drawn up a figure to predict what would happen to Benjamin Crawford.

Sixty-six. The percentage that defined the chance he and all the other first round picks had at making the majors after years of collecting data to estimate such a thing. Although he had been a big deal in high school and an interesting topic to discuss among the baseball writers, who often try to pretend they know what will become of some kid from the Texas panhandle, his opportunity would be starting at the very base level of competition. Just like all those clutch moments where he found himself with a bat rolling between the fingers of his powerful hands, he looked at the situation and smiled. In Yakima, his future awaited him and the rest of the 2006 draft class.

But today, Benjamin Crawford had other business to attend to. Today he had to go and say goodbye to someone else.

Ben drove down 35W and turned towards the West when he got to Waco. Following U.S. Highway 84 he got to Gatesville and after the few necessary incorrect turns and reroutes that befitted the navigation style of Benjamin Crawford, he arrived at the Alfred D. Hughes Correctional Facility. Exiting his car, he approached the visitation office, and after a brief encounter with a strangely kind staff, he waited for Daniel Westboro in the lobby.

"Mr. Crawford please approach Window 4," said the host in the lobby.

Ben stood up and walked to the window to meet the apple-pie faced and smiling Daniel. Daniel was ecstatic to meet his best friend; the sight of Benjamin was the first happy thing that happened in the life of Daniel for two weeks. Benjamin smiled back and spoke in the telephone.

"How are you Daniel?" asked Crawford.

"Alright, getting kind of tired of the color orange though. Makes my ass look fat," said Daniel as he kept on the jovial roll.

"Did you hear the news?" asked Benjamin.

"Yeah, I heard about David…" said Daniel with a now somber appearance on his face.

"No dumbshit, about what happened with me," said Benjamin.

"I got drafted. Firs' goddamn round West! I'm goin' to the big leagues!" said Ben.

"Really, they need horseshit catchers that bad?" asked Daniel.

"Fuck yeah, I could be the next Bill Bergen," joked Ben.

"That's cool," said Daniel. Daniel's mind had drifted off course and gone in the direction of David again. He wondered where the little man could be.

"That's all?" asked Ben.

"Sorry, I'm just thinking a lot right now," said Daniel.

"The fuck man, I did it, I got where we both said we was goin' to," said Ben.

"Look Ben, it's not all about you all the fuckin' time," said Daniel with irritation in his voice.

"For fuck's sake I've seen sad hand jobs receive more praise than whatchoo are givin' me," said Benjamin.

Daniel froze as a sneer broke across his face that curled his upper lip and bared his teeth.

"HALLEFUCKINGLUJAH! Congratulations! Kudos! All honor the great Ben Crawford! Jesus Christ man, do you not see what you are doing! I am never going to be able to live that dream I had. I'm going to sit here and look at you and think of how I was supposed to be there instead of you. You ever think maybe someone else can have some goddamn oxygen? Where the hell is David? What did I do to deserve this?" hollered Daniel who had aroused the guards who were beginning to grab at their Tasers in the event of a wild demonstration of Daniel's anger.

"It's your own damn fault, Daniel," said Crawford as he rolled his shoulders looking at David with an uncharacteristically unenergetic face.

"You did whatchoo did and that put you here. I don't know where David is, but thankfully he isn't around you," said Ben.

"My mama told me not to talk to convicts and she was right Daniel," he added as he stood from the chair still speaking into the telephone.

"Look man, I'm done. I don't need you in my life no more. I've got better things to do now. Bye," said Crawford as he hung up the dangling receiver.

Daniel willingly went with the guards back to his cell with the fury towards all things relating to Benjamin Crawford still clearly pulsating through his body, and shown with the throbbing of the prominent veins in his neck. Benjamin drove the four hours home and proceeded all the way to the graveyard to look at the headstone of June Winters.

Benjamin thought of Daniel's girlfriend, with sorrow in his heart.

Chapter 37:

David found himself sitting in the household of Jacob Clubber and looked out to the Florida landscape, thinking about how a mere two weeks ago he was near the Oklahoma border lost and alone. Here in Lake City, he found something he swore he forgot a while back, sort of like a pocketknife someone happens to forget on the bumper of a truck before it plummets into the recesses of a ditch, a pleasant surprise with a sort of warm feeling if you can imagine it.

In Lake City, David was happy. In the home of Jacob and Sarah Clubber, he was little more than an elongated stride from the outside edge of the Osceola National Forest. David adored the serenity in this environment, the way his voice sounded in the wide expanse of these fields, and he liked that someone finally appreciated him. He thought back to that night when the giant straw-like cowboy kicked his size fourteen cowboy boot on to the North Texas soil. He remembered the fear that coursed through him as he thought Jacob Clubber would be the man to end his miserable existence.

"And what is your name, partner?" asked Clubber on that night.

"What the hell does it mean to you?" asked David defensively, much like a dog above a slab of fresh meat.

"Well, I don't know. Must be some kind of important because here I am asking you for it. I guess I just wanted to see if you were lost. It ain't normal to see such little ones struttin' about at this hour," said Jacob.

David looked straight ahead, arms crossed and deducing what he could from the situation.

"You need a lift?" asked Jacob.

"No," said David.

"You sure?"

"Yes."

"Well where in God's name are you goin' or can I ask that?"

"I don't know."

Jacob Clubber looked at the boy and thought to his childhood, when he was a much younger man and was in a similar predicament. When he was younger he too had run from home and for some peculiar reason that surely God only knows he could see the look in David's eyes. The look of depravity, the look of neglect, the look of being chewed up and spit back on the tainted Earth like you were a plug of Copenhagen is what Jacob saw in David's eyes. Jacob could see all these things in the way David carried himself, from the way his arms drooped to the way he bent his head to avoid being noticeable, even here in the presence of an audience of one.

Jacob then said, "Come on, at least let me give you a lift to the next town."

"Fine," responded David.

It is strange how the lonely highway can become such a bonding force between two individuals. That is how it was along U.S. Highway 287 on that night in June when David climbed into Jacob Clubber's truck, the sickening yet oddly satisfying sound of some incessant yodeling ebbing forth from the stereo. No words were spoken for the longest time, but there was a noticeable draw between the two, a feeling of belonging for David and a feeling of guardianship for Jacob, a man who had tried and failed several years to have children of his own with his wife Sarah.

"Where are you from?" asked David, the first question of the night that finally broke the silence.

"Me? Well, I'm from Freedom, Oklahoma," said Jacob.

"What brings you all the way down here?" asked David.

"I was on my way to Amarillo, had to go and pick something up for my ma from there," said Jacob.

"You live there then?"

"No, I moved a while ago. I was just out here for the Fourth of July. I live in Florida now," said Jacob. "Had the privilege of marrying the prettiest girl in Tulsa."

"How'd you end up in Florida?" asked David.

"Well, sometimes you don't rightly know. I mean I never thought I would be makin' this trip with anyone but myself, but here I am with you in the passenger seat asking me 'bout my life," said Jacob. "I guess the way it goes is that we don't get to really know everythin' all the time and anyone who ever tells you that is straight bullshittin' you partner. Even us old men who try to say we know it all really don't."

David suspended his questioning for a good thirty minutes following the exchange before he finally had enough courage to ask the kind stranger, "You look at the stars very often?"

Jacob replied, "Of course."

"What do you see?" asked David.

"I dunno, buncha pretty lights I s'pose. Why? What do you see?" asked Jacob.

David paused for a moment and then said, "My granddaddy used to tell me he would look at that great big sky on them nights when not even the coyotes would make a sound and he would always wonder, is there someone up with all them stars lookin' back at me?"

Jacob thought about this momentarily and responded, "I don't know, but I'd sure like to know your name first."

David pondered for a moment, as he thought about the implications of revealing his true identity to this stranger and what that could do to him if he were to be handed over to the authorities. But, he did owe this man some sort of identification at this point.

"My name is Christopher. Christopher Hart," said David.

"Nice to meet you Chris. Now are your parents expectin' you back at some point tonight?" he asked as the road sign passed by announcing that Amarillo was a mere ten miles away.

"No," he said looking at the floor confirming the aforementioned suppositions by revealing the cigar burn on the back of his neck; a sight which caused Jacob to clutch at a similar scar on the back of his own neck.

"Well, Christopher, I'm not going to let you sleep on the street tonight. You coming back to Ma's with me?" asked Jacob.

David smiled with his boyish grin emitting the spark and jubilance of life that only emanates from the grins of youth.

"Alright. The name's Jacob by the way."

From there all the way back to Freedom the two laughed and talked like two friends that hadn't seen each other for years.

Chapter 48:

Daniel Westboro woke from his cell and dreaded the sight of yet another day behind these iron-clad bars. He felt like a caged bird, but he had neither a song nor a prayer. On the 25th of November Daniel looked at those walls and felt the clutch of the shackle. In places freer than this, there would be a celebration with golden turkeys, a plethora of stuffing, and mashed potatoes with their smooth texture gently meandering through the gullet in a bath of gravy and butter. He swore he could taste Mama Hart's corn pudding from the deep recesses of this decrepit institution, and could still hear the voice of Kyle as he spoke of all the crazy things he did growing up. A 32 year old Daniel was writhing in the pain of looking at his life and realizing he was really nothing anymore.

It had been fifteen years since the last time he saw his brother, fifteen years since he saw his former best friend, and it seemed only Ruth and Pastor Thomas managed to come by anymore to say hello to him and even that was on infrequent occasions. Thanksgiving just didn't feel like it anymore, no matter how much the prison attempted to raise morale by providing a meal reminiscent of what was served outside the gray walls. Holidays thus became less important over the years as Daniel began to become institutionalized.

No longer did he care about what day of Christmas it was, who's birthday was coming up, or when the country would celebrate yet another Fourth of July. To Daniel, the easiest thing to do with all of these holidays was do his best to pretend they didn't exist. He remembered all the random passers-by back home when he was a free man, and it seemed the entire country knew his name in those days. They gathered so cheerfully and competed to wish him well, to say Merry Christmas and Happy Thanksgiving. The girls would sheepishly coax him into an encounter under the mistletoe which he would avoid, for that hallowed ground was only intended for June to occupy with Daniel.

June. How he thought of her, and the regrets he had for the poor decisions he made with her. He often dreamt of her, how she moved through his thoughts, the way that light reflected off that girl being the greatest occupation of his mental capacities. He truly missed every part of the brunette he was lucky enough to call his. Daniel hadn't cried for years since that day with June where she fought with him for the right to love his broken self, but he could feel the tightening of his chest when he thought of her now. It was when Daniel thought of what he did to June that he could fully convince himself he deserved every part of this treatment by the state.

So, Daniel chose to make himself suffer. He used the hours of vacation afforded him by the state to brood and think about all that had been wrong. In his eyes, the only way to make himself feel right was to fully feel the pain of his incarceration. To feel the pain of Ben hating him, The pain of the loss of Luke Hart, The whereabouts of David, and the thought of the six feet of dirt above the head of Ms. Winters. It wasn't good enough for Daniel to just be imprisoned when he was in a mood like today, it was important that he punished himself worse than these walls ever could.

"Get your ass to the mess hall, Daniel," said Sergeant Redford, who had been promoted since Daniel began his imprisonment.

Daniel remained in a recline upon his bunk, staring upwards at the ceiling without a thought in the world but making things as miserable for himself as he could.

"You get that ass in gear or I will do it for you," said Redford. "I am not putting up with you feeling sorry for yourself today."

Carl Redford stood and was infuriated. He hadn't taken this job to be some kind of babysitter for the convicts of Texas, at least not in this sense. Not to mention he was upset with himself that he ended up working this dead-end job and fifteen years later he still found himself working holidays while the warden continued to assure him, "Don't worry, we'll give you next Thanksgiving off." Even more infuriating was how the state made him mollycoddle these killers, thieves, liars, and cheats. Instead of this being the fullest punishment of the law as the court promised unto them when that gavel struck guilty, the government had slowly turned into a nanny-state hodgepodge of "collective interest" and "rehabilitation". In the good old days he would leave this "sorry asshole" poking around in his blankets all day, as long as he showed up for roll call and took care of the duties dispensed him by the state. Redford was disgusted that his job now entailed trying to make this low-life enjoy his day off. He took this job to make sure a criminal paid his debt to society, and on this day he was instead forced to insist that a full-grown man come down and eat a Thanksgiving supper that the state paid extra for.

"Daniel, you better be fucking sick, or I am sending your ass to the hole. You listen to my goddamn orders!" said Redford

Daniel remained completely and totally non-plussed, instead fixated on his determination to hate himself.

Redford knew he delivered an idle threat. The state had taken that from him too, the ability to confine the rebellious and naysayers in the bleakest of dungeons without expressed written consent of his superiors. It was pathetic. In an institution designed for discipline, the prisoner had now reached a point where they had a choice in whether he'd listen to an officer. Redford shook his head as he knew the circumstances of the shifting of the Overton Window, to this new world bent on helping every hurt puppy it sees. Daniel would do whatever he damn well pleased on Thanksgiving for the state said it was his, and there was nothing Redford could do about it.

"Fine Daniel, but you better bet I'll work that pathetic fucking body of yours like you never have before tomorrow. I'll make goddamn sure of that," said Redford as he poked the chest of Daniel with his baton.

Daniel eventually joined the other prisoners in the rec yard and tossed a ball to the flashing leather of Simon. The old man didn't move as well as he used to, and he often joked about the deterioration of the body. He found it extremely amusing how life has this tendency to endow one with so much capability when one is young, only to have it stripped away when one finally becomes wise enough to properly maintain that most beloved machine, the human body. At fifty years old he was already beginning to feel the onset of senescence, from the discovery of the lining underneath his once beaming eyes to the way his arm that once had an eighty mile an hour fastball was beginning to wing forward with less and less vigor. It felt like life itself was draining from him as time began to take things away from him. His fastball, his speed around the base pads in the prison yard games he and Daniel would play in, now realizing there are more important things than some little ball snapped between two pieces of flashing leather. Simon's mama died years ago, his oldest boy Austin was heading off to college, and within the past couple years his wife Juanita had left him. It was hard to believe one could smile looking at fifteen years spent behind frigid bars, and more, looking at what little was left when a van finally pulled one out of this entrapment, but Simon somehow managed to find a smile. On this Thanksgiving, Simon was thankful for the friendship of Daniel Westboro.

Meanwhile, Daniel also felt the pull of time on his body. His lankiness had been eliminated as the metabolism and activity level of a seventeen year old major league bound pitcher had disappeared and had been replaced by a thirty-two-year-old man down on his luck. Daniel tried hard to keep in the shape of an athlete, and had worked the entire time since he got stuck in prison on making his way back to the national stage when he got out, but as usually happens to the incarcerated, two forces strained and perhaps eliminated such a dream.

Time and complacency. Time whittled away at the pristine bands of long and tough muscle fiber that rippled in his forearms and pushed back the shoulders of his jersey, and the life of looking at a number of years between himself and freedom had worn away at the drive and the passion. Daniel remembered that day in the prison rec yard throwing with Simon Juarez six years ago, when for the first time he felt nothing on the mound. No happiness, no sadness, no rage. In fact, Daniel thought perhaps on that July day that he was bored. On his thirtieth birthday, he faced harsh reality that perhaps baseball would never be his career, that maybe mama wouldn't look down from heaven and see the Westboro name printed on the back of a blue jersey for the Texas Rangers, and that maybe, just maybe, he would have to do something he never really intended on doing and grow up. It was depressing then, but at this point Daniel had accepted his reality. He studied with the Jaycees and developed quite a mind for business, thinking that when he got out he would be some kind of salesman or

something. It didn't have the same ring as "the man
they trembled at the sight of" named West, who when
he climbed that 20 inch high mountain towered over
the rest, but it was something. It was the future. It
was what has always happened to all old men who
decide they are, time took things away.

Chapter 49:

Back in LeHigh County that Friday, things
were much the same for most of the town as Sheriff
LaGrange began moving into the office that was
finally his. Robert Westboro had succumbed to being
an old man, and felt himself incapable of properly
enforcing the law in this little county.
Arteriosclerosis, diabetes, and arthritis began to wear
at the hardened man, and it was with a heavy heart
that Robert Westboro handed the office to Deputy
LaGrange; the boy the good sheriff told them would
uphold the laws of God and man to the utmost of his
capabilities.
They pitied the old man, he had lost his wife,
both his sons, and now he was at the threshold of
death where no longer he would have family to
mourn his passing which seemed to be approaching
ever closer by the day. It was a hard life for Robert
Westboro, having one son who killed the prom queen
and another that ran away. With hushed voices
people discussed the shaking of his hands and how
the stress and strain of losing his family so early
seemed to be wearing away at his body. His once
powerful voice had become a sort of crackle, a cane
in his once massive hands supported the frame of
his aging body, and one couldn't help but think
maybe the smile that so often came out when
children came up to say hi to "Sheriff Robert" before
he would produce a piece of candy was just an image

to give them the false reassurance that he was alright.

Still, it was a happy day for Samuel LaGrange as the chairs and books he owned were being carried in by a gracious city hall staff that prepared the new office for their new sheriff who would be the first to conduct business in the new addition to city hall. He was welcomed with open arms as the man who would continue to enforce the law in the way Robert did. Not to mention, his wife Anna was easy on the eyes.

A long blonde girl from the southern reaches of Texas; she was as good as the first lady to these people who seemed to honor this man of the law as if he were the president himself. Her glowing blue eyes and radiant smile paired well with the likes of Samuel LaGrange who had changed from a boy fresh out of school into a man. LaGrange smiled at all the people who greeted him by name and gave him tokens of gratitude like free coffee and donuts.

Behind these closed doors, he found himself rather saddened to realize he would be without his mentor and colleague Robert, the man he had come to hold in reverence for delivering him an education in law enforcement that stuffy books and classrooms did not. He found himself alone that night with the old desk of Robert in front of him and little else, except the sound of his own thoughts in the autumn quiet of city hall. Samuel took several postures trying to decide which one was best for the photograph the papers would be taking tomorrow, and out of curiosity went shuffling through the drawers to find the last of Robert's belongings. The usual suspects of paper clips, pens, and mini-calendars with scantily clad and buxom women adorning them were produced. Samuel thought he'd found everything until his knuckle came in contact with a weird ridge at the bottom of one drawer which wasn't at the bottom of the identical one on the other side. In his curiosity, he moved his fingers across it and jostled the distinctive node. He then felt the shifting of the bottom of the drawer.

"Hmm, that's strange," he thought.

Samuel LaGrange, being the officer he was, continued his sleuthing until the cover lifted. It appeared it was some sort of secret drawer that not even Westboro had been fully aware of. There were random pieces of lint, hair, and pieces of parking tickets that Samuel knew were probably documents Robert tore to bits after he got whatever teenage driver that happened to be speeding to promise not to do it again. Then he found a tissue.

"Jesus, Robert, clean up a little bit," said LaGrange as he chuckled pulling the napkin out. Red stains seemed to wrap the napkin and it looked like the remnants of a bloody nose, but a black B was clearly legible when examined in the right light. So, at the risk of exposing himself to aged mucus, LaGrange carefully opened the tissue with a pair of latex gloves, being careful to minimize the tearing as it unfolded.

Unwrapped and clearly saying what he thought it did, Samuel ran to the phone and dialed the boys in Austin.

Chapter 50:

Benjamin Crawford was at the Dallas International Airport shooting the bull with his teammates when a sudden rush of officers entered the airport.

"Shit, this ain't somethin' you see every day," said Ben to the second baseman standing next to him.

"Put your hands up!" shouted an officer now pointing his gun in the face of Benjamin to the surprise of all his teammates, and those in the airport that stared at the commotion with the constables taking place in the main lobby.

"What fer sweetheart?" asked Ben jokingly as he extended his hands to the air at the orders of the officer.

"Benjamin Crawford, you are under arrest for the rape and murder of June Winters."

Camera shutter flashes sparked from the laminate floor tiling while Benjamin was being cuffed and Mirandized.

Chapter 51:

"All rise for the honorable Judge Taylor," said the bailiff.

On this day in December, with Christmas shopping taking place outside the walls of the courtroom, Benjamin Crawford, in an orange jumpsuit, sat beside his attorney, Jerry Tiner. Jerry had gone to Harvard and while there he became thoroughly educated in the law. He was as much a superstar in the realm of criminal defense as Ben was a star on the ball diamond.

What typically took students eight years of continuous effort took the incredibly gifted Tiner four to accomplish. From that day forward, he was seen heading the legal defense of some of the most notable cases of the day from multi-billion dollar corporate fraud cases to freeing the accused from crimes he convinced the jury they simply could not have committed. From arson to wire fraud, Jerry had handled it all. Today, in the interest of saving his best friend from prison, Tiner was in the LeHigh County courtroom, the first time Jerry Tiner had been back to this little blip between Abilene and Amarillo since high school.

"You may all be seated," said Judge Taylor as the multitude of reporters and citizens remained standing to observe the nightmare they all thought had concluded fifteen years ago.

"We are here today to hear the case of Benjamin Crawford vs. The State of Texas as related to the murder of June Winters," said Judge Taylor.

"The jury has been selected and informed of their instructions as to how to proceed with the discussions at this hearing. I will let it be known now that no cameras will be allowed inside my courtroom, and I will remind the jurors once again that discussing the case or any evidence related to it outside of this courtroom is strictly prohibited. I know the visibility of these proceedings, but I will not bend justice to accommodate public whims of wanting to view this trial. Counsel, do you have any opening statements?"

"Yes we do, your Honor," said Jerry Tiner.

"Understanding the propinquity of this trial to the hearts of many in this community and nation, I would like to make them aware this foudroyant espousing of accusations against my client may beleaguer him presently, but it is not to be expected that the imprimatur of this great and honorable court will be bestowed upon any documentation besides the stationery to pronounce the impeccable character of Benjamin Crawford as continuing to be wholly and completely unfettered. This trial is about the murder of a girl named June Winters, who was killed at a time when my client was penurious in all senses of the word. As he is upon this day, Benjamin Crawford was a good man with not a single villainous component of his physiological or psychological being. A man who upon the death of Mary June Winters was identified by his parents as slumbering at home, while the likes of the man already tried and convicted by this court, I may add, was obscure in nature, with no sufficient evidence that can conclude what he was doing that fateful night, beyond the procured bat and hat that belonged to the aforementioned convict. That is to say, a guilty plea was made for this crime and through this and the following hortatory, I hope the jury can clearly see that the blood of Mary June Winters may not be placed upon the hands of Benjamin Crawford, and furthermore observes that this very proceeding is a complete and utter waste of time," said Jerry Tiner in his refined vocabulary.

"Okay," said Judge Taylor. "Are there any opening statements that the prosecution would like to make?"

"Yes, there are, Your Honor," said John Zachary. John had also graduated from law school, but with not near the success of Jerry Tiner. Instead he graduated from the University of Texas on the "C's get degrees" track of college life. Still, much as he was years ago, the new district attorney of LeHigh County found himself in this courtroom dressed in a cheap patched up suit and disheveled hair. The idea of disorganization emanating from his body, and further suggested by the stack of papers he had thus far dropped three times, he was now prosecuting for the first time an actual case with implication.

"See, Your Honor, I know that there's all this song and dance from the defense shouting that justice was served, but I refuse to accept the guilty plea of Mr. Daniel Westboro as the end of this case," he trailed off as he drank some water to calm his quavering voice.

"I know the defense is well-educated and well-allowed by the Constitution, but I think justice will be served correctly if this ruling is reversed. The state believes it has found sufficient evidence to convince the jury that the first convening of this court was wrong," said District Attorney Zachary.

Several minor witnesses were thrown back and forth between the questioning and cross-examining of each lawyer over the course of days, when finally Jerry Tiner said, "We would like to bring Robert Westboro to the stand."

"Mr. Westboro, do you swear to tell the truth, the whole truth, and nothing but the truth, so help you God?" asked the bailiff.

"Yes," said the aged Robert Westboro.

"Robert was Daniel Westboro a problem youth?" asked Tiner.

"Yes."

"Would you describe the actions of Daniel as violent?"

"Yes."

"In what ways did he harm you?"

"He used to hit me in his anger."

"Was he known to be violent while angry?"

"Yes, he got in trouble at school for it all the time."

"And would you, Mr. Westboro, be willing to believe that Daniel may have been the killer?"

"Yes," said Robert with disappointment in his voice, as the whole of LeHigh and all reporters in the courtroom caught sight of the sheriff speaking against his son.

"And do you think, knowing the clear rumors of Mary June Winters sexual immorality leading up to her death, that Daniel would have the capacity to be a killer? That he would have clear motive to kill his lover?"

"Yes," said Robert looking even more saddened.

"No further questions, your honor," finished Jerry Tiner.

"Mr. Westboro, are you a man that likes to drink?" asked John Zachary as he stood up and futilely tried to groom his off kilter hair.

"Yes, a little bit," said Robert.

"Would you perhaps say an alcoholic?"

"No."

"Mr. Westboro, are you aware how much alcohol you have bought the past 25 years?"

"Objection! Your honor, this is irrelevant," said Jacob Tiner looking agitated.

"Overruled, but get on with it Mr. Zachary," said Judge Taylor.

"In your bank records, we found an outstanding debt of $10,000 to Jackson Crawford with a majority of that balance coming from liquor sales. What the state is wondering is how did you repay such a large debt in such a short amount of time when the month prior your savings balance was $0?"

"Objection! Your honor, this has absolutely nothing to do with the case! How can you allow someone to fill your courtroom with such unnecessary air?" asked Tiner.

"Overruled, Mr. Zachary, you may continue," said Judge Taylor.

"Mr. Westboro, please answer the question," said Zachary.

Robert was stunned. He couldn't believe what was happening to him. All eyes gazed at him as people waited for the good sheriff to deny any nefarious actions, but he was cornered. John Zachary had him before the eyes of God and all of LeHigh sweating nervously as he spoke his answer.

"I stole it from the bank," said Robert.

"All of it, I forced their hands to repay the loan," said Robert as the crowd gasped and his head went into his shaking hands.

"No, you didn't," said John Zachary.

"There is no evidence of any transfers taking place between your finances and Jack Crawford besides the elimination of a debt which Jack consented to in notary. Mr. Westboro, why did Mr. Crawford write off your debts?"

"Your Honor, this is inflammatory. I refuse to watch my witness be badgered," said Tiner.

"Mr. Zachary, are you going anywhere within ten miles of this case or are you trying to bring up an entire new lawsuit? Because I might have to uphold Mr. Tiner's objection if you don't get somewhere soon," said Judge Taylor.

"Your Honor, jury, and the guests of the courtroom, the state has sufficient evidence to prove that Jack Crawford forgave the debt three days after the murder of June Winters. This would be ignored, except for the fact that exhibit A, the tissue with "Ben did it" written in Black Sharpie, and semen with DNA identifiable to that of Benjamin Crawford, was found in the desk of Robert Westboro, in a compartment located in the bottom of a drawer in his desk he said he didn't even know existed. However, considering the shelving was not an original feature of the piece of furniture, it is deducible that Robert installed the "secret compartment" himself, and was fully aware of it. Mr. Westboro, did you or did you not hide the bloody tissue in your desk from the authorities that came to investigate the scene where June Winters was killed?"

Robert Westboro looked forward with a snarl.

"Your honor, this is highly speculative and clearly badgering the witness," said Jerry Tiner.

"Sustained, Mr. Zachary you will not launch any speculations in my courtroom," said Judge Taylor.

"Bullshit, Your Honor! Robert Westboro clearly hid the incriminating document in order to save the son of Jackson Crawford from paying for the crime of the murder of June Winters! Mr. Westboro, did you hide evidence to protect Benjamin Crawford from suffering the penalty of the law for the crime he had committed?" asked John Zachary. The bailiffs prepared to remove at least one of the individuals from the courtroom as all present could feel the palpable tension and anger.

"Fuck you, you little prick!" said Robert. He stood from the witness stand and ran at John Zachary with the jagged edge of his water glass that he shattered on the front part of the lectern. His old achy muscles and bones fired in a fashion that only adrenaline could bring about as he chased after John Zachary. The bailiff, who sprang into action in response to this violent chase, had a hard time grabbing onto the old man and preventing him from attacking the District Attorney. After Robert was cleared from the courtroom, John Zachary unveiled the DNA lab report that was never released during the first trial which was also traceable to a bribe by Robert Westboro of the forensics department to create a fake lab report indicating Daniel's DNA was the only DNA present. The honest report showed that the DNA of Benjamin Crawford was found on both the cap and bat that belonged to Daniel Westboro as well as fingerprints on the gun in Daniel's car that was used to shoot June. The trial may have not been over for no verdict was read yet, but the jury had heard enough and deliberated for a mere fifteen minutes before the foreman said,

"On behalf of the people of LeHigh County, we find the defendant, Benjamin Crawford, guilty for the rape and murder of Mary June Winters."

Chapter 52:

The course of the following weeks brought about several events consequent of the results of Crawford's conviction. The beloved sheriff of LeHigh was revealed to be nothing like the man that they wanted to believe in. Old lovers came forward and spoke of his promiscuous behavior he participated in while Mrs. Westboro was still alive, and old teammates of Daniel's appeared from the woodwork to record on microphone their observations of the frequent bruising and cutting on the person of Daniel Westboro.

Coach Carlson, who after years of being persecuted by the community for being the man that so violently assaulted Robert, was finally understood. His tale finally seemed more believable than the one Robert always told; the one where Carlson allegedly pounded on him in a drunken stupor and was forgiven because "he was good to the kids".

Ruth and Kyle Hart were once again respected by people instead of being viewed as a couple of softies who sided with Daniel because their first born son was practically a brother of his.

The legal system went to work as Robert Westboro was sentenced to 20 years in prison for his role in obstructing justice and keeping Daniel locked away. Furthermore, a deeper investigation as to his handling of crime showed a long history of corruption as multiple cases of theft were thrown out shortly after upticks in the margin of Robert's bank account, and certain assault cases were dismissed as domestic disputes from the same cast of characters.

Enemies of Robert in high school just happened to get the fullest penalty of the law from the bench of Judge Brown, and his friends usually incurred no losses whatsoever. For that, Judge Brown, who had then presided over the federal district five court, was summarily removed from office in a 100-0 vote in the senate, a vote which served more as a formality than anything else for it was clear that the Judge had violated the one clause of his employment which demanded that he operate "in good behavior".

Jack Crawford lost his restaurant and received a short sentence for his crime in paying off the sheriff to hide evidence. He was left by his wife Judy, and he'd never return to Holt for no man continued to respect him. He would serve a prison sentence as well for bribing a government official and for aiding a fugitive of the law, along with a host of other tax evasion crimes.

It was also discovered that Robert had paid off the director of the statewide manhunt he had very publicly ordered for, for the search of his son David. People felt a bitter taste in their mouths as they thought back to the situation where they imagined Robert and his glistening crocodile tears and how he would cry for the cameras to show the mourning he experienced for "his lost son." To this effect, people deemed him the lowest of the low scoundrels. Of all the sins of the man who most clearly sinned in every walk of life when someone wasn't looking over his shoulder, the idea that a man would pay to be rid of his last-born son and go on to pilfer the money from several donation drives in the interest of finding him again to finance his alcohol habit was outright despicable. It vitalized the innermost sections of the collective penetralia of LeHigh when the citizens thought of the pain they all thought that Robert experienced and how much it moved them to think of a man they thought was down on their luck, only to be proven incorrect all these years later.

After the court proceedings, Robert would never apologize for what he did. He would never have the chance to. On Christmas day, the day before his final sentencing hearing, Robert Westboro was found slumped in his bathtub with a twenty-two caliber round in his head and the soft swooning of an Andy Williams Christmas album playing in the background. In the rusted out porcelain, that one could find in only the deepest recesses of the deepest corner of the most tired house in all of LeHigh County, sat a coward who would never pay his debt to society but rather accelerate his sure condemnation to the pits of Hell. The man all had loved so much in life became a decrepit and despised pile of deteriorated bone and flesh in his death.

Robert Westboro's ashes were buried in a pauper's funeral officiated by Pastor Thomas, and for the sake of police custom in LeHigh, attended by Samuel LaGrange. Pastor Thomas kept the service short and said little of note beyond the hope that God would forgive him for all he did wrong. Deputy LaGrange walked away glad to be freely departed from the man and drove back to the Sheriff's office seconds after the conclusion of Thomas' oratory on the life of a man who fooled everyone.

"O God, by whose mercy the faithful departed find rest, send your holy Angel to watch over this grave. Through Christ our Lord."

Daniel stood up and was walking back to his car when Pastor Thomas approached and said, "Daniel, are you sure you're alright?"

"Yes, I am," responded Daniel, the years making an impact on his voice.

"Are you sure?"

Daniel paused and looked to the puffy clouds above the cemetery with too many familiar names, and pondered whether he should tell his pastor the truth. To most, this appeared the redemption that Daniel had been searching for his whole life, the final opportunity to watch the man who hated him plummet deep into this Texan soil never to be seen again. To many, this appeared the chance for Daniel to watch all the bad things in his life go away, and in some ways this looked like the end of the story.

But life doesn't work that way.

When Daniel looked in that grave, he saw the one man he wanted to make peace with, for if he could ever find a way to love him, he would find a way to love himself. He thought if he could ever win the pride of his father, he would be happy. Daniel did not love his father when he died. That is what bothered him. He felt that he failed. That is what was killing him.

"Father, I swear, I'm fine," insisted Daniel.

"Just know, Daniel, that it wasn't your fault. That God loves you and will always keep you close to his heart," said Pastor Thomas.

"Father, that is straight bullshit! If God loves me, then why in the hell am I here! Why am I a 32-year-old man that has not a single tangible skill for the real world?! If fucking God has got my ass like you say he does, and I am so close to his damn heart, then why did he do this shit to me?" asked Daniel, clearly infuriated by the prior fifteen years of wrongful imprisonment for a crime he didn't commit. He was outraged at the years he lost thinking he was a nefarious man as much as the years he concluded that he was violent and lost the love of his life because he killed her. The question was fueled by this fiery passion and hatred for being put behind iron bars for something that the man that was once his best friend did.

"Daniel, I have no words. All I have is faith and I know it is challenging to see sometimes what the grand devise of the Lord is, but sometimes we must accept it. Sometimes, h e has plans for us we will never understand, and I have no idea why he would test you so," said Pastor Thomas.

"Fuck that! Nobody would do this to anyone. If this is what your "god" deems is right, then I don't want a fucking part of it!" shouted Daniel.

"Daniel-"

"What? Am I supposed to be thankful for what has been done to me? Am I supposed to be goddamn happy that June is gone? Maybe throw a whole fucking celebration because I have not a single friend in this world," said Daniel as he looked at the urn, "and I don't even get the chance to tell him I forgive him. Father, you couldn't understand, but I can't believe this bullshit anymore. I'm done."

Daniel pulled shut the door of his car as the eighty-year old pastor watched a previously devoted and loyal member of his congregation go elsewhere.

He had no words, for there simply weren't any. So, Pastor Thomas left the graveyard, and when he got home prayed for Daniel to find his way. At the same time, the good pastor wondered himself if his prayers would ever be answered.

Chapter 53:

Daniel tried to work his way back into the community, but the transition was not smooth by any stretch of the imagination. People looked at him with a curious eye and questioned what his next action would be. The eyes that gazed upon Daniel were reminiscent of the glances imposed upon wild beasts encased in the concrete and glass of zoo walls. They made superficial glances at his much changed complexion and mistook the roughness for guilt, and the sad droop of his eyes for regret. Like some sort of creature, they examined the specimen of Daniel Westboro and saw a man that had undergone the metamorphosis wrought by serving time in a prison. As the caterpillar enters the chrysalis as a worm and departs from the silk confines as a beautiful butterfly, so did Daniel emerge from his own cocoon made by the cohesive water and aggregates of Alfred D. Hughes as a cold hardened man from the lively optimistic boy he was.

It is noted in biology that most butterflies enter the world near a flower, or some sort of sustenance to nurture themselves appropriately into this new stage of life. But Daniel was not entered into this world near all the nectar like the aforementioned lucky bug. Instead, he was brought out with work restrictions, background checks, and prejudice for his existence among those who still believed the gunslinger named West did it. Doors would slam in his face with ease and old friends would pretend he simply didn't exist anymore. The few who tried to reconnect with him felt disconnected by all the years that had passed. Like a dove released from a cage, he originally found the absolute joy that comes with having bars come undone about you, but quickly realized the true lack of sunshine and roses in the cold cruel world. Daniel may have found freedom, but justice had destroyed him. No company wanted a man who's only real occupation the past fifteen years had been scrubbing toilets and lifting weights. No friend of a criminal that did something as cruel as Daniel was accused could remain one. The simple fact he had been accused meant several decided they could not associate with a man that evil ever again, and the few sympathetic would quickly be brought to that persuasion to avoid the persecution of the community.

Here in Holt, Texas there was nothing for Daniel Westboro except this house that belonged to his father, the house where he had last felt the embrace of his mother's loving arms before she left that fateful day so many years ago. The house where hallways formed magnificent spaceships traversing the galaxy when he and David had played, and where he had read the letters from the multitude of people interested in his right arm so many years ago. Sadly, no mortgage payment could be paid in memories, nor restructured by reminiscences. In inheritance, Daniel did not get a single dime from his passed father, only the long ledger lines bleeding profusely of red ink, and the name on the title of this house that contributed mightily to it. Daniel had no future in this city, in this house, or with all these people. Only a past.

Daniel had come home after a long day knocking on every business' door and ended just where he started. People who had loved him now hated his mere presence, and even more hurtful were those who tried to pretend he wasn't a man. The judgmental stares and personalities of this community thoroughly united in hatred had made it clear to Daniel he was no longer welcome. He no longer had anything to call home. But Daniel was tired. He didn't have time to think of all the people who hated him.

No, for now Daniel would sleep on this tattered old couch. Together they would look a perfect embodiment of one another.

Chapter 54:

Meanwhile, in happier parts of the world, David Westboro awoke from his slumber and slipped into fleece pants and a t-shirt with "Rebels" written across the front in bold lettering, the blue letters accented in their block fashion with a logo for the Lake City Rebels baseball program behind the letters. A tall green tree stood in the living room of the house which was perfectly sized for the little family of fate, and upon the branches were ornaments with everything from "Freedom Oklahoma" to "Miami Marlins" written on the sides of the spheres that encompassed just about every cause, destination, and date important to the Clubbers.

It is a wonder why people buy these little glass balls, why these decorations are manufactured and then paid for by people, why something so insignificant can be seen as a necessity in a world where we often feel so depleted of monetary resources. To someone like David, these glass balls meant everything in the world. All was right and good with the world when he was within spitting distance of the Osceola National Forest, for in these simple and quiet walls of Jacob and Sarah Clubber, David found love. He found hope. He found peace from everything he came from and a destination to everywhere he could go. At 25 years old, David found this part of Christmas to be the best one. Getting up early and watching Sarah Clubber busily prepare a turkey for company that would be coming later, watching his dog Spike beg for the gizzards and neck, and smelling the notoriously strong coffee made by Sarah on Christmas morning to power through the day were all special in their own perfect ways. David swore he could feel his entire body lift from the ground when he thought of what this day meant to him, and overlooking from the bannister on the edge of the staircase a warm smile spread across his face.

"Christopher, I don't care how much beggin' you do, you ain't gettin' a single one of those cookies until the rest of them are here," said Mrs. Clubber.

"It's all good, you need any help Mrs. Clubber?" said David.

"Well, if you can keep yourself from eating all of it, I have got some brownies that need frosting," said Mrs. Clubber, who felt like telling David once again her name was Sarah, but this time resisted saying anything for she knew she wouldn't change him.

Sarah watched the 6'2" 190 pound man standing in her kitchen and looked at him in the way mothers do when they look at their children and don't want to show them their adoration. Much like a mother smiles softly at her boy behind his back as he brings home a muddied set of clothing after an afternoon of rambunctious play, or a bouquet of dandelions picked from the backyard, Sarah smiled at him. Sarah knew that her boy had grown up, but still loved the displays of innocence in a kid that took care of his mother. Sure, she may have been wary of this dirty boy plucked off the plains of North Texas by her husband without consulting her, but she'd come to love David as one of her own. David was a sweet boy, who had difficulties getting along with the other kids at first, but had become quite a gentleman.

"Mrs. Clubber, who all is coming?" asked David.

"All of the Clubbers today," said Sarah.

David was very excited to have all of his family arrive at the house today. He thought of the fun that would take place telling his cousins, aunts, and uncles about what coach said about possibly being called up to the Majors next year after a successful season at Triple-A. He looked forward to playing cards with the men of the Clubber family and being teasingly referred to as "Big Shot" and "Hollywood." David would feast heartily upon Sarah's cooking on this day, and not regret the gross overconsumption of calories that took place during family holidays outside of the baseball season. It was one of the few times he was allowed to indulge in life like "normal people", and it made him feel gratified in the rewarding feeling of being surrounded by good people and good food. Christmas brightened David's face like no other thing.

David then heard a doorbell ring and left his duties to welcome their beloved guests. He wrapped his arms around each individual member hoisting the children into the air in grand bear hugs which made them giggle as they reached a height that tall men were well aware of, but the vertically ungifted were not. The altitude pleased them while the feeling of someone who loved him against his chest and in his arms made him melt on the inside. David would hug everyone who entered those doors extremely hard for he knew what not having that ability felt like, and because of that, he held on to Christmas with all the might in his muscular forearms.

On that day that David Westboro celebrated Christmas with his family.

Chapter 55:

Coach Carlson awoke from his slumber, and hoisted his cancer-ridden body from the bed he'd purchased for this little house so many years ago that he never thought he would be dying in. Regardless, John Carlson was at a point where he couldn't think of what he didn't do anymore, for old men have too many memories to begin analyzing them towards the end of their lives. It was for that reason that John Carlson did not think about his former dreams, but rather the rest of the day ahead of him.

Last year when he was diagnosed, he finished the season, and then, and only then, he told his team he had but perhaps a year or two to live. He had to. A man must tell the most important people in his life when things like that happen, and so he did his duty. There were no tears. There was no grandstanding. He spoke in that Coach Carlson way of his and told the straight truth.

"Boys, I don't want you to remember me for this," he said.

"It would mean a lot to me if I could just live in your memories as a man that I hope made you all a little better than you were before. That and I just want you all to know a little something, now that I'm old enough to be right about everything," said Carlson as some nervous chuckles broke out among the boys.

"Whatever your dream is, chase it. I want you to run after it and grab it with both hands so goddamn tight that you can't tell the white of your knuckles from the top of the clouds. Keep your eyes plastered to that son of a bitch and never take them off of it, for there is nothing more valuable than having something to wake up for. One day you're going to wake up and be forty years old and swear just yesterday you were listening to this crusty old codger barking orders at you, and you're going to wonder what the hell was wrong with you for wanting to keep coming back. You're going to look at those hands of yours with the callouses still well-worn into the palms, and then you will remember why. You'll remember your teammates. You'll remember your games. If you're like me, you'll look at kids like you and wish that God gave old men just one more chance to do it all over again because you want to be out there under those lights. They told me I'm going to die. So what? At least I can say I lived happily having the privilege to call you all my sons," said Carlson as tears started to break across his player's faces.

"I loved every damn minute of it, and I hope you can say the same," said Carlson.

When Carlson awoke this morning though, he could feel the disease eating him, and the sneaking in of self-pity for his condition. It may have been some cellular process where his cells engaged in mitosis at an inappropriate pace and only a microscopic cross-section of him could reveal the true destruction, but like the many stricken by the horrible disease before him, he could feel the weakness setting in. He didn't move the way he used to, his body was being robbed of mass, and his complexion had mostly faded away. Pale and thin, Coach John Carlson was a shell of the man he once was. He fought hard, but it was becoming clear that the fight was lost, that the years of tobacco had destroyed him, and that's what pained him.

The cigarettes were like a staircase of death, they told him. Although he finally purged himself of the guilty pleasure, the risk of lung cancer remained elevated to the floor he left at. The 30-year habit he had before he finally separated from the most unrequited of loves was what brought him to the state he was in right now.

Carlson went to church that Sunday morning like always, and like always endured the strange glares of the children who could see the ailment destroying him. It wasn't their fault, they could never know how their stares would make him feel, but he always viewed their rude peerings as more respectable than their parents' attempts to conceal their spying. Carlson sat in the back of the church and looked for Daniel all morning. He had heard he was still in town and thought for sure that he could find him here, for what else could he be doing on a Sunday? But, Coach Carlson did not see Daniel that Sunday morning and proceeded back to his car to check around town. Carlson went to Dee's which in the absence of Crawford's had become the only bar in town. When he got inside, he saw West in the back corner nursing a beer with what was presumably his last dollar in his right hand, thoroughly intoxicated already.

"Long time, no see, West," grunted Carlson.

"Coach?" asked Daniel. He looked up shocked to observe the man he hadn't seen for so long before his very own eyes.

"Well, are you going to make me buy my own goddamn drink, West?" said Carlson jokingly as he struggled into the booth across from him, chuckling the entire time.

"Of course not, Coach! Dee, one more round for me and my friend here!" said Daniel.

"Actually, make that one for him. I'm good," said Daniel correcting himself, realizing that Carlson's drink was the only thing he could afford.

"So, how's life on the outside?" said Carlson in his best imitation of Al Capone.

"Pretty goddamn great, pretty goddamn great," said Daniel as he handed over his last dollar bill to the barkeep. "You know what the best part of being out of there is?"

"What?"

"I can take a piss whenever the hell I want. Shit, I could go right now and no one could stop me," said Daniel.

"Well, Dee might not appreciate it that much. I hear she mops these floors every once in a while," said Carlson loud enough for the namesake waitress to hear him.

"Rumor has it she sometimes brings the customer's beer over for him, too," said Carlson laughing at his wit.

"You might be the only man in LeHigh that thinks you're funny, Coach," said Dee as she placed the beer in front of him.

"Damn, ain't you being a sweetheart? That's one more than usual."

"You know, it ain't right to swear on Sundays, Coach," said Dee to the crusty old man in his red-checkered shirt.

"Well, I guess you're right... I'm really fucking sorry," said Carlson in a sarcastic apologetic voice which accented the foul language intentionally as Dee continued to roll her eyes and Daniel continued to try and suppress his laughter.

"Maybe you two should get married," said Daniel.

"That would be great for him, I think he owes me more money than anyone else in this whole county by now," said Dee.

"Nonsense, she just knows I am more man than she could ever handle," said Carlson as he chuckled a little more.

Dee walked away with a slight tick of a grin. As much as she and Carlson made fun of each other, he truly was the only customer she had that she could shoot the bull with. That and when among conversationalists like Dee and Carlson, wit and inappropriateness were two things that enhanced dialogue, and Dee couldn't help but have the hinting in the back of her mind of what misery there would be when Carlson finally kicked the can.

Carlson watched her walk back up to the counter to resume putting together silverware before he looked back at Daniel and began speaking to him again.

"Well, West, I'm gonna talk straight with you. Doc says I only have a year or two left, and I ain't got much but I want you to have this," said Carlson as he pulled a pocketknife out of his coat.

"What is this?" asked Daniel.

"It's a knife I got from my pops. I'm not gonna get all gushy or nothin', but I think you should have it," said Carlson pushing the knife closer to Daniel's hands.

"I wanna know about that curveball of yours, too," said Carlson.

"Why?" asked Daniel.

"Because I got a friend that owes me a couple of favors and I think I could give you something, if you're willing to go get it," said Carlson.

"Coach, you're making no sense," said Daniel.

"I mean, I know a guy that coaches single A out west, can you still throw?" asked Carlson pushing the matter.

"Coach, I don't think you understand, I can't anymore. I'm too old, I won't make it and I just need to get a job. I need to move on with my life," said Daniel.

"I appreciate the offer, though," he added sincerely.

Carlson drummed his fingers on the bar table. He looked around for a short time, but knowing what little time he had left he thought it best not to waste it, and instead began speaking to Daniel again.

"Look, Daniel, I know you ain't the typical kid they're gonna look at for this, but I know it's your dream. You worked harder than any kid I ever coached and you gave every team I saw you on more than they deserved of you. I'm giving you the last of what I can give to you, because you deserve it, and it's time someone actually did something for you. You don't have to go, but I'm giving him your name. I want you to be happy, and if it isn't for you, it isn't. Just don't make any decisions you'll regret," said Carlson before he finished his beer.

"Lord knows I have."

Chapter 56:

A phone call rang from downstairs on December 29th, a day of importance to Daniel for two reasons. One, today was the birthday of Mary June Winters, and two, it was two days until the bank would remove him from this house, whether he was prepared to or not. It didn't make much difference to Daniel, however, for he had already liquefied most assets he had left in his possession except the Yugo out front and the guitar that he discovered hidden in the recesses of the attic of this old house.

It was a shame he had never before run into the instrument, for it was Daniel's lifelong aspiration to master the six-string one day. To pluck strings and create life in the dead of the sound, or in better terms, to do as the musician strives and make life just that much more worth living. When he pulled out that old Alvarez from the beaten leather case in the attic, he had reminiscenced about the songs his grandfather used to sing about Sunday morning going down, and the way Felina twirled in the West Texas way. To many guitar players, to scratch a simple tune by Johnny Cash or Marty Robbins was not a great accomplishment, for the songs were composed of perhaps three or four different chords, and the melody was sung over a repetitive and predictable strumming pattern. Daniel, however, could still hear the of out of tune notes and muffled strings, and even this many years later found the beauty that was present in a guitarist who sung about things straight from his heart.

Daniel was sitting on the lonely chair next to the dining table that his mother used to put supper on. When she was alive, supper was never very much, but the thought of her filled his heart and he caught himself thinking back to that time when things seemed so perfectly imperfect. He thought of those days so long ago when he was a ten year old boy wanting to make his mother proud, and she would be so happy to see him succeed, never missing a single game, going to every elementary school choir concert, and kissing him goodnight every night. Daniel wanted to find a way to somehow say all these things, but he lacked in magniloquence and was not attuned to the art of writing a melody. The poetic nature of lyrics eluded him, and he was frustrated by his struggles in trying to write something for her. He knew if she was around, she would want to hear something about herself.

The phone rang and he went to answer it.

"Daniel Westboro residence," he answered.

"This is Jeff Bentley. I was interested in talking to you, Mr. Westboro," said Mr. Bentley.

"I'm sorry, who are you?"

"Jeff Bentley, I am the general manager of the Texas Rangers. I heard from John about you. He said you had nothing better to do, and I'm giving you something I heard you've been short of. I'm giving you an opportunity," said Bentley.

Daniel couldn't believe what he was hearing. He had been removed from the game for so long. How could anyone possibly put faith in him? He was old and a convict, two things he was sure would have precluded him from this offer. Daniel didn't believe Carlson when he told him what he did, and now he felt ashamed that he'd questioned the authenticity of what Coach had told him.

"Look man, I am just calling to see when you're going to come out here, because I need to make arrangements. Have you been keeping in shape in the doghouse?" asked the fast-talking Bentley.

"Yeah," responded Daniel shyly.

"Good, when am I gonna see you out here?" Bentley quickly retorted.

"Um, coach I don't mean to trouble you or anything, but I don't know if I can," said Westboro.

On the other end of the line Jeff Bentley had a pen in one hand with a roster sitting on his desk where he was penning the tentative plans for the team he was going to field the next year. He was preparing to sign the former number one prospect in baseball, and he felt excited being the only manager that even reached out to Daniel and all the negative baggage his notoriety would carry. In fact, he was so excited by the situation that he had already made the decisions necessary to bring this stone-age relic to his ball club, and had also drafted the email to send to the boys in Texas telling them about his pick up. He knew what he was doing was ballsy, for it was uncommon for someone so advanced in baseball years to start a professional career, and even more rare was to find a team willing to sign a fossil like Daniel, but Jeff Bentley saw opportunity for himself to prove his managerial skills. He had a reputation for his high-flying bold decision-making and he thought if Jim Morris could start a major league game at 35, then Daniel Westboro could do the same at 32. The only thing surprising Bentley was that he'd just heard someone turn down one of his phone calls for the first time ever. He responded,

"What was that, Daniel?"

"I said I don't know if I can Mr. Bentley. I don't think there is any hope left for me, and I feel like I've got to move on with my life, sir. I'm done with baseball. I've run out of bullets."

Jeff couldn't believe what he had to go through to try and give a man his chance at the life of professional baseball. Most young boys he called in this same manner already were packing their bags and yelling "Mama!" in the background before the receiver was even hung up. Then again, Daniel was no longer a young boy.

"Look Daniel, I'm a busy man, and I don't have time for chit-chat. I either hear back from you tomorrow, or I fill the spot with someone else. I really don't care which."

Daniel heard the words, processed the situation and responded, "I don't blame you Mr. Bentley, I'm sorry to disappoint you."

"Do you really think I care? It is your loss. Call me back by tomorrow, or I just forget we ever had this conversation."

"Okay Tha-"

"Bye"

Daniel returned the phone to the receiver and pondered the conversation momentarily before once again dismissing it. What the hell was he thinking? Old men don't play baseball. No, that was a game for children. It was a part of the Daniel that was, not the Daniel that is, and he had no reason to answer that rude man. Why would he? Prison had already killed that dream for him, and he was ready to move on from that dream to a new one. Maybe become a salesman, a construction worker like Simon, or better yet, go into business.

"That's it," he thought. He was going to start a company from scratch and sell things. He didn't know what, but he was pretty sure it would be commodities, something like gold or oil or silver or perhaps shares in the trade of these goods. He thought he would make money off the idea of silver, by selling silver certificates. After all, the Jaycees had told him how some of the most boring areas of the market are the most profitable. So Daniel completely dismissed the conversation and found himself chuckling based on the fact he even pondered the idea. What was he going to do? Earn the minor league minimum salary while he treaded water for three years just to conclude that his dream was as dead as he thought before he even started his pointless journey? Really, life wasn't like the movies, he wasn't made to become some sort of Cinderella man. He wasn't anything at all like James Braddock. No, he had his life planned in front of him, and nobody in their right mind would try to fight with the decision of Daniel when he made one.

With his life mapped in front of him, Daniel began pegging away at the exercise he found in a guitar book his grandfather had bought him years prior, a beginners manual where it demonstrated the proper grip of the plectrum and taught him the correct posture. It was a simple song he was learning, a hymn he knew the words to. Daniel was playing Amazing Grace on that old Alvarez, just trying to get his fingers to hit the correct part of the neck at the right time to let the flowing three-four melody pour forth from the instrument. However, he got frustrated.

The guitar was making deadened sounds where his fingers weren't properly holding the string against the fret and it enraged him, for the book was clearly written with a much younger reader in mind. It annoyed him severely that somewhere out in this great big world there is some pretentious child of some privileged family playing this song, and he can't even sum a single note. It annoyed him to think there was a little girl out there that tickled the keys much like his grandmother used to and not only could play this song as written, but probably in any other key someone asked for too. He was frustrated to think of all the people out there with their privilege and how they probably didn't even realize it, how they were probably moaning to their mother that they didn't have the right guitar, lunch was not to their standards, or yelling at their father for getting them the wrong toy train at the most recent Christmas celebration. Rage filled his heart as he thought of the entitlement, and then compared it to everything he had come from. How Daniel wished upon these souls that they saw the mere rags and binds that his soul had entered the world into, how he wished impoverishment upon the wealthy. He viewed that as the only justice that was possible in this world; the whiners deserved to live in as horrendous a condition as they complained.

Furthermore, the thought of this song enraged him as he analyzed what the words were saying. He despised this thing that he now called religious psychobabble, this thing which once swayed him in his shoes and served as a theme song for his love of God, how this did stir the demon of anger within him. Why did he believe in God? What bullshit did he let himself play party to? What caused him to be poisoned so, and why would he worship the same imaginary force of the universe that his father did? Daniel was fuming when he put the Alvarez down and let the riot rise from his soul as he produced the bottle of whiskey hiding in the back corner of the kitchen cupboard and uncorked it.

He guzzled a most full gulp of the spirit wishing it would imbibe him wholly, for he had no desire of this world anymore, nor did he believe that the Lord above would frown upon him for using these mind-altering chemicals. No, Daniel let the spirit enter him, not to quell the spirit of anger but instead to supply it, to give food to the beast which is only satisfied when it consumes a person entirely. He sent his right fist sailing through the wall as he screamed and threw the glassware that was on the counter on to the floor of the house those over-entitled men were taking from him. He kicked the door with such a tremendous force that the thing was freed from the hinges and flung heavily to the Texas soil. Daniel began tearing to shreds the couch that his father used to sleep on and threw the pieces of foam and upholstery to the dirty floor where they piled up only as remnants of something that once was. Daniel continued to consume the liquor as his temper caused him to wreak havoc upon the rest of the house until his drunken self had decided it had enough.

Daniel was done with all this, he was done with all these masquerades, and he would make himself the loser life set him out to be. With that, he grabbed the revolver sitting on the kitchen table and ran upstairs to the bathroom to look at the mirror. He needed to; he felt the only right way to dispose himself of this world was to do just as he had done with his dog and look him straight in the eyes before sending a hot piece of lead through his skull.

"Fucking do it!" he yelled at himself as tears ran down his beat-red face.

"You motherfucking coward, finish the goddamn job!" Daniel's heart was racing as the trigger tightened and he became more pissed off with himself.

"I'm going to count to motherfucking three and you will do it you goddamn pussy!" hollered Daniel as he bit down on the barrel so tight that he could taste steel on his tongue, and feel the coolness of the metal on his front teeth.

Daniel's finger tightened on the trigger. Slowly, slowly now. Death was approaching, death was liberty, it was freedom... how the hell was it taking so long?

And then he stopped.

He looked at himself in the mirror, and saw what he was doing and could only think about his mother. He thought about his brother and what he meant to him and how he promised over her dead body that he would protect him. Daniel decided if he was going to kill himself he needed to ensure that David was alive first, not for himself, but for his mother.

Angrily swiping at tears, Daniel removed his father's service handgun from his mouth and put it on the kitchen sink adjacent to the basin while his hands shook. He balled up his fist and hit the reflective glass shattering the mirror into several pieces. Daniel then went downstairs, and sat at the kitchen table for a good twenty minutes before dialing the number Bentley had left him earlier.

"I'll be there in two days," said West.

Chapter 57:

Simon Juarez was on the streets of El Paso on January 4th, free from the binds of probation, and as long as he obeyed the law, sans some restrictions for former felons, he was a free man. He could come and go as he pleased, and that made him very happy. He was working and paying for school and by all accounts was the man that the world wanted him to become.

Never did Simon envision himself getting a college education. While in prison he had finished several years of his public school education and after being released to find no wife, kids, or pretty much any family to speak of anymore, Juarez went to El Paso to build his dream.

Simon was a man who loved children and his dream was to teach them so they didn't become the same mess of a man he did. He never again wanted to turn on the news to hear some kid caught between a rock and a hard place had committed a crime to support his family, because he was the only one trying anymore.

Simon was not resentful of the justice system for doing what it did to him. His crime was violent and did deserve the penalty imposed upon him. At the same time, he knew if he could've changed things, he would have. Simon never wanted to hurt that poor kid, he just wanted to help his mother and family, and the life of the roughneck means going through droughts of unemployment that the salary simply does not allow. But he was going to do something.

With his new Associate of Arts degree in teaching, Simon had dreams of working at a school like the one he attended in Travis County and unlike his teachers, he was not going to hate his students. No, Simon was going to give his all to his students, and he was going to love them for he knew what it was like to stand in their shoes. He knew the pain of not having enough to eat. He knew the struggle of not having a father to stand up for him. He was all too aware of hustling through life. Unlike the messages on the radio and television that kept endorsing this life of crime and hatred, he would be different and give to students the rare commodity of an instructor who had felt the full plight of giving in. Simon by all accounts was unremarkable in his skill with the English language and an even worse mathematician, but the one thing he did know how to do was stand by his friends and family until they left him.

It is for that reason that when he read the paper in the slum apartment he shared with three other men that his eyes stared so intensely at the headline of the day in the sports section of the El Paso Times. In bold lettering and all caps the line read:

"Daniel Westboro designated for High Desert Mavericks, A Rangers Affiliate"

Simon continued to read the story about his friend and the rediscovery of the famous pitching prospect by Jeff Bentley.

"A man once mired in the mud of murder has been employed by the Texas Rangers in the wake of a sensational once-in-a-lifetime trial where he was betrayed by his closest friend. He is said to be reporting to Adelanto, California within the next couple days, Jim Travis reports," read the vital content of the article.

Simon called over to his friend, "Hey, Jose!"

"What's up, Simon?"

"Did you see this?"

"What?"

"That Daniel kid, you know the one I was in the big house with?"

"No man, that's baseball I don't pay attention to that shit," said Jose chuckling.

"He's playing in the minor leagues."

"So he's getting paid for it?"

"Yes."

"Well, when are we going to start getting checks in the mail?" chuckled Jose.

"Maybe your friend could help out, get enough money for Austin over there to wash his balls every once in a while," laughed Jose as Austin looked at him momentarily and then shrugged knowing how true it was.

"I don't know man, I think that kid will go far," said Simon.

"At 32? He might as well start pumping gas already, Simon," said Jose.

Simon folded the paper and thought about his friend presumably living out his dream, and couldn't help but think back to the hours he and Daniel had played catch in the confines of Alfred D. Hughes. He thought of how much it meant to him when Daniel told him it would all be alright when he left that cage to face life without Juanita, how Daniel used to tell him he should chase his dream, how he was sure Simon could find some way to work with kids, and that he should accomplish that in any way possible, just like his baseball coach used to tell him. Simon thought of how much he could sympathize with Daniel and how both had risen from nothing to the men they were today, especially West's impeccable work ethic that inspired him to finish his education at El Paso Community College. Simon smiled as he filled out the crossword that morning beaming from ear to ear as he was getting prepared to go and interview for a job at a local juvenile detention center that needed a new English teacher. Simon thought deeply about what Daniel had inspired within himself; the will to become successful and live a life beyond the oil rigs, and have purpose beyond watching the drill plummet deeper and deeper into the face of the Earth.

"I don't know man. I think he'll make it," said Simon.

Chapter 58:

Daniel pulled into Adelanto as he was instructed by Bentley to do, and just in time. The moment he crossed the city limits, he heard the timing chain in his Yugo finally go in what appeared to be the excruciating end of his vehicle's life. Steam billowed forth from the hood as Daniel steered it to the shoulder of the road, and when it finally stopped, put it in park.

"Goddammit anyhow!" screamed Daniel. He kicked open the door to go and lift the hood and check what was wrong. Daniel threw the hood up and continued to cuss while pulling out a flashlight to look at the engine and assess the damages.

"Car trouble?" asked a man who had crept upon Daniel.

"Yeah, I think the damn timing chain blew," said Daniel as he kept pointing the light into various crevices and caverns that were visible from the top of the engine block.

"I'd just be glad to have a car like that go on me," said the man looking at the outdated, ugly, and now unusable automobile.

"Me too. What's your name?" asked Daniel as his fingers had found the loose end of the chain.

"Well, she's a goner," the man said as Daniel pulled out the broken car part.

"Why would you say that?" asked Daniel.

"Because these old Yugos have an interference engine. When the belt goes the pistons and poppet valves smack into each other and get absolutely positively ruined," he said.

"Damn, are you a mechanic or something?" asked Daniel.

"No, I'm just as dumb as you for buying a piece of shit like that."

"Hey, at least it is my piece of shit," Daniel retorted.

"Damn straight. Sorry what is your name?"

Daniel told the man his name and discovered that the man's name was Andrew Thompson, a guy from Ohio coming into town for some corporate niceties and paper work or something like that.

"Who do you work for?" asked Daniel.

"I don't work for anyone. I am the most employed jobless man in the world man. I play baseball right here in Adelanto."

"Damn, I guess we're teammates," said Daniel.

"What do you mean," asked Andrew as he raised his prominent athletic shoulders in curiosity.

"I mean I'm in town to sign, too," said Daniel.

"Aren't you kinda old to be in single A?" asked Andrew.

"Ain't you kinda young to be disrespectin' your elders?" asked Daniel as he grinned.

Daniel and Andrew laughed for a little bit and continued their banter.

"You ever heard the story of One Stone?" asked Daniel.

"Why no, I haven't. Regale me, ye olde wise man," said Andrew in his best attempt to sound medieval.

"Well, see there's this caveman, right? And he was born with one testicle. For that, by the namin' customs of the time, his father gave him a name and said 'My son, you shall be named One Stone'. So, he goes through life and everywhere he goes people ask him his name and he always angrily says 'One Stone' while the people of the village laugh knowin' where it came from, you know? And so, one day when he grows to be the strongest man in the whole village he says, 'All you who call me One Stone shall die'. But Blue Bird, a girl in the tribe, thinks she is funny and calls him 'One Stone'. As punishment for her crime, she is taken to the woods by One Stone where he makes love to her night and day, night and day, night and day, until finally she dies from it, and 'One Stone' shows them the body and says 'This is what shall happen to all who disobey my command'. Then a few years pass and Yellow Bird, an old friend of One Stone, comes up and says 'Oh God! Hi, One Stone,' and she is whisked off to the forest with One Stone where he made love to her night and day, night and day, night and day, until finally he could make love no more and Yellow Bird survived. And so the moral of the story is 'You can't kill two birds with One Stone.'"

Andrew fell to the ground laughing at Daniel's joke and once regaining his composure said, "You'd be one to know, bet you and One Stone were best pals through elementary school!"

Andrew was consumed with laughter at his own comment and the old joke that Daniel had once heard from Bob Tiner. Daniel couldn't help but hear Benjamin Crawford laugh in that voice, and for a brief moment, it saddened him to think of what Ben would've done had he been here at this moment. Then he went back to remembering why he hated Crawdaddy and started laughing with great bravado in chorus with Andrew over the course of the evening, trading off-color jokes with each other that typically tied Andrew to recently departing puberty, or Daniel, in the words of Andrew, having no venom left for his own affairs with womankind. It was clear from that day in January, along the road leading into Adelanto, that Andrew and Daniel had become great friends.

It was convenient that both had the same unlikely profession, as Andrew let him climb into his Ford and ride to the front office of the High Desert Mavericks. Andrew parked the car in front of the building and both thought rapidly about what entering those revolving doors meant. For Andrew, it would be the start of a dream, the founding of a new purpose in life, and the beginning of chasing down the lucrative major league contract that spun past his wild eyes for so many years while his long hair stretched behind his sprinting body on the base paths.

For Daniel, this was the resurrection of what he had lost, but he was unsure if he was ready to rise from his crucifixion. Daniel was still unsure, even after the elongated trip that brought him here if what was behind those revolving glass doors was really for him. It may be small-town California League ball, but Daniel couldn't help but think of how vulnerable he was truly making himself. He thought of how old he would be compared to his teammates. He thought of all the years between him and his last start. Furthermore, he thought of how he lost the game for Luke Hart; how much he disappointed all of his fans, teammates, his coach, and most importantly himself when the Abilene Arrows had cut through the center of the lineup and he gave up the one pitch he simply couldn't give up that night.

All of this would be put up to public scrutiny when he signed that piece of paper with his name already typed on it. This was not the glamorous entrance into professional baseball that Daniel envisioned for himself when he was the best prospect in baseball all those years ago, yet, he knew the significance of being among the fraction of a percentage that make it this far. For a moment, he considered leaving that car and never looking at anything that said Adelanto ever again, because if he did, at least he would've played his last game as the best pitcher in state that just didn't have the right stuff on one night; if he were to sign, there was the potential of underperforming and leaving baseball a total disappointment.

"We aren't getting any younger, let's go," said Thompson.

"Alright, you firs'," said West.

West and Thompson walked cautiously through the front entry way and proceeded upstairs to the office of the general manager where Jeff Bentley was waiting.

"Nice to see you could finally show up," said Bentley in a disapproving tone.

"Sorry, Mr. Bentley, had a little car tro-"

"I don't care. Look, here are your contracts. I could read you what it says, but I'm pretty sure you can figure it out," said Bentley.

"Take the calendars on the back page home with you; that is your schedule with the team."

"Than-"

"Bye," said Jeff as he went back to tapping away on his keyboard.

Daniel and Andrew walked out of the office to the front lobby where they unceremoniously signed their contracts pledging their lives and baseball talent to the High Desert Mavericks for at least the next three years. Andrew's eyes lit up bright as the sun staring at that piece of paper that had only one word upon it in his eyes, and that was opportunity. Daniel thought momentarily about the implications of his decisions, and once again found himself pondering the end of his baseball career. But, Daniel felt the lightness of his wallet, and thus the main motivation for Daniel was to once again get paid.

It was on that day in a dusty lobby that the baseball career of Daniel Westboro rose from the ashes. Time would be the sole determinant of whether or not it was a good decision.

Chapter 59:

David Westboro wasn't your typical first baseman. He was rather lanky, and his coaches at every level of his baseball career questioned the smallish frame. It was a mystery how the ball got pounded past the outfield fences with his small arms, and people often wondered what the real story behind David Westboro and his Panhandle mannerisms. Teammates at Osceola High often watched him walk onto the diamond and say no words; it was almost the end of his freshman season before his team knew he had a voice. They knew that Jacob Clubber was watching over him, but no one really knew why. Theories stretched from abduction, to a child out of wedlock, to a long lost nephew, but the kid who chose to be known as Christopher Hart was truly mysterious in origin. When people asked him who his father was, they would be met with the

concealment of his eyes behind a red brim of a
baseball cap and the departure of the young man
who would then walk away and engage in work.

Apparent to many, David just liked to bide his
time or at least avoid questions. David was a very
happy child, but predictably through his teenage
years his friends knew he griped about Jacob, but it
was for much the same reasons as any boy stuck
somewhere between manhood and childhood. The
only complaint David had about his guardian of
strange acquaintance was that he didn't let him stray
very far off at night, but it was well apparent to
everyone around David that Jacob and Sarah
Clubber were good to him, and they loved the shy
boy with a strange drawl. It was with pride that the
Clubber's took a family photo with David
brandishing his bat over one shoulder and his glove
upon the other hand. David looked into the shutter
of the camera that his Uncle Bruce owned and
smiled, displaying for the whole world his handsome
featured face and long curly black hair.

"Goddamn, Christopher, I think you broke the
damn camera," said Uncle Bruce.

"Hey Bruce, there are children here," said
Sarah.

"Sorry," responded Uncle Bruce who
concealed his face to hide the grin he had for his own
joke. It was moments like this that let David know he
had made it. Right here, right now, David had found
family.

Despite this, David felt torn inside, for he
knew the boy they accepted as their own was not
Christopher Hart from the orphanage, but rather
David Westboro, a kid who was abandoned by his
own father who, as he had learned a month or so
ago, framed David's older brother to save himself
from debt. David missed Daniel when he was out
behind Jacob Clubber's house throwing into peach
crates, trying to imagine how the leather used to

snap when Daniel's hand caught the flying projectile. David often found himself wishing he could play catch with Daniel again.

David also missed the days when people called him David and not Christopher, because he had come to learn that the moniker had a meaning to him, and it felt wrong to deviate from the name his mother had given him. It was a simple name; it stemmed from one of his mother's favorite books of the bible as a child, the book of Samuel. In that story, a young boy took to combat with but five stones and a sling taking on a Philistine named Goliath. The Israelite youth was off to do something no man dared try: attempt to kill Goliath of Gath for he felt that the Lord was on his side. To the surprise of everyone, Goliath was smote by a lone stone to the forehead from the sling of David.

Several years later, this story motivated David's mother to give him a name from this book, symbolizing he was greater than himself, and through following God, anything would be possible. She wanted to make sure her son, long after she was gone, knew how special he was, and she prayed that David would be like the one in the Bible and never doubt himself even when the challenge was at a point where he could convince himself it was insurmountable.

David felt terrible whenever he let himself be addressed as Christopher because he knew he was lying, and an entire web of lies thus surrounded his manufactured existence. In direct violation of what King Solomon had written in the book of Proverbs, Daniel not only committed the sin of lying with one's tongue, but had a perpetual cycle that looped around itself creating a knot; a knot that was beginning to resemble a noose wrapped around the very idea of life for David. If anyone found one of the loose ends and discovered all the lies necessary to make himself who he was, he would no longer be anyone. With that fear, he was like many dishonest men who have their own knots waiting to be unbound by a curious eye.

The thought of reputation was not the crux of David's dilemma, but rather the fact that then he would have to tell people the real truth. He would have to reveal he was the brother of Daniel, and furthermore, the son of the now notorious Robert Westboro. He would have to tell everyone that he was not an orphan, but instead abandoned, or in his own interpretation, deemed so worthless that even the man that made his existence possible resented him. This would cause people to question who David really was, and how much of his abandonment was due to Robert's villainous character and how much was due to David's flaws as a human being. Perhaps people would think "perfect Christopher" was just a futile attempt to rectify all the wrongs associated with his true identity. Simply put, David had an entire new identity and as far as he was concerned he was bound to being Christopher Hart as long as he may live. In a perfect world, David thought that David would be dead and Christopher would live on.

On this day, however, David would be obligated to be Christopher Hart, and other than baseball, living out the lie that was Christopher Hart seemed the only thing David was truly good at anymore.

Chapter 60:

"This guy's got some heat," said Oscar Detmer, turning to Jeff Bentley as they watched the first practice of the year. Oscar was the head coach of the High Desert Mavericks. He'd put together a moderately successful major league career mostly based on stealing base pads, putting a total of 84 through his 6-year flirt with glory, his career ending due to a combination of underperformance in fielding and injuring his wrist by being hit by a pitch in his last game. Still, when one looked up his stolen base count it was more than Roberto Clemente, and because of that Oscar often joked that he was a "man among the greats," which often aroused laughter when one noticed he only had 84 career stolen bases and little else for statistics in the major leagues.

Detmer was hired by the High Desert Mavericks for two reasons. One, he was a valuable asset being a coach who had played the game at the professional level, meaning he could talk to his players on an equal footing. Two, he was cheap.

Detmer was paid a measly thirty-thousand dollars a year annually to coach his little team in Adelante, and he took it graciously. Taught when he was younger to not look a gift horse in the mouth, Detmer found happiness in stretching out his attachment to baseball just a little bit longer. Besides, he had made wise decisions with his money after baseball and profited mightily from a string of McDonald's franchises he had pinned up around the area. In this way, Detmer was part of that expansive list of millionaires who no one knew possessed such great sums. He instead chose to carry himself quietly, and tried as hard as he could to have people first recognize him by the content of his character rather than enumeration of his wealth. From the streets of the dying port town of Sanchez in the Dominican Republic, Oscar had found much happiness in Adelanto where he had the ability to continue his love affair with baseball and not have all sorts of unwarranted attention directed at him or his money.

"Got him for a bargain, too," said Jeff. "Up to you to get my golden boy to work."

"Well, the season is a couple months away, but I don't know if that'll be long enough to get him back where he was," said Detmer as a fastball flew out of the reach of the catcher Andrew Thompson. "I'll do my best," added Detmer, the lack of confidence clearly audible in the hollow delivery of the sentence.

Daniel was on the mound and threw his head to the sky as if the elevation of his jaw towards the horizon might counteract the early release of the baseball from his fingertips, but sadly, the ball continued on its poor path and crashed into the fence behind home plate, causing Andrew Thompson to display the pop time that got him into this entire world of professional baseball and race to retrieve the poorly thrown ball.

"Come on Daniel," thought Andrew Thompson as he went back to retrieve yet another errant throw.

Over the past couple months, he and Daniel had developed a rather sound friendship working on their respective position requirements before this day in February, the first day of spring training when all pitchers and catchers were required to show up at the Spring Training complex in Surprise, Arizona, to show the coaching staff of the Ranger organization the best of their abilities in hope of getting their shot at the ten percent of the one percent. That is, to make it to the major leagues and play in the same league that had once hosted names such as Ted Williams, Stan Musial, and Ty Cobb. In this sports complex in Arizona, were some of the most elite athletes in the country. All of them were just trying to make a name for themselves in the next two weeks of team practices and the month afterwards with about fifteen officiated games. Little did they know that the managers had already decided who would and wouldn't make it months in advance.

The fates of these youthful dreamers were chosen in smoke-filled backrooms where minds dedicated to spotting serious talent put names on whiteboards and shifted magnetic placards until a roster for each level was agreed upon, with the players "on the bubble" well known to all in the room. A spreadsheet full of numbers strewn across an otherwise white sheet would be in front of every coach as the statistics were poured through and a host of old men attempted to do as Billy Beane did: construct rosters with the host of sabermetrics bestowed upon them by Bill James. It was a heartless and cruel process, but that was the way it went. As in any profession, to get the best of the best, the underperforming must be rooted out and eliminated. "Dog eat dog" was a light term for the amount of competition and politics that played into the roster decision-making process.

Andrew Thompson was worried that his new and only friend in this whole city of Surprise was going to be eliminated because of all his mistakes. In contrast, Thompson continued to impress, fielding the bouncing balls to perfection, framing every pitch better than Leonardo Da Vinci painted the Mona Lisa, and hitting well in the batting practice following these bullpen sessions. An undrafted free agent from the middle of Ohio, Andrew Thompson was bound and determined to make an impression on this team. His agent had pored over the several organizations that overlooked his college career at Louisiana State University and called all of them looking for anyone who would take his prospect, and through the process hopefully make both of them richer men. Texas was the only team that called back with any interest. The wide-eyed boy from Ohio and LSU product quickly drove to the West Coast to sign his deal. Andrew Thompson knew entering camp that he was one of the men deemed "on the bubble." It wasn't like high school where in Ohio he was deemed the belle of the ball and a sort of baseball debutante to the Division I baseball programs strewn across the country. Here, he was merely another kid with wide-eyes, crazy hair, and a mission to let the little boy inside of him see those sodium lights they were always sure they could find one day. He had worked hard for this moment, harder than he'd ever done for any reason before.

"Daniel," said Thompson as he walked to the mound.

"What?" asked Daniel. He was stretching out his arm as if the action was removing kinks, sort of like when one unrolls a garden hose and pulls down the length of the rubber sheath to straighten it and open the flow of water from the spigot toward the end of the hose.

"Dude, you gotta settle in! Come on give me hell!" said Andrew with the full exuberance of youth trying to ignite a flame that wasn't in the eyes of Daniel on this morning.

"Alright," responded Daniel blankly in a perfectly neutral manner.

"Westboro!" shouted Detmer from the dugout.

"Yes, Coach?" replied Daniel.

"Show me that curveball," said Detmer.

Daniel cocked the ball in his fingers in the manner of the Get-Me-Over curve and launched a pitch resemblant of something the old Frying Dutchmen Bert Blyleven may have thrown for the Twins had it been thirty years earlier. It was a thing of beauty the mere moments it was in the air; Thompson barely moved his mitt as the rapidly rotating laces were halted by the pocket of the glove.

Detmer grinned at the raw ungroomed talent dispensed upon him by Bentley as he was reassured he could do something with this sideshow project. The team broke from practice at about noon and were thus free to partake in whatever a minor league ballplayer may find himself doing in February on the streets of Surprise.

Baseball is a sport riddled with hours of free time, and to the surprise of many ballplayers who had recently left high school, or in the case of Daniel, his first team since departing LeHigh County High

School, many are shocked at the sheer amount of hours afforded for ballplayers to be independent. A mere three hours into the day and all the players were headed off to God knows where until the next morning's call time at nine o'clock. Daniel didn't really know what he would do having been so long without a dime to his name, and with all this free time after several years of incarceration he didn't really know how to live anymore. Blankness. That was the word that would describe Daniel's expression looking at the thermometer that read 78 degrees Fahrenheit on the dash of Andrew's Ford pickup.

Thompson, however, was not confused as to how to be a young man with a recent signing bonus and free time.

"Hey, Danny boy," said Andrew. "The other catchers and I have decided that we would like you to come with us even though you are a dinosaur."

"To where?" asked Daniel.

"To the bar"

"Why?"

"Jesus, Daniel, to get bitches," said Andrew. "Isn't it obvious?"

Daniel kept resting his head on his balled up right hand looking out the window into the desert of Arizona.

"Look I'm pretty sure we can find you a nice redneck girl looking to get cradle-robbed if you just tag along. I mean for Christ's sake, you're a professional athlete, there's gotta be some cleat-eaters in Glendale!" said Andrew punching the arm of Daniel trying to elicit a response from his new friend.

Daniel kept looking forward, still unmoved, and still without any sort of countenance to express anything except that one word yet again. Blankness.

"Do I have to pay you to have fun?" asked Andrew.

"I think you should just go without me, Andy," said Daniel.

"Alright, but it's your loss, Daniel," said Andrew.

Andrew Thompson pulled the truck in front of a hotel that the team had rented for all minor league players reporting for spring training. A red-clay structure reminiscent of the way pueblos were constructed in yesteryears, the place had served as a milestone for Daniel being the grandest lodging his body had ever been housed in. His eyes lit up looking at the three-star establishment as the luxury of the place caught his eyes. From the white railings constructed in a Greco-Roman fashion in front of each balcony to the pond in front of the main entrance where a fountain sprayed water straight up trying futilely to touch the heavens before plummeting back to the face of pond creating a beautiful rippling across the surface of the water, it was all spectacular.

If the Apache that once inhabited these deserts saw this monstrous structure built for pampered humans, one must believe they would be struck with awe. Water, seemingly out of nowhere, quelled from the surface of these dry plains, and the very building itself was a work of art. In this way, Daniel was much like them as he gazed at the hotel, and wondered what other magnificence he would be exposed to.

"Well, here it is, Daniel. Keys are apparently waiting at the desk for you," said Andrew in reference to what he'd read on the itinerary that was sent out to all players in the Rangers organization for Spring Training.

"Alright, see you later, Andy," said Daniel as he exited the car.

Inside, Daniel was guided to his room on the third floor by a teenage boy in what he called "a funny-looking jacket" where he was handed the key and allowed to open the door to where he would be living for the next month and a half. Daniel walked in and examined everything from the granite sink basin to the patterned rugs and the fresh fluffy white towels neatly arranged in the bathroom. Star-struck was a light term to describe the feeling Daniel was experiencing. He dropped onto the bed, and when his head hit the pillow, he felt a rush of relaxation extending from the outermost edges of his peripheries to the innermost knots of his thirty-something-year-old muscles. In the middle of Surprise, Arizona, where most middle-class families would dismiss this residence as some sort of budget lodging, Daniel Westboro felt like a king. On that day, Daniel rested.

Chapter 61:

Daniel Westboro had had enough of the humdrum that was the bullpen sessions before the first games of Spring. He eagerly awoke to see the circle on his calendar had finally reached today. The Los Angeles Angels of Anaheim were coming from Tempe, Arizona, a group of Californians foolish enough to think they could quell the wrath of the Rangers, at least as Daniel put it.

He put on the blue jersey with his team name so proudly emblazoned on the front, a number 21 printed on the back and his last name across the shoulders in a similar font.

Westboro; a name that had traveled through so many forefathers and was listed on his driver's license, birth certificate, and now the back of a uniform that belonged to a professional baseball player. Daniel thought of all the moments that lead to today, the hours practicing his pitching, the years under the tutelage of Coach Carlson, the time he spent behind cold iron bars where he had convinced himself his dreams had died. He thought of the friends he had made and lost, how Benjamin Crawford almost made this day impossible, how close he was to throwing away this opportunity, and how proud his mother would've been to watch him slip on this Rangers uniform.

"Look, Mama," said Daniel as he looked in the mirror.

"I did it, Mama," he said again smiling while tears came out of his eyes which still stared at the magnificently deep blue fabric.

But Daniel was in the industry of athletics, and in this arena, weakness was the last thing anyone would ever let another see. So Daniel quickly abandoned the thoughts of all of this and moved to the task at hand. This was the first game of Spring Training, the first opportunity to "prove his ass was worth this damn job." Daniel had finally come to accept himself as a professional athlete, and finally let himself believe his dreams were coming true. At this moment he was a matriculate of the infinite university of baseball, where tuition was his hard work, and his degree would be a ring from the world series. It is very lofty for such an old pitcher so far removed from the game to think about that seven game ordeal that has been happening for over 110 Octobers, where the best prove to the world who is entitled to call themselves the greatest, but Daniel was similar to everyone else on that field in that regard. His dreams were set on something much greater than himself, and finding a purpose such as that is a rather beautiful thing.

At the same time, there was the thought of today. The first step on the journey to getting a ring to commemorate his marriage to baseball a good twenty-some years after the day it happened was to do well in any and all appearances he may have over the next month and a half and to take every opportunity as if it were his last. For him and the other older men donning a jersey for the Rangers or one of its affiliates, that notion was becoming a little more believable each and every passing day.

Shortly after Daniel got to the stadium, he began warming up as is typical of the pitcher. When pitchers warm up, it is almost a religious affair with everything from the manner in which they stretch to what types of throws they make being a highly sacrosanct procedure that usually had persisted with them since the first days they began playing baseball. For Daniel, he would put his left shoe on first, and perform a variety of arm circles to open the shoulder capsule, fifty of each the small, medium, and large variety in each direction. He would then grab the back of his arm and pull to feel the stretching of the four muscles that composed the rotator cuff. Like the burning of incense in an ancient temple, only after this could Daniel think to hoist the ball even to his ear and begin throwing at Andrew Thompson.

One. Two. Three. Over and over he would repeat these numbers staring at the black stamp in the palm of Thompson's glove. A little faster, a little harder, each throw warmed the joint a little more until it was finally primed for battle.

It seems silly to some to see such a dedicated practice of ancient ritual, for it was such meaningless game. Certain celebrities were known to participate some of these contests; in the case of a perfect game, the players themselves were rarely aware of the occurrence. For the established ones such as Sergio Vasquez and Randy Carter, these games were barely worth showing up on time for, merely opportunities to get extra exercise before the start of the next season.

"Ready, Daniel?" asked Oscar Detmer as he walked out to the bullpen to hand him the ball.

"Always," responded Daniel.

The Angels took to the field batting first as is a typical nicety on the baseball diamond. Eddie Trinket, the much awaited Los Angeles prospect, would hit lead off. Poised as if he were about to run in his stance and leaning over the plate as if he were asking for an errant fastball to strike his elbow, Eddie looked straight at Daniel with a grin. He was met with that kind of smile fit for Wheaties boxes, and the perpetual rise and fall of the ball in the pitchers right hand.

"Play Ball!" shouted the umpire.

Eddie threw up a hand and called for time.

"Coach, I thought this game was for rookies," said Eddie deliberately speaking loudly enough for Daniel to hear.

"Like maybe his son is supposed to be pitching," he added.

"Play ball!" said the umpire again, with annoyance in his voice.

"Hey, it's not my fault Blue, it's not every day you see them dig a piece of shit out of the gutter and put it on the hill," said Eddie Trinket.

Daniel stared back unwavering in his composure, the ball still being tossed lightly up and down, up and down, over and over like the gentle metronomic monotony was to instill a sense of discordance. He cocked back a fastball and delivered it over the plate up and in towards the arm that was dangling over the strike zone.

"Damn, you need some glasses?" asked Eddie as ball one was called.

Daniel was unphased and threw another one in near the same spot, this time a little closer to his arm.

"You wanna go, old man!" shouted Trinket as he began removing his gloves and walking towards the mound.

"Eddie!" shouted the Los Angeles bench.

"Get back in the box!"

Trinket picked up his gloves and looked back at Daniel with the rage clearly showing in his face. Daniel was still unmoved.

Daniel wound up and delivered a low curveball that Eddie hit straight to the shortstop, and that same shortstop delivered to first in a routine groundball play. Daniel smirked as Trinket angrily went to his dugout realizing that Daniel had completely owned him. Daniel was extremely confident when the PA system sounded for the maybe seven thousand fans in attendance the name of yet another promising Angel's prospect and first basemen.

"Batting Second, from Lake City, Florida, Chris Hart!"

Many applauded the name for he was a boy they had all come to love and know; a man, who even as young as he was, was considered destined for baseball greatness like Lou Gehrig or Rod Carew. A kid that could play anywhere, he had the thundering power of Harmon Killebrew and the swiftness of George Sisler, a true master of the batter's box and a real dominant presence on the field that only played first so as to get his bat in the lineup as often as possible. It may have taken him three years since leaving Ole Miss, but Christopher Hart was going to be a real force to reckon with as all the baseball pundits would say.

Daniel prepared for Christopher as he would any batter. He treated them all as nameless ever-changing objects. However, he found it necessary to first look in their eyes, the only thing he needed to remember, the only exchange he found necessary between himself and the man in the box. Daniel looked at him, but he noticed something.

He had seen those eyes before. That eye black pattern was something he knew from so many years ago, and that curly black hair belonged to...

"No... It couldn't be," he thought. "There is no chance."

"David?" said Daniel in a questioning tone as he lowered the glove to his side.

David Westboro looked at Daniel and realized who was on the mound. He lowered his bat to look face to face at his older brother. Daniel looked at his jersey again and saw the name on the back. He read Hart, and thought of what the name once meant, quavering as he put the glove on the mound.

"Is it you?" asked Daniel.

David Westboro stared back at the mound motionless, as Daniel stretched out his arms and began approaching home plate.

"David," Daniel said as tears started to leak from his eyes.

David looked at him inquisitively and backed away, brandishing his bat as if to defend himself.

"Can he do this, Blue?" asked David Westboro.

"21, back on the mound!" shouted the umpire.

"He's my brother; I haven't seen him in so long, I..." Daniel was struggling to find words as he approached David trying to get a hug.

"What the fuck?" said David.

"Blue, I don't know what he's on, but he's freaking me out," David added still retreating from Daniel's attempts to feel his hands and wrap his arms around him.

"Goddammit!" said the umpire under his breath so as to avoid losing his job.

"I can't take this anymore. Get out of here twenty-one!" he shouted while making a hand signal which was meant for ejecting players.

"David!" said Daniel again as he kept approaching. The police on the edge of the stadium began to approach Daniel to apprehend him.

"My name is Chris!" said David.

"You're my brother!" said Daniel.

"No, I am not!" shouted David.

"I love you David," said Daniel between sobs as the policemen tased him to try to quell his wild attempts to feel his brother, to make sure that it was real; that David Westboro was alive.

"Time! Detmer, get your team back in order. I'm letting you warm someone else up," said the umpire.

Detmer called upon another arm from the dugout to begin warming up to pitch the three innings Daniel Westboro was supposed to pitch, and David went back to the dugout to calm himself down following the very unique situation that had just played out on the field.

"They don't pay us enough for this job," said Eddie Trinket.

"No, they don't," said David. He then watched his brother be drug out of the stadium trying to just steal one more glance of the only family he had left.

Chapter 62:

"Why?" asked Jeff Bentley as Daniel sat at the desk opposite him. "Just why, Daniel? Why do you throw away every opportunity someone gives you? What was this? Some publicity stunt? Been a little too long since the papers have been talking about you? What?!?!" shouted Bentley who was getting more and more animated.

"Congratulations, you're the first person to ever make a spring training game interesting! At the expense of the Texas Rangers! No, not them, me. I sign you on as a long-shot prospect because I owed my buddy John some money, and what do you do? You make it look like I sign emotionally unstable maniacs!" he added now throwing things off his desk for added effect.

"You're suspended for two weeks, Daniel. That's from the bigman. The Commissioner! That's worse than God punishing you, Daniel! You made God come down on you, because you looked at the golden-boy of the major leagues and decided in your fucked up head that he is your younger brother. Guess what Daniel, he's dead," said Bentley.

"I don't even know what to say to you, but I'm taking half your check this month. You're getting cut, and if you ever want a goddamn chance at baseball again, you're going to apologize to Christopher Hart..."

"His name is David," said Daniel.

"What?" asked Jeff.

"His name," Daniel spoke louder, "is David."

Bentley stared down at his desk and sighed heavily trying to get all the anger out of himself without further damaging the contents of his office.

"Get out of here and do what I told you, because I don't have time to deal with this," said Bentley as he went back to answering emails.

"Go on. Get," said Bentley as he waved him out the office doors.

Daniel Westboro walked the streets of Surprise destitute and out of a dream that had only lasted a mere two weeks. He was not allowed back in the clubhouse or team hotel. His teammates were discouraged from talking to him, or even of him, for the managers and coaches saw him as a toxic force much like Ryan Leaf was on the San Diego Chargers in the NFL. It happens all too often with the young and successful; they lose all sight of what being human is and let fame overtake them and change them into monsters. For several who end up in professional athletics, the spotlight ends up burning deep holes into young boys who know of nothing but a game with no tangible value to society beyond entertainment, and from these holes lose the better parts of themselves to an unforgiving world.

Many looked at Daniel with an inquisitive eye and wondered to what extent he would be consumed by the limelight. It was reasonable for everyone to question his mental health as the men on the streets of LeHigh would do after watching the replays of Daniel's apparent nervous breakdown and sobbing affair caught on the camera of a fan's phone. No one bothered to question why he did what he did before he was cut from the team to remove "unnecessary baggage", but that is how society works. Much like the office of Jeff Bentley, it forms conclusions on a limited sample size and doesn't consider the fact Christopher Hart was Daniel's younger brother, a brother he loved more than life itself. It doesn't have time to worry about who the real victim is with all the dollar signs there are to grab.

Daniel at one point thought the loneliest island on Earth was that 20 inch high mountain at the center of the baseball diamond, where the pressure is and always will be greatest. He thought that being in a cage where the songbirds never speak was the lowest canyon of them all. He thought life in LeHigh County was the worst one he would ever live, but today Daniel found that there was in fact a place lower than all of these and that was on the backside of an old retirement home where he looked at yet another pond that was never supposed to be there.

"Maybe I was never supposed to be here," thought Daniel.

On his left and right was a wide expanse of unyielding soil that would bake in the scorching heat of an Arizona July up to the edges of suburbia, where the expanse of sand ceased and was replaced by lawns that had no right to be green, but by some wild form of biochemistry found the ability to. He had no home, and the Rangers organization was doing all it could to prevent Daniel from see his only friend in the middle of this desert. This was what life was now, though. Daniel looked at that water and felt as out of place as it did, and as he ambulated along the shore could not help but think about life again.

Across the road he saw a church house and coming forth from its doors were a new husband and wife, young and prepared for the world in front of them knowing that forever they would have someone on their side, knowing with the utterance of "I do" that even in the worst of times, it would be alright all the time. Daniel pulled a photograph from his wallet and looked at the sweet face of June Winters, and wondered if life was worth living. He wondered why God, if He somehow existed, seemed to devastate him at every turn. On that day, Daniel decided he was going to purge himself of love. All it ever did for him was tear him and that old photograph apart.

Chapter 63:

Samantha Lawson was a pretty woman. She happened to be on the streets of Surprise that day to visit her aging father in the retirement home that Daniel Westboro was pacing behind.

A woman of the desert, she came from the sand of Arizona, commanded by a destiny forged by God to be like her father and roam the expanse by horseback or maybe simply saunter upon it in leather boots. She was a girl obsessed with the way the sun kisses the Earth as it settles down for rest on the western horizon on any given night and made it a point to see it happen every single night. Tall and thin, wearing jeans that clung tight to her legs and a leather hat her father had given her several years prior which let tangles of her thin blonde hair protrude in such a way that the wind pushed her locks, she gazed upon the desert. She had an angular jaw that gave her a sort of heart-shaped face and beaming blue eyes which surveyed the high desert when she rode. Some had told her long ago a career in modeling might be more suitable for someone of her appearance, but she was not interested in being stared at by millions of people. Samantha was a woman who would guide her own destiny. But as with all decisions, there were costs.

"Ms. Lawson, I'm sorry, but there are not sufficient funds to continue his housing here and the state is not going to pay," said Mr. Cox, the owner of the establishment who was kicking her father out today.

"Bullshit, you can't go kicking my pops to the road! The only fuckin' thing this man has ever done is be an honest one!" shouted Lawson behind the frosted glass door.

"Look, I understand entirely, but we are running a business here," said Cox.

"Medicare won't pay for his stay, your father lacks the sufficient funds, and your check bounced. You have until next week to move him out," said Cox.

"Well, fuck you, too, then!" said Samantha as she walked out the door.

Samantha proceeded down the hallways of the nursing home and thought of her father at the end of this hallway and his failing memory. He had been diagnosed with Alzheimer's a few months prior and the condition was progressing rapidly.

"Hi, dad," said Samantha as she walked in the front door.

"Hello, Sam!" said Mr. Lawson as he stood quickly from the chair.

"How are..." he pondered trying to figure the last word out.

"You! How are you?" he said, feeling accomplished in solving the sentence.

Mr. Lawson was a very optimistic man. Someone in a similar position as he would have been very miserable and frustrated in that sentences had become puzzles and leaving his keys in the fridge had become almost a regular mistake, but Lawson somehow managed to find the bright side in the situation, taking triumph in each task that was now difficult, such as remembering the names of some of his favorite baseball players on the Diamondbacks.

"What do... you....uhh...want...to do?" asked the elder Lawson.

"Papa, I want to take you back to the farm," Samantha said with a smile.

"Really!?" said Isaac.

"Of course, Papa, let's get your things," said Samantha as she helped her father stand up from his chair.

Isaac and Samantha were lugging his few possessions out to Samantha's truck and one couldn't help but smile when they saw the happiness in Isaac's eyes when he knew he was going home. He made it a point to tell all of the staff that walked by him how happy he was, and they weren't lying when they said they were going to miss him at the old Oak Ridge retirement home. They would miss most those eyes that always seemed like they were laughing and the smile that lit up a room. Even in his old age, the former cowboy found something to smile about no matter how bad things got.

Samantha wished she could share the same optimism as her father, but she was the one who had to take care of him, and although she loved her father, she was not quite sure how to take care of an old man with the condition he had. Thus the reason the normally self-reliant Samantha had paid for his tenure at Oak Ridge. She was not going to see him die on the street or hurt himself back on the ranch due to some failure of his memory. With hardly a dime to her name, she worked hard in order to stay afloat being the only Lawson to take care of good ol' Ike in his ripened and wise years, for she was the only one left that cared. Isaac climbed into the front seat and buckled himself, as Samantha put the car in drive and began moving down the city streets. She came upon Daniel who was sitting on the curb, head in his hands.

"You," said Samantha.

"Me?" asked Daniel wondering why this car was slowing down on this busy side street.

"Yes, you. Do you need a job?"

"Depends, what are you paying?"

"More than your sorry ass is making sitting around there. Come on, get in," Samantha said as she unlocked the doors to her pickup truck.

Daniel climbed in for he figured whether this was opportunity or some twisted way to kill a man that either would be the solution to his current miserable situation if he was to enter the doors of the red Dodge that appeared as old as he.

Samantha grabbed a pair of sunglasses from the overhead compartment and put them on, an act which further accentuated the bone structure of her face. A perfect combination of ruffian and femininity graced the face of Samantha Lawson, a stark contrast to her mannerisms and conduct.

"So, where the hell did you blow in from?" asked Sam as she continued driving south with her eyes on the road, but still producing a satisfactory smile of acknowledgement to her passenger.

"Texas,"

"Nice, so why are you around here?"

"I'm just a baseball player, down on my luck."

"Hey, I don't hire no bullshitters. So what are you, a ranching man, some sort of city-slicker what?"

"I play baseball. For Texas," said Daniel staying steadfast in his stubbornness.

"Like fuck," started Samantha as Daniel produced a jersey from his backpack.

"Well, fuck me," said Samantha realizing he was, in fact, not lying.

"So why the hell were you lookin' so lonesome?" she asked.

"I just got cut."

"I see. So you musta not been a very good one."

"Yeah... Somethin' like that," Daniel said as he looked out the window.

"Well, if it's a piece of ass you're looking for, you might as well kick that door out. I just need someone to make sure my papa doesn't go on hurting himself, understand?"

"Of course."

"I can't give you much, but I can at least feed and clothe you until you get on your way again. There's no way I was leaving you to do nothing because last thing this town needs is more unproductive assholes," Sam said.

Samantha pulled up to the bounds of the Lawson residence, turned the key from the ignition, and placed the car in park.

"I don't know how much I'm going to pay you; we can talk about that later. For now, you just do what I say, alright?" said Sam.

"Wouldnta thought any different," said Daniel.

The trio got out; Daniel and Sam began hauling in items for her father. She brushed hair that was dangling in front of her eyes to the side and couldn't help but notice with her now unobscured vision the muscles of Daniel's arms protruding as he gripped a stack of books of great mass. Samantha quickly blushed and looked away when Daniel looked up to see what she was looking at. A combination of Daniel's blindness to the situation and Samantha's quick concealment made the flirtatious glance wither away and remain unrecognized by one party and unacknowledged by the other.

Samantha was not normally a shy girl. She was the kind of independent that hated people like Daniel with their smooth accents and stubborn nature to ascertain the most difficult tasks possible before anyone else could try them. Samantha was busily convincing herself this was a vagabond man who was just being given a home so that her town would stop being populated by all these hitchhiking losers that rode in and festered the streets as the panhandling leeches they were. However, proof that Samantha was smitten was the sheer amount of denial that tried to refute her emotions. On that day, the hobo on the corner of Surprise was already beginning to invade Samantha's heart, and in spite of all resistance, the parasite was winning.

Chapter 64:

David was in Tempe, Arizona when the squad decisions were made. On this day, the third of April, decisions would be made over who should be on the twenty-five man active roster, the forty man reserve list, and who would be assigned to the other levels of baseball throughout the Angels system. In the case of David Westboro, he was hoping for his minor league contract to be purchased, a term that was rather archaic as it was pretty obvious no money actually changed hands during these deals. If his contract were to be bought by the major league organization he would be placed on the forty man roster, which, although not a guarantee that he would be on the field, would at least grant him the ability to play major league games, and gain more rights in negotiations. But David did not care much for the money, or rights, or what he called "the bullshit", he only cared about getting a chance to live out his dream and play under those lights. When he was called to Coach Dewey's office and informed of his promotion he was rather ecstatic. Beyond the wildest stretches of his imagination he was signed to the 25 man active roster of the Los Angeles Angels.

"I made it, Mr. Clubber!" screamed David into the telephone. "I'm an Angel!"

Jacob Clubber was standing out on his back porch looking at the tall tall trees of Osceola State Forest, and couldn't help but smile as he heard the boy he had taken as his son laugh and scream having accomplished what he set out to do. He remained quiet while David screamed into the telephone about all that had happened.

"I'm proud of you, Christopher," Jacob Clubber said warmly.

"Thanks! I have a couple other people to call, Mr. Clubber!" David continued. "Bye!"

Jacob Clubber heard the phone click and relaxed deeper into the rocking chair on his back porch, staring at the piece of woods behind the house he had built for Sarah and himself. He thought of the day Sarah and Jacob were sure they would never have children because she was barren, and his history precluded him from adopting children for the state thought at first that he was too poor to support a child, and later decided he was too old. He remembered the hours he spent praying that God would one day give him a child, and how he found him on a lonely highway stretching to Amarillo. Upon first sighting, Jacob would not have known that this was the answer to his prayers, but since that day his unyielding faith in God had become further solidified. Jacob smiled when David smiled, for Jacob had taken David as his son, and on that spring day, the trees of Lake City seemed a little bit greener and the sun a little brighter for Jacob's son was happy.

Meanwhile, David had taken to the streets of Tempe with a smile on his face. David had fought long and hard to get to this point, and all was right and good.

That is, until he remembered the encounter he had experienced about four weeks ago with his brother. The truth is, from the moment he saw the name Westboro written on the back of that blue jersey, David knew who he was standing before. When he was in the dugout watching that unique pawing of the ball as it rose and fell from scarred and calloused hands, he knew who was firing that ball in the air. He knew he was looking at an honest man that day: a man who just wanted to know that the boy he was seeing was truly the younger brother who he left so many years ago. The little brother he protected from a horrible man for the duration of the time he was around him. As he looked at a reflection cast back at him from a storefront window, he couldn't help but see a liar.

When people came up to get an autograph from the young prospect, he would write in swirling handwriting the name "Christopher Hart," and he would feel a little more remorse every time he attached the false moniker to yet another card or article of clothing. Thousands of young boys in Florida knew his name, the way he would be addressed on the news and in papers as "an International Man of Mystery," the way he possessed an aura of "cool" as many feel when they think of James Bond or a host of other popular culture spies. The greatest contribution to his popularity was the fact that no one knew who he was. That sort of mystery, combined with a reserved persona that only shows toughness and the will to succeed, draws people in. The only problem was David no longer knew who he was, either.

Most days he was able to just accept David Westboro as being dead and Christopher Hart as his new identity, but the surprise in Surprise had rattled him. David had taken the character of Daniel and assassinated it, making him look a weak man with a damaged psyche, all for the cameras to absorb images of someone pouring out their soul while they were most vulnerable, only to be shunned by who they opened their hearts for. David was a liar, and he knew when he read that Daniel had been placed on waivers that it was his fault. He was responsible for ending Daniel's baseball career. It was context that the ever pounce-ready sects of society didn't have that made what would've otherwise been accepted as totally normal, totally abnormal. Unlike the man he stole a last name from, he failed his family when it needed him most.

"Nice job, Chris!" said Coach Johnston, his baseball mentor for the last few years who would soon be departing for Utah to take care of the Triple A team housed in Salt Lake City.

"Thanks, Coach," said David.

"Just so you know, Hart, it was a privilege coaching you, and I know you got big things ahead of you," he said. "Go light their asses up for me."

David proceeded to drift around the streets of Tempe preparing to head back to Los Angeles for the home opener, and even if he wouldn't be starting opening day, at least he would have the assurance that if a hole needed to be filled he would be the first one asked. Later, after perusing the city for the better part of the day, David returned to his hotel room and looked at the ceiling realizing that he was living the life the real "Hart Attack" should have.

Chapter 65:

Daniel was at the Lawson residence on opening day; a month later, he still was in the same place. As was expected by him and everyone else who was aware of his story, he cleared waivers and was released by the Texas Rangers organization on the basis that he was too much of a liability to the team in terms of negative publicity. Daniel had come to accept his fate and had decided his professional baseball career might as well be forever held at the one out he recorded in a Spring Training contest. Daniel Westboro now was a ranch hand, and had come to like this line of work where no one bothered him. On the ranch, he was responsible for very fundamental chores that Samantha taught him very quickly and making sure that Isaac didn't hurt himself.

As promised, the job did not pay well. Other than being allowed to sleep in the barn and being fed, Daniel was pretty much unpaid for his labor and was often reminded that he could find another line of work for Samantha didn't believe in enslaving the former pitcher. Samantha was almost wishing he would move out, for in her eyes what she originally was doing as charity was turning into a nuisance. She appreciated the help in taking care of her father, but Daniel in no way was good at being a cowboy.

When he tried to lasso, he tied himself in knots, with a rifle he was as worthless as glasses on a mole, and when it came to the task of herding cattle he was about at successful at organizing them as he was at balancing the checkbook he didn't have. It did afford him several hours of the day alone with Isaac while Samantha went about fixing her cheap ranch hand's mistakes, and being early in spring it afforded the two several hours to bond over the Arizona games played on the old JVC TV that sat in the corner of the room, a piece of furniture that at one time was rarely put into employment, but now became something Isaac interacted with almost every day.

"Goddamn, Harvey is pitching well," Isaac said, smiling for the lack of pause that was necessary to deliver the message to Daniel.

"Yeah, he is," said Daniel, who was busily washing dishes for Isaac.

"Daniel, what was I supposed to... do today?" asked Isaac as he looked at the calendar strewn with his handwriting which was too messy for his old eyes to decipher. Daniel took the calendar and tried to figure out what the old man meant by the note he wrote for himself, but couldn't quite work out anything. He kept moving the piece of paper around until he saw a cursive "A" and tried to fill in the rest. It came to him slowly.

"Two n's... or maybe an m? That's an i, okay... r?" and then Daniel could see it for sure.

The word was "Anniversary". It was the pain of such a disease that things left so easily that at one point were so hard to forget. Often times people complain and talk about how they wish they could forget certain things, make certain pain go away, watch it drift into nothingness like a ship on the horizon. The problem with Alzheimer's is that one begins to realize how much they miss remembering it all. For Isaac, it was easy to forget the silly things, like math, telephone numbers, and his schedule, but it always brought pain to the face of Isaac when he heard of the things that left him. He clung tightly to the memory of his wife, the name of his daughter, and sometimes even found happiness in remembering the face of the first girl that broke his heart. Daniel could see Isaac looking confused as he stared at Daniel waiting to tell him what was written on that day.

"Mr. Lawson, I believe today is your anniversary," said Daniel.

"It is? I guess it is..." said Isaac who looked at the ground saddened that he had forgotten the day of his own wedding.

"Daniel?" he said, half-sure and half-wondering if he was saying the right name.

"Yes, Ike?"

"Can you... uh... you... promise me... one... thing?"

"What?"

"I love... uhh.... uhh..." Isaac began to well up in tears as he was trying to remember the name of his daughter, the happiest thing that had ever happened to him in this cruel world.

"Samantha," said Daniel as he wanted to make sure Isaac said what he was going to before his mind left its train of thought as it so easily had so many times before.

"Take... care... her," said Isaac. Daniel looked back at Isaac.

"Please," Isaac pleaded. He couldn't grasp the words at that moment, but what he wanted to tell Daniel was he knew he wasn't for this world long and he had seen all the bad things all the bad men that roll through this one-light town did to her. How Sam had learned to live without a man for no man had ever been good to her. How it seemed when Isaac left she would be on her own and how he knew she knew she could handle everything by herself and how little he wanted her to do that, because no one should have to go through this merry-go-round we call life alone. Isaac saw Daniel as someone who would be good to her and was hoping in the bottom of his heart that Daniel would be the man he could leave her with. Daniel saw all of this in those eyes that spoke where Isaac's decaying brain failed him.

"I will," Daniel said. "I promise."

Isaac leaned back in his chair and went back to the piece of paper he had been scribbling on all day. Perhaps the saddest part of all of it was that Daniel would be the only one to leave the conversation remembering what was said.

Samantha came back later that day from work to relieve Daniel of the duty of watching her father. As always, she thanked him and gave him whatever money she could spare and once again told him the house was open to him, but as always he insisted on sleeping in the barn. Samantha sometimes grew frustrated that he wouldn't take her offers to escape the poor living conditions of the outdoors, and even more so felt the pain of an unrequited love she could not express to Daniel. The feelings had burned inside her for the past couple months causing her suggestions to find work elsewhere to change from simply being good will into a desire to rid herself of this god-awful wonderful feeling. She hated emotion. Many men had played her heart, and they had to try very hard, but Daniel required no effort, for that unexplainable catalyst of affection somehow sprung when Samantha saw Daniel. Samantha hated herself for being susceptible to such a thing.

Outside, Daniel looked at the stars for the better part of an hour feeling the oppressive dry heat of an unseasonably warm May in Arizona. The dust sifted outside as cows mooed, making noise for no other apparent reason but to remember they were next to each other, that they had something to lean on. Daniel remembered the vow he made to Isaac in the living room, but dismissed it. Daniel remembered what happened the last time he gave himself to someone, and there was no way in hell that he was going to get the sweets for some "bum and stumble tomboy". He went through the list of reasons to hate her, the book of why he was meant to be alone, and reminded himself once again that his heart would die in the ownership of June Winters, wherever the hell she may be. Daniel had killed love, and he decided that in the morning he was going away so as not to tempt that hellacious spirit to bother him ever again.

The next morning, Daniel was awoken by shouts emanating from the farmhouse. When Samantha awoke that morning, she had found Isaac's armchair empty with a note laying on it and his horse missing from the stockade. In sloppy handwriting the piece of paper read:

"I love you, Sam. Goodbye."

Meanwhile, miles from the farm on a gallop, a confused Isaac was in the saddle destined for somewhere he hoped was beautiful when he started the mission but had forgotten a few times along the way. The purpose of the journey was to leave Samantha after a night when they played cards, danced Texas Two-step, and in all had a very happy time together. Isaac knew what was happening to him. He was losing that optimism he had even a month ago, and beyond that was forgetting the stories that Samantha liked to listen to. He forgot the words to old cowboy songs passed down through generations of renegades and frontiersmen. Isaac was losing who he was and he didn't want Samantha to go through the pain of watching the good in him die.

It was for that reason that he chose to leave, for he was getting to a point with his disease where such a voyage would not be possible and after months of being looked after and supervised in everything he did from going to the bathroom to walking around his abode, he wanted his freedom. Isaac knew nothing about the man he left behind for his one and only daughter, but he did know that he was a better and more loyal man than he had ever seen around her, and that was good enough for him. In a point of Isaac's life where he was starting to forget the most important things to him, he left before Samantha would ever hear him struggle trying to figure out her name, because he didn't believe his child should have to do that. At a point where he was confused all the time, Isaac found happiness as cactus whipped by him and he stared at the red stacks of rock before him, knowing he would die in God's country.

But none of that made sense to Samantha who was on her knees still clutching the note which contained quite possibly the last thing he would ever say to her.

"Come on."

"What?"

"We're gonna go and find him, Daniel!"

"You mean you are going to," responded Westboro in a cold voice.

"What did you just say?" replied Lawson, looking at him with the deepest expression of twisted fury imaginable.

"You will. I'm leaving," said Westboro again.

"Fine," said Samantha as she stormed to the stockade and threw her long legs over the saddle atop her fastest horse. Daniel felt no remorse as Samantha rode off, although a younger Westboro may have decided to give into those excitations he experienced looking at the cowgirl.

"Just a set of pins and tits," whispered Daniel to himself when he felt the slightest tinge of feeling to perhaps help her or have some grandiose scene of affection. Daniel was an embittered man and even in the case of Isaac, his only friend in Arizona, riding off to God knows where he still couldn't muster up anything to go and save him. Daniel dismissed love as some carnal wrath which riots in the loins for the sole purpose of promoting the advancement of the species. When he looked at Samantha and felt his chest move, he believed that it was some biological facet of himself just trying to procreate, and because of that, he refused to administer care or protection to anyone but himself because he felt no desire to bring another into this world. Daniel climbed atop an old dirt bike stashed in the corner of the barn and rode northward, knowing that there was nothing left for him from whence he came.

Behind him, Samantha wiped a tear from her eye as the only two men she could consider having a part in her life left.

Chapter 66:

A clock hung on the wall in Bardy's saloon, with the hour hand directed westward and the minute north. As was almost a law of this time at any bar that had karaoke, a man that had too much to drink was busy "singing" the words to Piano Man into a microphone like the one mentioned in the rock classic, an object which served as the sole similarity between this bar and the song. No waitresses practiced politics, no bartender had any aspirations of being a movie star, and nobody who had served in the Navy had been through those old wooden saloon doors in what seemed like forever. Still, the song liked to hint that perhaps there were people like that trapped in this bar lost along the highway, and the patrons were too busy worrying about getting inebriated on their low salaries to really care about what message emanated from the speakers. Here was Daniel, sitting in the corner proceeding to get stoned.

"Hey man, could I sit here?" asked an elderly black gentleman who approached Daniel.

The man had a visible milkiness surrounding the iris of each eye and was dressed in dingy attire. His breath stank of cigarettes and his hands bulged at the knuckles where the arthritis affected him most. He had just come into the establishment to start his own journey in becoming summarily hammered, but he found a newcomer and thought that the appropriate thing to do was to first approach the stranger and ensure his welcome in the selective club of low society.

"Sure," mumbled Daniel, in the middle stages of his imbibement.

"Where you from?" asked the old man taking his seat slowly as the old joints resisted the motion.

"Why the fuck do you care?" asked Daniel as he started swaying in his stupor.

"Because you're interesting; all my father's children are interesting. I've never seen you here before."

"And probably never... will again," said Daniel, pausing to hiccup and hold back the Irish flu.

"Maybe not, maybe I will. That's the beauty of life; some people get to be friends and stand by us forever. Some come and go, and that's okay too. Never get to know unless you start talking to some."

"Will you shut up, you fucking nigger? I'm trying to get a bit tipsy," said Daniel who now was feeling the anger stir within him from the alcohol.

"Seems you are fairly sauced already," said the old man ignoring the derogatory term.

"I didn't tell you how to fucking live your life you goddamn porch monkey."

"No I guess you didn't. May I buy you a drink?"

"Why the hell can't you figure out I have no time to bullshit for your goddamn banjo-lipped jigaboo ass? Huh? Just shut up and let me drink, I have some shit to forget."

The man looked at Daniel with his presumably glaucoma-ridden eyes and sighed, and then upon the moment scooted his chair closer to bring his face closer to Daniel's.

"Daniel, why are you so cold?"

"Because, I don't fuckin' need anybody. Jus' leave me the fuck alone."

"I know a lot of people from my life that have said that before. It's okay to believe that. People are awful sometimes, and I know that too. But, they are also good."

"Bull fucking shit Satchmo, they all suck like your eight ball ass."

"No, they don't. You don't even believe that."

"Just leave me the fuck alone, please."

"I can't, though. You need someone right now and I can help you."

"No, you can't, you can't bring my reason for living back to me. She's fuckin' dead. Thank you for figurin' that out. Now leave me the fuck alone."

"I won't. You're right, I can't bring back June. Nobody can. However, I guarantee you if you still love her she wouldn't want to see you like this."

The man stood up and drew closer as Daniel looked more and more saddened thinking about the weight of the world.

"God works in mysterious ways, man. Sometimes you can't tell why he does what he does, but someday you will know-"

"Oh, now Uncle Tom is gonna drop some scripture on me. Like that shit means anything."

"I think it did once to you. Otherwise why would you wear that cross around your neck?" said the old man pointing to Daniel's chest where a crucifix made for him by June hung loosely to overlap his heart so that whatever piece of her was left on it could creep just that much closer to the deepest parts of him.

"Dude, you are not a bad man, and I think you know that. I know this isn't you, because what you are right now is nobody. You loved her, and it was real, and now you're scared to feel that ever again, aren't you?"

Daniel looked up and got heated

"You don't tell me what the fuck I am!" screamed Daniel in a voice that elicited a rise from the bartender preparing to take care of his second job at this establishment as the bouncer. The old man waved him off, and the bartender respected his wishes going back to washing mugs while a curious eye was focused on the table of so much interest on this Tuesday night.

"I don't need to. You know who you are. Man, life is wonderful. It's the most beautiful thing I've ever seen and life is great. You don't have to believe in a God above to see that."

"Quit lying to me. Life is shit. I wish I could've just died already."

"It's okay. Sometimes people feel like that. There's absolutely no way I could ever know all that happened to you, but just to humor an old man why don't you pray with me. Even if no God is there to answer it, at least you can be assured that you have one friend in Arizona."

"Fuck you."

"Man, please, it might make you feel better."

Daniel looked down at the table and remembered what he had done that day in leaving Samantha Lawson to go searching for her father alone. He also thought about the vow he made to himself after the last time that he was hurt that he would never love again. He was conflicted, for this man in the face of his hostilities refused to turn his back on him and seemed the only person left anymore that actually cared about him. He was annoyed, but to have one friend in Arizona he decided to take hands with the old man and pray.

"Lord, bless this man and heal his heart. Let love flow in his heart and guide him on his way, for he is the one who needs you worse than anyone else I know right now. Lord, hold him close to you and forgive him for his sins in using your name in vain, and Lord forgive him for the things he has done, in the way I hope you help me forgive him for what he has done to me. Amen."

"Happy?" asked Daniel.

"I am. Barkeep, his tab is on me. Make him sober up before he drives off," said the elderly gentleman to the barman behind the counter.

"Dude, just follow your heart and always do what feels right. I guarantee you you'll be a much happier man thataway, and I hope someday to see that you have made it. God bless."

"Goodbye," said Daniel as the old man walked away.

"Fucking prick," he thought. "What the fuck does he know, anyways."

Daniel turned around to look for him, but it appeared as if he had never been there. He finished his drink in solitude and had formulated a plan before drifting off into a drunken slumber in the alley outside of Bardy's. In the morning, Daniel would look for Samantha.

Chapter 67:

On this day in Texas, the people of LeHigh were as they normally were, living with the passage of yet another uneventful day as they watched the ground dry more and more. Ruth Hart watered her plants in a futile attempt to keep them alive, but the ravages of two years of La Nina conditions took their toll on these fields here and elsewhere in the state. Ruth was an old woman now and knew that the climate changed with the cooling of winds over the Pacific and the reduction of rainfall would make people panic, worrying that rain would never come again. Then, El Nino would return and the heavens would open releasing the true elixir of life to the ground below. Ruth had grown accustomed to the drought and become desensitized to the multitudes who called the sporadic rains the beginning of the end of viability of farming here. Ruth and Kyle watched the drought come and go, and prayed for Bob Tiner, the people of LeHigh, and lastly themselves to not go out of business before the water returned.

However, it was also true that Ruth had watched things leave her and never return, and in that regard, no amount of age or wisdom could prepare her. Sometimes when she drove past the old Westboro place she hung her head low as she thought of the tragedy that happened there. Often she prayed someday she would see the Westboro boys again, and just as often she wept realizing that in all likelihood she would have to wait until getting to Heaven to see them with her boy playing baseball in the backyard like they did in everyone's younger years.

It depressed Ruth that Joey had moved away to Michigan to be a mechanical engineer. She was happy that Joey found a woman to make him happy and a job that made him wealthier than his father ever could have imagined, but she missed waking up in the morning and having her two sons beg for breakfast. She missed when Joey was okay with being a little bit chubby and indulged on the extra serving of pecan pie she made. Ruth was getting old, and she didn't like seeing things leave her.

That was life, but she had no option to dwell on such things all day because there was a more pressing matter and that was visiting John Carlson in his home to make sure he was alright.

Coach Carlson was a stubborn man, and being someone who made a very low salary his entire life as a baseball coach and gym teacher, there was not much for him to retire on as neither profession paid much. Now at old age, the sentimentality of being a mentor to hundreds of young kids and a positive influence on their life was not going to pay for the essential medical costs to keep him alive. Chemo was an expensive process, but because his lung cancer was inoperable he had no choice but to take the route of utilizing this radioactive material. The prognosis was based on the median, and because of such he may live longer than the one year mark, or he may not. Put simply, if he was the average man, he could expect death on that day a year from now. His doctors wanted to explain to him the statistics involved in prognosis and how the numbers weren't absolutes, but Carlson didn't obsess over the what-if's. He had grown to accept he was going to die.

"Hello, Ruth," said Carlson from his chair, looking up from the newspaper in his hands where he was busy reading about the state of the Rangers.

"Damn, Texas sure is gettin' old," he thought to himself as he folded up the paper containing an article on how Texas was by far the most veteran team in the nation which came with obvious benefits of experience, as well as the handicaps of age.

"How are you feelin'?" asked Ruth to a man who seemed to appear in pain all the time.

"Feel like shit, so I am doin' just fine," Carlson said as he chuckled a little bit to try and add humor to the rather sad statement.

"You know, last time I was in Lubbock I had this real hot nurse, made me feel like a man if you know what I mean," he suggestively said as he lit up a cigarette.

"John, why're you smokin'?" asked Ruth.

"Because I'm an old man and can do whatever the hell I want. Besides, it's not like I can get worse," said John.

"I guess... I was just swingin' by to see if there is anythin' you need," said Ruth.

"Well, the doc is pretty much having me live on lettuce at this point. Maybe I can go and join Bob's cows and graze on his pasture with them," said John cheerily. "Like I keep tellin' the guy, what I really want is a nice T-bone. You know, tons of pepper and mushrooms, and coat it all with sea salt. That would do it. Fuck, you have to imagine that a hunk of meat would do me some good at this point," said Carlson as he lifted his bony arms, and couldn't help but think of some of the middle-school boys he had taught over the years when he made this pathetic flex. Ruth sort of frowned focusing on the pain that could be seen in John's pale face. John couldn't help but notice the anguish Ruth's face as she looked at the anguish in John's.

"Jesus, the last thing a dying man wants to think about is dying, Ruth. It was supposed to be a joke," said Carlson as he slumped back into his chair now thinking about how little people understood him. Everyone thought that since he had such a devastating terminal illness that the only thing he would want is sympathy, while in reality the only thing he wanted was someone to laugh with. A simple smile. Hell, he would deal with someone not looking at him with saddened eyes for once. He wished someone on the street might pass him wishing Godspeed not because he was ill, but because he was a man. John Carlson just wished people would treat him like they always had, and his best friend Kyle's wife was not doing that right now.

"I'm sorry," said Ruth. Although she was not a very observant parent when Luke was still alive, she had taken up the practice of noticing more things, for it would help her smile if she smelled the roses more. Ruth could see John hurt, and she knew exactly what he meant.

"John, whatchoo want to do today?" asked Ruth.

John momentarily tried to maintain his glum mood, but he then reconsidered as he couldn't stop thinking of that clock ticking ever so stiffer as he neared the end of his life.

"I'd really like to go shootin'. Like go and get some squirrels or somethin'," said John.

"Then we'll do just that," said Ruth.

Into the truck and off to the fields went Ruth and John, the most unlikely pair to ever go squirrel hunting.

Chapter 68:

Daniel Westboro did what he had decided he would do and drove that night to the wide reaches of the Arizona desert in a direction that he figured would be somewhat resemblant of the heading Samantha may have taken to find her father. It was a mission of fate, a journey where the destination is clear, but the navigation is not so well-founded. The road had no bounds, pavement lay miles behind him and Lord only knows what kind of environmental regulations were being violated as tires churned the dust. Daniel didn't much care if he buried his car up to the axles, for within himself the doggish loyalty that made him so valuable to his comrades in LeHigh guided him. The blazing sun beat upon his brow but Daniel disregarded it, holding his mission in higher regard than his own comfort.

By some miracle, Daniel found her.

With the wind duning sand and a red paisley handkerchief covering her face, Samantha's eyes squinted into the distance as the tracks that might guide her to her father vanished with the arriving dirt. She felt her heart sink as she watched the likelihood of finding Isaac disappear with every gust which resurfaced the broad expanse of desert sand, making any possible footprints disappear. Each rush of air made the trail lie about the tragedy that occurred upon it, and even as skilled a cowgirl as Samantha could not track in these conditions. Like the disappearance of a coyote's howl into the summer air, so went Isaac.

Samantha knew it was true and accepted that trying anymore was futile and simply a poor plan, for Isaac decided he was going to die in this way and nobody could stop it at this point. Her lips and teeth ground with the compression of her jaw, the tiny rocks popping between her teeth causing a sensation of sandpaper on her tongue. She lowered the handkerchief and did an about face to spit with the wind, and in the process caught sight of the truck Daniel had stolen.

Daniel opened the door and stood alongside the vehicle looking at Samantha as she stared right back at him in a chess match of stares, competing to see who would be the first to talk.

"Why the fuck did you come?" asked Samantha, as her face turned from blue sorrowness to red fitful rage.

"Because."

"Why?"

"Because, I thought you needed a ride home," said Daniel.

"I've got one," said Sam coldly as she swung her leg over her horse.

"Samantha."

"What, Dan?"

"I spoke to your pa before he died."

"About what?" asked Samantha.

Dan continued looking at her and responded, "You." Daniel coughed on the collection of sand in his throat, then asked, "Can I take you home?"

Samantha and Daniel locked eyes in the desert, the fullest extent of both characters' stubbornness glaring, rays drawn between two sets of eyes. Eventually the gaze broke, and Samantha said nothing as she guided her horse into the back of the truck and lashed it down to the protruding gate about the rail box. After ensuring the safety of the old mare, she climbed in the front seat, shut the door, and looked forward.

"Go."

Daniel obliged and began driving the truck back toward the Lawson residence as Samantha remained silent. The miles wore away bleakly as both thought about Isaac.

Daniel was busy questioning why he would do this to himself; for what reason he would come back and help this Arizona cowgirl who was foolish enough to take to the high desert looking for her father in the middle of nowhere. Was this friendship? Foolhardiness? Perhaps love. Daniel couldn't tell anymore. Maybe Daniel took to the family business and became a quality liar like his father and he too could tell himself he was a better man than he really was.

Daniel remembered the wishes Isaac and how he asked him to take care of the woman sitting next to him. At the same time, he thought of who he really was. An ex-con who got another chance at the majors, and like every other opportunity he was ever given, he found a way to lose that one too. He couldn't see in himself the ability to carry out the orders of the dying fellow and he wondered if he really wanted to. The way Daniel figured, maybe only God could tell why he was here, but as the life of the rambler is, that was the best he could hope for, and perhaps wish that he may die in his sleep.

Samantha didn't think much. It wasn't that she was dumb or uncreative, but she had nothing to think about except the setting of the sun seen through the windshield and where her father may be standing as he watched it fade away. That, and why a man she barely knew would come back for him, and why she felt grateful. She figured it was because this was the first nice thing any man except her father had ever done for her.

All the while, Isaac watched a red Dodge stretch towards the horizon, smiling as his eyes closed, and he died peacefully in his sleep.

It was late when the car finally stopped in front of the Lawson residence, and the engine hummed to a halt shortly after the key was turned and released from the steering column.

"Thanks," said Samantha as she opened the door.

No other words were spoken as Daniel began his saunter towards the barn. Samantha had been walking just as proudly, but a mere twenty feet later, the world brought her to her knees.

Tears were something she couldn't find on her driveway, never in her life had she allowed herself that luxury. She didn't allow herself the weakness of grief , for the idea of surrendering oneself to the whims of the world was deemed selfish, pitiful, and ultimately deplorable by the people like her. In a lifetime of being told to brush things off, and to not tolerate grief she was confused what was really meant by the tugging feeling in her chest when she thought about her father. It was selfish to miss him, and it was selfish to forget him, and that is, was, and may always be the story of the range. Having a heart that can love someone, but somehow not feeling sad when they are gone.

In this way Daniel knew exactly how Samantha felt; he wasn't sad, but his feet just changed direction and he went back to her. The faded denim brushed the Arizona dirt and her hat flopped back as a wind uprooted it from upon her head. Daniel rested a hand lightly on her shoulder and looked at the stars. The Southern Cross reached down from its great place in Heaven causing him to think about himself and the world around him.

He thought about God and how that name once stirred something in him. He thought about how Pastor Thomas used to tell him that all good men may have the opportunity to get to that great big ordeal in the sky if they were just righteous. Hell, Pastor Thomas didn't even say they had to believe in God. Then again, what was a righteous man? Would a righteous man be sitting here right now with no words to say, or are there more important things in the world than dealing with one woman who lost her father? Was he a righteous man for coming back, or was he devilish because he had run. Daniel didn't know. He may never know. The one thing that was known is that on that night Samantha Lawson threw her arms around Daniel and held him as a tear slipped out of her eye, taking a long confused path to the ground. Daniel stared straight ahead the entire time thinking nothing of it, only about those stars and why they had brought him here.

Chapter 69:

In August, Andrew Thompson felt he was playing the best baseball of his life. The glove he wore was cracking unlike any other, his swing level and striking the ball with more force than he even knew he was capable of, and every game he had this year had only been violated by poor execution by his pitchers. Thompson was riding high on the life of the rookie on an upswing.

Thompson was convincing himself with each passing day that life was but a progression and the prior day was going to be forever worse than the next. Andrew laughed heartily with his teammates in victory and found a place where he could feel okay losing because at least he left everything he had on the field every time. Andrew Thompson was no Ben Crawford, his slight frame didn't allow for such a punishing reputation in the batter's box, but he was consistent. When Andrew took to the field he may have not hit three times a game or sent rockets over the center field fence, but people could put faith in him. Like the starter in a car, he may have not been the sexiest piece of machinery, but he was important to making everything else happen, and as anyone who ever had the misfortune of watching Bob Uecker while he still was dragging along the most pitiful major league career ever seen, or Clayton Kershaw in the playoffs, that was a thoroughly undervalued part of baseball.

"You've been traded," said Jeff Bentley from across the desk with Coach Detmer.

"What?"

"We have enough bread and butter on this team, Thompson. You're a good kid, but we don't want you. I'm sorry, you're headed to Minnesota," said Bentley.

Thompson panicked. His parents had already bought plane tickets to come and watch him play, he had already made arrangements to move in with his buddy near Frisco, Texas, to have a home after his expected promotion.

"But sir, I have my mom coming-"

"Kid, I don't really care. Okay? It's business and you're really not hot shit alright? I made sure to get you a job, but we found a kid we like better. Should've given us a reason not to get rid of you if you needed to stay in Texas that bad," said Jeff now filing his fingernails while dismissively uprooting a kid from what he thought was going to be the first step to a successful major league career.

"Why do you hate people?" asked Andrew.

"What do you mean?" asked Bentley now pulling open the drawer to put away his fingernail clippers.

"You don't even care. And neither does Coach Detmer. You told me that you guys liked me and wanted to keep me around. I just paid rent this month, dude! And now I'm heading to Minnesota?"

"Well, somewhere in the Twin's system."

"Why?"

"Because I'm a businessman and I need to sell a team, and those people out there don't care about teamwork, or dedication, or consistency, or brotherhood, or whatever the catchphrase of the day is to describe all of you rolling around in the mud. You know what they want to see? Numbers; because numbers make fucking sense, and you don't. As far as this world is concerned, Kid, you're just another entertainer that is getting paid to put on a show. Look, you're a nice guy from Ohio with pretty good knowledge of the game and competence to play at the Double A level, but I've seen other kids like you walk in this office a thousand times, and turned a thousand other kids like you to the wind, so they can go and play for every team in the majors and feel good telling their kids that when they were young they were the guy everyone on the team adored. You know what, Andrew? Nice guys don't win. They never do," said Jeff Bentley, looking at the corner of his desk at a picture of the girl who left him on his wedding day with nothing but a letter saying she was never coming back.

"This is a lesson. Coach Detmer tells me that you take the blame for the wild pitches and all that ballgame stuff I don't know and/or care about. If you want to be good at anything you have to force everyone around you to believe it, and I'm sorry that it took until now for you to figure that out. I hate people because they make this job hard because every time I get rid of one of you I end up having to tell the same story and half the time write up this bullshit narrative that you were 'a valued part of the team' and 'it was a difficult decision.' Fuck that, I get rid of you because there is more money somewhere else, and it is my job to find it."

Thompson looked across the table his face flush red as he listened to Bentley. All he heard was that he was worthless because the only thing people wanted was pennants and they didn't care who the man was. It finally made sense to him why all this garbage is so pervasive in professional athletics. He thought of the twenty-nine other Jeff Bentley's scattered across the country and how they did the same thing and generally less honestly.

"Do you have anything to say coach?" asked Andrew as he looked at Coach Detmer.

Coach Detmer still had his hands folded on his belly leaning far back in his chair reclining to such a degree that slumber seemed the only appropriate proceeding step if one were to be taken. There was an utter disinterest in Detmer's eyes as he said, "No."

Andrew Thompson then stood up from his chair, and turned towards the door before looking back one last time at his coach.

"You're gonna regret this."

"Probably not," said Bentley.

With that, the baseball career of Andrew Thompson in Texas came to a close and he made his way towards Minnesota. Like the fur-traders that preceded him by hundreds of years, he too hoped he would find success in the star of the North built on nothing but a hope and a prayer.

Jerry Tiner strolled around his office in New York around that time. He was a well-established man and well-respected even in the loss of the landmark Benjamin Crawford case. Jerry hated the small town at this point. He thought of his younger self and how stupid he was to embrace such a raucous culture. Moonshine, hoedowns, and the like, how despised were these pillars of Jerry's previous existence. How he dismissed his former friends when the Christmas cards from the likes of Christian Vier and Randy Bowman crossed his desk. The one time in the past fifteen years he had gone back to that little "shit hole" he came from was when he went to defend Benjamin Crawford, the last man he had any semblance of faith in. God no longer mattered to him. The baseball diamond was but a sifting of dirt on a plot of land better made into some industrial setting that was "actually worth something." Jerry hated even thinking about what he was when he was younger.

Instead, he found himself much more comfortable occupying this gigantic mansion with a long oak table, a leather volume in front of him, and lights placed evenly across the entire fifteen foot long surface. A younger Jerry would've complained about the rich bastard who lived on the hills in New York thinking he was better than everyone else and how much that kind of arrogance annoyed him, but now,

Jerry was that man and as often happens he had changed. The once gun-toting, mud-wheeling, freedom-waving man of the Panhandle had taken to being isolated in New York far from any friend who could hurt him, far from anybody he would have to defend in a court of law and vouch for every time a reporter asked him anything for it was nearly always a question about Benjamin or Daniel. How he hated those two.

By means of time, Jerry had become a man without a heart and placed the value of everything instead in his brain. Long ago he abandoned from his initial wish to establish justice and free innocent men, and became a hateful carrier of the law who pursued only the cases in which he could profit to further furnish this lonely home full of luxuries. From the outside this palace looked like a place for a king, but on the interior sat but a man dead on the inside.

"Mr. Tiner," said a young boyish butler who entered the room.

"What?" said Tiner dryly, not breaking the stare he made towards his novel.

"I have a letter for you."

Jerry maintained eye contact with the passage he was reading and extended his small bony finger towards the desk indicating to the boy where to leave the letter. Jerry often treated his employees like this. He had gotten this persuasion typical of men in power that his time was worth more than anyone else's and monetarily, this was true. As for the kid who took care of Jerry's mail for him, he was not going to try to fight for respect, for the paycheck to pay for his small apartment was far more grand than any stand against the wealthy he could make. So, carrying out the orders, he dropped the small letter on the table, and the boy quickly evacuated the room before Jerry could do as he typically did and judge him for the volume of his breathing threatening rhinoplasty upon the boy if he could not rectify that "insufferable tone of his nostrils".

Once Jerry grew tired of reading Faust, he put the book back on the table and grabbed the letter seeing a haphazard scribbling on the back which read "Papa". Jerry paused for a moment as he could see the shaking present in the writing of his father in his old age. He remembered how in other cases he had worked on that handwriting analysts mentioned how such a shake from previously pristine handwriting may be the indication of deteriorating mental faculties and quite possibly the onset of Parkinson's. Jerry looked at the letter for two minutes in solitude staring at the name and thought of where that paper had come from. That paper brought memories of all those people and their mange, the filth of their barns like the one that was in the same yard as his first home, and everyone who he convinced himself merely pretended to care about him. It had been so long since Jerry cared about anyone. Tiner thus examined the letter and proceeded to extend his hand over the wastebasket where he dropped the entire envelope. Jerry had no time to worry about that drunk town anymore; he had convinced himself he was capable of living alone forever.

Back in Holt, Bob Tiner sat wondering what his son was even up to anymore.

Chapter 70:

"Goddammit, Daniel. I always tell you to put away your razor," said Samantha from the bathroom upstairs while Daniel was lacing up his shoes, "and you always leave the damn thing out."

"Sorry, Honey," said Daniel.

He had taken a job in town as a clerk at a local hospital. The work was mundane, but easy, and available. Every day the stack of claims for everything from X-rays of little Billy's broken leg to Grandma's pain medication went through the office where Daniel would check each form to make sure it was correctly filled out, which in this day and age essentially meant checking the numbers. Some of the more common numbers, 6705, 42-98, and 219-87, were stamped in the upper right hand corner of the documents indicating circumcision, hip replacement, and arthroscopy respectively. There was nothing in the job description that demanded that Daniel dress as he did every day, but to Daniel this was him protecting his livelihood, his first time feeling happy in quite a long time. There was nothing special about Daniel anymore, and he liked that. Nobody knew his name, and to his employer he was simply a number responsible for handling other numbers that people who are really good with numbers would play with until the almost inevitable audit that always resulted in a mistake being found in the chain and one of the higher ups in the company being fired.

There had been a point in Daniel's life where he would have been enraged by a man who was anything like this. He used to hate complacency, and now it seemed the best word to describe the hairstyle he donned which found structural integrity by means of the cohesive properties of pomade. His shoes shined, a pair he found on Palm street in the middle of Phoenix made of steer hide and being sold in the used bin with just a minor scuff on the heel. His skin sparkled as the sun radiated off his face and the sheen of his hair bounced light back unto the world.

He had become one of those city-slickers, the kind that reflect the sun so prominently unto everyone else, but who in most cases just used that to hide the real darkness inside. The way he would ignore people talking directly to him, forgo throwing money in the bagel money jar at work, and just the general lack of concern for any other human being. It wasn't that he looked a bad man to the world anymore, but that he had become someone the world wanted. That shine gave the superficial impression that Daniel was a positive influence in the world, but it would be questioned in a greater context, for what he had gained in manner and class, he had lost in drive and ambition.

His greatest goal was no longer those grandiose dreams of taking a baseball between his fingertips and lasering it past the best batsmen in the game, but rather it was held within the idea that he could die with more toys than he started out with. Gadgets of all sorts dotted the house and were around the living room, from insulated coffee cups to instructional books on learning the bongos that he would never use. Daniel smiled when he looked at these things and his greased-back hair taking a sense of pride in the man he had created.

Meanwhile, Samantha exiting the shower upstairs was not so happy to see the evolution of West. Samantha could see the loss of the ruffian edge, the killer spirit, the things that made Daniel who he was. Samantha had all the reasons to hate Daniel in the world, but that indescribable force of nature which dictates the way of people had remained with her. God only knew why Samantha loved the man who abandoned her in her time of need, but the truth was that she did.

"Yes, Sam, I'll put it away next time," said Daniel lacing his Oxford shoes.

"Damn straight," mumbled Samantha now placing a hat on her head.

It was a peculiar arrangement in several regards for each of them. Perhaps the greatest challenge for Samantha was looking at that cross on her chest and thinking about what God may think of this wretched cohabitation. Sex was not a part of the living arrangement, but still, for months on end she had lived with Daniel in violation of that phrase in Thessalonians which said that appearing before the world as sinful was wrong, for it was against the word of God to be his follower and make one of his people appear immoral in this way. Furthermore, she knew Daniel was a man who had little faith, for every time she had gone to church she noticed him staying away from it. Samantha was troubled because her heart rested with a man with an issue with faith, which challenged hers. At the same time, she was sad to remember who he was, and who he had become. She wanted to make Daniel a righteous man, but could see the hypocrisy in trying to do it in the sinful way she was. With that, Samantha took to the range to herd cattle as Daniel went to a car he had bought to drive to the hospital.

The presence of routine in the life of Daniel had changed little, but the pawing of stitching was now the pawing of a mouse in his right hand moving files from place to place and gently swaying his head back and forth to show the satisfaction he had in his job.

"My supervisors will love that!" he always thought.

It disturbed others to look at the countenance of Daniel bouncing back and forth and how it shined too brightly for someone changed to this legally condoned imprisonment called clerkship. The other clerks were honestly terrified, for they had a sort of prejudice against happiness and any form of optimism towards the future. Daniel had chosen this line of work because even this recently since the most bizarre departure from the game of baseball ever, many of these uninteresting shells of men and women were as thoroughly disinterested in his wild past as he was in their boring histories. No one was able to tell if he was in prison at one point and per the labor laws of Arizona, only his employer was

entitled to his record of servitude, which in its very
unique case allowed him to work such a high-
security risk job, for it was deemed not his fault that
his former friend had plotted to destroy him. A man
upon a mountain had found a way to become a
hermit within its deepest valley, and Daniel was to
all intents and purposes, a happy hermit.

No one knew anything about Daniel, and he
chose to help them lose trust in him by repeatedly
lying about from whence he had come and what he
did to lead to this very day. West wanted to see the
destruction of that young boy with a fiery passion
and a granite conviction, for like many men who
decide they are old, he wanted to deprive himself of
that livened boy. He never wanted to look back at the
decisions that were made and the effort lost in what
he now thought of as a stupid dream, so Daniel
didn't. Punching time cards and doing a good job at
his mundane occupation was more important to him
now.

Daniel proceeded with the rest of his scripted
morning, pouring a cup of black coffee to be left in
the rightmost corner of his desk, and pulling out the
keyboard which rested upon a sliding board. He
extended it to the same distance he always did before
starting a program made by someone better with
computers than he, where he would finally type in
the appropriate keys for the billing information on
the variety of claims pouring through the claims
department. Daniel would break for lunch to eat half
a sandwich and then after a few more hours of
prescribed button mashing, he would call it quits
and shut off his computer ready to go back to the
residence of Samantha.

Samantha had returned from the fields
around that time, covered in mud and straw, with
cash in her pocket gained from a variety of odd jobs
she was hired to perform. Samantha worked hard in
the mud with her hands, the way her father did and

his father did, and his father before him. They toiled relentlessly in God's country holding His word close to their heart and the dream of becoming something worth bringing into Heaven forever persisting in their memory. Samantha was not entirely sure that the current situation was conducive to meeting her Heavenly Father, so it was with a heavy heart that Samantha said, "David, you can't live here anymore."

"Why?"

"Because it ain't right for an unmarried man and woman to share the same household. It is wrong in the eyes of the Lord."

Daniel listened as he nonchalantly kept on unlacing those Oxfords of his and removed right shoe first, the proper inverse of always placing the left shoe on first. It was in this action that Daniel couldn't help but have a flashback to who he was. His platonic conception of himself may have tried to kill all parts of Daniel Westboro the baseball player, but the ritualistic methodology incorporated into putting on his shoes was something which brought back the terrible memories. Daniel knew at one point he had believed in God, but it had been nearly a year since he was even able to say His name. In fact, at work Daniel would speak with his other coworkers and refute the idea that there was a God above in favor of thinking that no supreme deity was existent. Truth be told, there is no way to know if Daniel was correct in his skepticism, but the pain in Samantha's eyes made it apparent that he had to do something to remain at this house.

He pondered marrying Samantha, and then the memory of June Winters and her red sundress flashed across the set of eyes all persons seem to have behind the ones we can see. The way she used to put flowers in her hair, how she showed up to cheer for Daniel, was there for him when he hurt, when he prospered, and even in death did all she could to save him from the fifteen years of prison he had to endure. Those black-eyed Susans pulled a little bit at Daniel's heart remembering how in one of the few times in his life he allowed himself to feel anything beyond determination and his outright stubbornness that he was trespassing in that sunflower field of McCullough's and dancing with her as left-footed as that waltz truly was. Daniel had tried to forget June so many times, but still held onto the cross he no longer had faith in because some strange part of his mental faculties led him to believe perhaps someday he would spend another day in August dancing with Mary June Winters.

"So, I'm leaving then?" asked Daniel.

"I don't know. I know it seems crazy as hell, but there is one way we could stay together and make this right," said Samantha.

"And what is that?"

"Daniel Westboro, will you marry me?"

Daniel stopped removing his socks and stared at the floor. Marriage? What a silly concept, a man and a woman decide to get all dressed for some inconvenient weekend when someone's aunt can't show up so a preacher can profess that in the eyes of God they are married. How does one know they can marry someone? Who can truly make a vow to last a lifetime with anybody, especially with the fickle nature of the heart? Hell, why is it that Daniel could even consider loving another woman when he still had the engagement ring he was going to give June in the glovebox of his car. Was it wrong to still love someone when you married another? Was it wrong that half his heart was wherever June was and the other half with Samantha on earth? Sure, he tried to lie that he had no feelings for Ms. Lawson, but one can only lie to themselves for so long before they realize who they really are is what they will be. How could he know that feeling in his chest for Samantha was not one of those lies? For that matter, he seemed to carry bad luck with him. His mother died when he was young, his father abused him, his brother refuted his very relationship to him, he lost a chance at baseball, served a prison sentence for a crime he didn't commit, and now pretended he was happy with some job where he pushed uninteresting numbers from one end of his desk to the other. Daniel couldn't even imagine wanting to bring that sort of negativity into the life of another for ending up with the same lot he had to deal with seemed a worse punishment than being hanged, for at least in the latter the misfortune came to a close. Even worse was, as evidenced by the false image he portrayed in this attire, Daniel was the liar he never thought he'd see himself becoming.

"I can't let you do that to yourself," said Daniel. "I can't let you pretend that all you deserve is me Samantha."

"Shit, I'll believe what I want, Dan. You think I get why either?"

"I bet you're as confused as I am, and that's why I should look for somewhere else to live and leave this place behind me."

"No. Daniel, that's exactly why you need to stay," said Samantha. "Like my papa said, marriage isn't about findin' someone perfect, it's about feelin' like you did. Daniel, you're the only man I've ever cared to talk to in my life. You took care of my papa, and he obviously saw somethin' in you because he asked you to take care of me. Again, Daniel, you're the only man I'd let believe needed to take care of me," said Samantha.

Daniel mulled over this, how he had told Isaac in his last conversation that he would take care of Sam, and he thought about how what she was saying was exactly true for Daniel anymore. Besides, in the weathered mind of Daniel he figured at least this would add some stability to his life.

"Sure," said Daniel.

"Damn, you sure know how to make a woman feel special don't you," said Samantha in reply to Daniel's dry hollow response.

"You know it," said Daniel, "That's why you love me."

With that, Samantha laughed, and she and Daniel embraced in the kitchen. Samantha knew she had found the love of her life and was holding him. Meanwhile, Daniel was looking at the refrigerator wondering himself if her love was requited or not.

Chapter 71:

David had had an admirable summer for a rookie, but failed to make the playoff roster for the Los Angeles Angels of Anaheim due to an injury. He'd broken his ankle when a third baseman from the Blue Jays stomped on the joint trying to reach the bag to the dismay of many Angels fans who envisioned the young first baseman being an integral part of a September playoff run.

As much as the fans of Los Angeles hated the predicament, David hated it worse. Reading the headlines which detailed his misfortunes, he was angered thinking of people who actually have it terrible, such as his own brother. David had at one point envisioned a life where he could forever be Christopher Hart and allow the death of David Westboro to turn from the fiction it was into the truth. David hated this injury for it meant he was obligated to think about life for the first time in many years. He had to think of all the people he lied to, all the people he ignored like the letters from Randy Bowman who talked about how similar he looked to David Westboro, the letters from Florida congratulating him for the pride he brought his little town near Osceola, and worst of all that thing which kept coming back to him. Every day he remembered ending the life of Daniel; he knew Daniel was dead. Without baseball, the man they called West had little purpose for living anymore, and David knew that. Because of this, David had spent many days sitting alone in his Los Angeles suburban home ignoring reporters who came by to interview him. One day David went to his basement to procure an old duct tape wallet containing a single yellowed slip of paper. Dialing the number on the card produced a ringing black telephone in the house of Ruth Hart, which was promptly answered by the now older woman.

"Mama Hart? Is that you?"

Ruth Hart held the phone, mouth agape, knowing exactly who that voice belonged to, albeit with a much deeper pitch and a timbre that befits the voices of boys after they have become men.

"David?" said Ruth into the phone once she finally found the capability to speak.

"I'm alive." said David, feeling tears start to form in his eyes.

"I'm all alright Mrs. Hart, I'm all alright."

Ruth couldn't believe what she was hearing.

"I'm comin' home, Mrs. Hart. I'm comin' to see you, and Joey, and Randy, and hell maybe even a couple of the Zachs, if they're still in town. Is that okay with you?"

Ruth smiled joyously as tears flowed from her face. "Yes David, come home."

David hung up the phone after a while and then went to the next order of business. A reporter from across town had always asked him to call this number if there was anything about his past he ever wanted to tell anyone, because they were all waiting and he wanted to write about it.

"Skip?"

"Yeah. Chris?"

"I want to talk to you. Bring your friends."

David got to the Angels clubhouse, finding a room full of reporters with their tape recorders out.

Their pens were ready to scribble whatever ramblings the ballplayer may have to say, since the world series was over, and in October there is little work for a baseball writer. They had showed for the next story to throw to the masses, hoping for some dark history and a juicy lead as to from whence Chris Hart had come, as is the nature of the reporter. The silence was palpable when David Westboro stepped to the front and a camera for ESPN pointed directly at his face to capture every nuance and sound for the viewers back home who found interest in hearing from the player who was bound to be Rookie of The Year.

"Y'all have asked me many times where I came from, and why my parents don't have the same last name I do. Y'all wanna hear me talk about some past that you haven't heard of before. Well, today, I finally am goin' to answer those questions,"

David then wiped the sweat beading from his forehead, and proceeded to speak under the scrutiny of a multitude of cameras.

"My name is not Christopher Hart. My name is David Westboro, and I was born in this town named Holt in Texas. Jacob Clubber is not my father. He is simply a good man who happened to find me as I was lost somewhere along a road near Amarillo. From that day I have been lyin' about who I am to all of you. Back in Florida, him and Sarah are probably as shocked as y'all are, and I blame none of you. I want to apologize to all the fans, friends, and family for never telling you, but I am simply a kid who ran away from home and became everythin' he always dreamed his older brother would be. Yes, David Westboro is my brother. I hope by the grace of Our Creator that you can forgive my dishonest soul, and I pray that the Lord forgives me for all the people I have ignored and lettin' down my brother when he needed me most. I hope that the good people of Los Angeles and the major leagues can forgive me for what I have done," said David as excited looks sprang back on the remorseful handsome featured face.

"Mr. Hart!"

"That is Mr. Westboro, and no, I will not be answerin' any questions at this time."

Tabloid writers' pens furiously scribbled out the remarks of David and a palpable sense of urgency was tasted in the air by the media in that small room in Los Angeles. Vans with the footage either raced to their news stations or the live streaming of the conference was already being sent out to the viewers back home. It wasn't every day that someone got to expose a hero for who he really was to the world. It was indescribable the kind of backlash that was received by David.

The pundits, teachers, students, parents, and grocery shoppers spoke in a variety of tongues and voices of their generation's Cain. Although he had not murdered his brother for the attention of God like the biblical man had, he had destroyed the reputation of one. A man who would've otherwise been considered completely normal was depicted on the television and in print as insane, and it was all because of the rookie all the kids wanted a card of for their collections. The boy in baseball that made the women swoon. The kid who arguably revived America's pastime for several who looked to him as a good man who got what he deserved, and inspired other kids in the middle of nowhere as to what they could do if they always just tried their best. But now?

Now it was a debate of if what he did was simply trying to make a guilty conscience feel settled, and what other lies a man like David could tell. Those toys he bought for small children who couldn't afford any looked like tokens for the public's affection, the autographs a way of cementing some personal connection with a few good men when they finally discovered the depths of what was wrong with him. In a country so infatuated with the destruction of the most integral parts of a man whenever possible, especially the destruction of those who appear positive influences on this world, David was mere cannon fodder.

Politicians used him as a way to elevate their own slimy histories by remarking about what kind of man could turn on their own brother like he had. Preachers threw away the cards he'd leave at the little churches he ran into along the way, and thousands of others simply chose not to believe that such an affront was even possible. In the end, it made David feel very lonely as it seemed the whole world wanted to isolate him, and the papers and talk shows wanted to help get everyone in on the game.

David held that jersey in his hands ready to light it for the lie that it was, and then remembered something far more important. He instead folded it neatly and placed it in the leather suitcase that Jacob had given to him so many years ago, and boarded a midnight flight to Amarillo. David might have had reason to hate himself so as to fit in with the rest of the people who knew him, but on that day, David smiled for he was finally free from being Christopher Hart.

Meanwhile, in a mahogany study in New York, Jerry Tiner looked for a number in the recesses of a leather notebook.

"Yes, I am calling about David," said Jerry speaking to a friend of his in Texas.

"I see no reason why we shouldn't be able to win an abduction case against Jacob Clubber."

Chapter 72:

One of the most convenient things about fly-by-night weddings is the lack of preparation needed for them. Between the bride and groom there was but one aunt, and she was a bit of nut job, and because of that, it was rather simple to choose a day to get married.

In a courthouse where a dusty clerk read some pre-written statement on behalf of the state, Samantha and David held each other's hands; he dressed in blue jeans and a flannel shirt and she a dress with an almost comical amount of design drawn on. Like many things in the life of these three gathered on this October afternoon, the idea of ceremony was abandoned for the value of practicality. No wine sat on the desk, no music was playing, and the adjective casual was an underperforming word in the attempt to describe how relaxed the scene truly was. Almost yawning as she said it the clerk uttered

"Do you, Mr. Daniel Ellis Westboro take Samantha Louise Lawson to be your lawfully wedded wife?"

"I do."

"Do you, Miss Samantha Louise Lawson take Daniel Ellis Westboro to be your lawfully wedded husband?"

"I do," said Samantha, her face producing an ebullient shine to accompany the bubbliness she felt in her heart holding the hands of Daniel.

"Alright," said the clerk who then stamped the document pronouncing their legal matrimony.

Daniel was kind of stunned the sheer lack of emotion behind the words of the toadish looking woman who passed that document so freely across her desk acting as if nothing had happened, when

Daniel had just combined his flesh with that of Samantha.

"Well, are you going to kiss me, Mr. Westboro?" asked Samantha with a chuckle to draw Daniel back in from his glance towards the clerk who surprised him with her complete dispassion for her job. Daniel then looked at his beautiful bride and needed no more coaxing. At that moment, God smiled down at the forging in the eyes of Samantha, and she looked at the groom with one of those looks of optimism that one only gets to see once or twice in their lifetime. Daniel could see the love in her eyes, yet somehow, even on this wedding day of his, he found a way to think of June.

He didn't quite know if this is what he was supposed to feel. He wondered if it was wrong that he married a girl who loved the Lord when he still couldn't find it in his heart to say He existed. All he knew was that being around Samantha made him happy, sad, angry, confused, and omniscient all at the same time and as any man who has ever felt love knows, that is exactly what it feels like. Daniel didn't make a big deal of his first kiss as a husband. It didn't seem important to him. He chose not to define anyone or anything by moments but rather by their collective worth. So it was with that that Daniel and Samantha went back out to Sam's father's old truck and started it..

"Where do you want to go?" asked Daniel, putting on his seat belt while the engine continued to whir.

"I don't care, I just want to go somewhere with you," said Samantha.

Daniel felt his heart blossom with those words, for it had been nearly fifteen years since anyone had said that to him. In those brief moments in the parking lot in front of the courthouse, a world of doubt about Ms. Lawson faded away in honor of a new faith in Mrs. Westboro.

On that day, Daniel realized that love was not a vector quantity. It wasn't some sort of force that man has control over. Love was something that chose the magnitude and especially the direction of itself. Daniel realized that Mary June Winters would want him to love Samantha Lawson because, if he could stop pretending he was clearly uninterested, maybe he could find happiness. After all, finding happiness only happens when one choose to leave their comfort zone. It was on this day that Daniel chose to become vulnerable to Samantha.

"We can do that," said Daniel.

"I've always wanted to go to Vegas," he said.

So the happy newlyweds went back to their small country home to prepare for the voyage ahead of them. It is a rather interesting phenomenon how when one is married they usually have the least amount of wealth they ever will, yet it is at this point in life that one tends to engage in the lavish activity of honeymooning. Then again, maybe it is the exuberance of youth and abundance of life that draws so many young couples to part ways with their limited financial resources. Nonetheless, that was the point this pairing was at, and several dances were shared in the kitchen, and smiles as the suitcases were packed haphazardly for the trip to Nevada. That was, until the phone rang in the living room. Daniel looked at Samantha and shrugged his shoulders as he went to answer the phone.

"Mr. Westboro on the line, how may I help you?"

"This is Trent Anderson."

"Oh. Are you one of Sam's friends or something?"

"No... I am the general manager of the Minnesota Twins."

Daniel looked worried and Sam could detect concern as Dan's hand busily tried to wave it away, for this look was simply trying to believe what he was hearing.

"The baseball team?"

"Daniel, what else would it be? I'm clearly not calling for your brains. I want to know how you would feel about coming up here and showing us what you can do."

Daniel's face twisted a little more and his eyebrows extended towards the ceiling at these remarks, thinking quietly to himself that people from Minnesota were supposed to be nice.

"Why?"

"Because, you're not bat shit crazy like we thought. Now am I sending a contract to your agent or not?"

"Sir, I have to talk to my wife."

"Feel free to call back, but don't wait too long, you ain't the belle of the ball you know..."

"Of course," said Daniel who hung up the phone and stared at the floor wondering how to put this to Sam.

"So when are you leaving?" asked Sam.

"What?"

"For Minnesota, they said they're goin' to let you play baseball again right?"

"Sam, I don't think I should. It's been too long, the team's not gonna want a headline on the mound-"

"Look, Daniel. You worked hard to get to this point. There ain't no way in hell you aren't gettin' on that plane. I'll make you go," said Samantha. Rolling up her sleeves and with agitation in her voice, it was clear that her words were entirely true.

"I've seen how you watched the game with my papa, and I could see that light in your eyes. I could see how badly you wanted to get back out there, and I've been prayin' for you that you get another chance. If nothin' else do it for your wife, Danny."

Daniel was hoping he was a better actor than he was, but of course, that is the problem with women: they always find out the truth. No matter how much he tried to show this reinvented Daniel, she could still see the man underneath those white linen shirts that wanted to get lost in the mud and pitch in a major league ballgame before he died. Even when Daniel had convinced himself baseball was part of his history, she could still see it in him and was begging for months for him to get his chance to redeem himself.

"Daniel, I want you to go. I'd be a horrible wife if I didn't tell you to leave."

"Samantha, will you come with me?"

"Dan, don't you go worryin' about me. I've gotta take care of the ranch. You better call me when you get there, though," she said smiling in that bittersweet moment while her brand new husband was heading for the door.

"Whatever you say, Mrs. Westboro," Daniel said with a grin.

Daniel was headed for the door, when he stopped and looked back and almost sheepishly uttered,

"I love you, Sam."

It was the first time since he met her that he believed in those words.

Chapter 73:

In Texas, the younger Westboro was in a different predicament. While Daniel was heading to South America to prepare for the season ahead over the long winter, David was busy searching for a lawyer to vouch for his guardian and mentor Jacob Clubber on charges of abduction. The last one had become frazzled in court when faced by Jerry Tiner for he knew the immense power carried by that little man.

Over the years, the once happy-face had been deadened with the presence of a thin pair of glasses and an air of adroitness. His gaunt frame had shrunk further making him appear the full realization of a devil on Earth; his sallow cheeks and bony hands stirring visions of the raised dead in people. He may have been a short man, but when Jerry Tiner entered the room everyone was entirely aware who the most qualified legal mind was.

Jerry was known to stare down witnesses and cause full-grown men accused of heinous felonies to crumble. Perhaps what terrified people the most about Jerry was the fact nobody could see life in him, only hatred and a pure drive for the unadulterated truth. People didn't concern him, they were simple pawns to his game of playing with the law. It was true what they said about nothing being more terrifying than a man who knew where he was going, and that is what Jerry was.

"Mr. Clubber, do you have legal counsel?"

"Yes, Judge Byron, he does," said Archibald Grieves, the man who entered in a suit as outdated as his own name.

"Okay, who are you?"

"Archibald James Grieves, attorney at law. I am here to represent Jacob Lloyd Clubber."

"Fair enough. Does the defendant have anyone to bring to the stand?"

"Yes, your honor, the defense calls David Westboro to the stand."

David was then escorted to the witness stand whereupon he would place his hand atop a bible and vow to tell the truth, the whole truth, and nothing but the truth, so help him God. Grieves would begin with the mandatory questions for the record.

"Mr. Westboro, is your name David Westboro?"

"Yes."

"Have you ever gone by any other aliases?"

"Yes."

"Which were?"

"I went by the name Christopher Hart for the past fifteen years."

"Okay. Mr. Westboro, when did you first meet Mr. Clubber"

"Seventeen years ago near the Oklahoma border."

"Mr. Westboro, wouldn't you have been around ten years old at this time?"

"Yeah, something around there."

"And for what reason would a mere child be stumbling about the northern side of the Texas panhandle in the middle of the night by a highway?"

"My father abandoned me there," said David as some in the crowd started to tune in closer.

"I attempted to emancipate myself from my father and he did not want his name tarnished by such. So, he instead told them all I was lyin' and ditched me in the middle of nowhere," said David as members of the crowd felt moved.

"And this is where you met Jacob Clubber?"

"Yes, it is."

"Mr. Westboro, would you say you were coerced into entering Mr. Clubber's vehicle?"

"No."

"Would you say that Mr. Clubber exploited you in any fashion?"

"No."

"Would you identify Mr. Clubber as your legal guardian when you were a child?"

"Yes."

"Mr. Westboro, would you say the decision was legal consent to accompany Jacob Clubber to Florida?"

"Yes."

"Your honor, the defense has no more questions."

Judge Byron shuffled his papers and in that man of the law voice said

"Alright, does the state have any questions?"

"Yes, we do, your honor," said Jerry Tiner as he slowly ascended from the depths of his courtroom chair. No countenance seemed to radiate from that face. In fact, the ashen look of his complexion lightened by years studying leather-bound books made Jerry look nothing like the kid that David had known at one point. Those angular teeth gave him the appearance of a vampire as the cold questions began to pour out.

"Mr. Westboro, is it or is it not true that you were under the legal protection of Robert Westboro when you disappeared?"

"It is true. I was the child of Robert."

"And is it also true that the state of Texas had a search party looking for you?"

"Yes but-"

"Mr. Westboro, does that not indicate that your father was in pursuit of his child?"

"It shows such but-"

"So, does that not mean that there was an adequate concern for your welfare when the official documentation of the search party shows that Amber Alert protocols were followed for twice as long as they are in normal missing child cases?"

"Jerry, quit bullshittin' everyone!" said David, the anger present in his eye. The courtroom feeling the tension in the air as a young kid looked at his old friend who now tried to vilify what he saw as his father. Jerry didn't even flinch.

"Your honor, may I ask more questions or does the witness need a recess?"

"That is entirely up to the witness, Mr. Tiner."

David was enraged, but there was no way he was going to afford Jerry the satisfaction of seeing him lose his composure.

"I'm fine," said David.

"Mr. Westboro, what evidence can you produce to prove to this court that you were in fact abused by your father and justified in your evacuation from his custody?"

"I have several friends who can attest a host of injuries they observed."

"Are these reports backed up by the police?"

David hung his head, for he knew there was no record. His father was the law, and if he even tried he would have suffered.

"No."

"Mr. Westboro, on what account can the court ascertain some credibility to your outlandish claims."

"The fact that he is a certifiable lyin' dirt bag that put away his own son for fifteen years," said David with agitation.

"David, are you aware that patterns in honesty can be traced genetically?"

"What do you mean?"

"I mean, hypothetically speaking, some psychologists profess that we can trace lying traditions down a family tree, meaning that if you and the court can refer to Robert as an almost pathological liar, could we not extend the same identification to you?"

"Objection your honor, badgering the witness," said Archibald Grieves.

"Sustained. Mr. Tiner, please tell me you have somewhere you are going with this."

"I do, Your Honor. After psychoanalysis of some of the certain behaviors David has shown in speech and writing, we have reason to believe that he is mentally ill with factitious disorder. We believe that Mr. Westboro was brainwashed in his young age by Jacob Clubber, and due to an underlying condition of Munchausen syndrome substantiated his claims with self-injury, which he would not confirm with the authorities due to bounds of his moral conscience which knew his father was a better man than the one he tried to show. It is for this reason that the state argues that perhaps the testimony of Mr. Westboro be discounted for his mental illness makes him prone to pathological lying tendencies, and we recommend treatment for the victim by a proper mental health care professional."

"I am not a victim!" shouted David as he stood from the witness stand.

"Mr. Westboro, the court orders you to sit down or I will hold you in contempt," said Judge Byron.

"Does the plaintiff have any more questions for the witness?"

"No Your Honor, we don't."

"Mr. Westboro, you may be seated."

David hated the bullshit of politics and law: the way these men in robes with titles that stretched across doorframes carried themselves and how they thought since they had just a little more opportunity than the next guy that they were the true arbiters of good and wrong. David seethed about this system and the many times it destroyed him and twisted his family into an unrecognizable knot. He remembered being a child and thinking the law was to protect people, but later learned it truly was just something that suited individuals play with for the entertainment of their over privileged minds.

When he looked at Jacob Tiner, he remembered how he used to speak of becoming a lawyer to save farms from the banks that twisted arms and pulled teeth from farmers as they severed their financial arms and legs. Now what he saw was someone playing a game. It was just chess to Jerry Tiner and Archibald Grieves and Judge Byron and everyone who played party to this crooked system.

He looked at his truly insignificant self and realized he was the pawn to these elites. No one here cared about Jacob Clubber quite the way he did. No, it was all just a fight to see who had the best technicality or bit of legal jargon to win over twelve people, more with pizazz than logic, reasoning, or the most important of all human tenets, morality.

The rest of the trial was a blur to David, as a series of psychologists, police officers, child abuse experts, and character witnesses went up to all pipe in their piece about what this world had done to him. All of that time he found himself wondering what the purpose was. If he was supposed to be the victim and he already said he wasn't, then what was the point of all these psychics and these doctors talking about all these esoteric subjects? Why couldn't they believe him? Most of all, David wondered how he had given them a reason to not believe him. He felt powerless, for his own identity was deemed untrustworthy. The only thing David could do was sit next to Jacob Clubber and pray that the closest thing he ever had to a dad would be free.

Chapter 74:

The sound of bachata music danced off the walls of the buildings around D'Aguila Lopez ballpark where Daniel Westboro was warming up for his first pitching appearance since a good five months or so ago during his first flirtation with the major leagues. Daniel didn't know much about this country and found himself concerned trying to have any dialogue with anyone in Santo Domingo.

On this day, Daniel Westboro realized he would be standing further from home than he ever had before. The southern reach of the ballpark being at a latitude no journey of his had ever come close to, but a place he would have to at least step on for

Daniel needed to "feel" a place before he pitched. Like the spreading of salts before a sumo match or the burning of incense in a hallowed temple, Daniel needed to complete the ritual of walking around every ballpark before he was ready to pitch.

He had kept in shape lifting after every day at work, partially to stay in good physical condition and mostly to stave off boredom while Samantha still worked in the fields. His teammates found great joy in hearing about his desert bride, and often jabbed at him with attacks on his masculinity because of the unusual predicament. Daniel took it in stride, for although a good number of them may have believed the arrangement was wrong, Daniel saw no problem in being the more homebound one, for he was happy the way he was. Besides, anyone who wanted to get too wise would be met with his ninety-three mile per hour fastball.

Oh, that aggression. How Daniel could feel it start to come back to him that day. When tossing a ball around with a bunch of teammates in what couldn't even be considered a bullpen session, it can be difficult for most players to find enthusiasm, and with the lessening exuberance Daniel found in his seasoned age, that was especially true. But even long after the last start the pitcher still remembers that extra bit of life that flutters in their chest when the ball rolls between their fingertips. The way game day went, how people ask if you're ready and you respond "always". That little bit of arrogance you need to take with you to the mound to be successful and the shutters towards everything that isn't propelling that small bit of leather sixty feet and six inches towards victory the approximately one-hundred times you'd be asked to do such. Daniel loved feeling that spirit of competitiveness rile up his heart, that raw emotion that all ballplayers try to pretend they don't have, but is the real reason why they play. Cocaine addicts habitually return to that destructive vice for a feeling like this.

The rush. That is what they call it. The feeling that nothing can stop you and the world moves so much slower because of how fast you are. Your vision goes a little blurry, but you can see so much clearer. That is the place Daniel was in.

At this point, Daniel took one last step to that southernmost reach of the ballpark and took in a mouthful of Caribbean air, now having walked about the place to a satisfactory condition.

Daniel stood on the mound of that little ballpark in that small little island country smiling as the Bienvenido Buccaneers sent the first man from the dugout towards home plate. Brandishing his bat high, and a persona that preceded himself, Sergei Guadalupe was a man to be reckoned with.

He was a boy that had arisen from Trou Basseux, a port town on the coast of Tortuga that floated near a lost island country called Haiti of which it was part. The country had been in shambles nearly as long as it sat there, the result of Toussaint Louverture leading a rebellion to free the nation from the grasp of a host of masters. He had been the first black general of the French military before he became successful in creating an independent republic in 1804 by some combination of militaristic genius and another part political wizard.

However, it was debated to this day whether such freedom was really wanted. Poverty and food insecurity had plagued the region almost as much as the consequences of corruptible men who had seized power by means of the thirty-two coups that had taken place since its founding.

Sergei was a man who escaped Tortuga. At thirteen years old, he left his family and his country behind for the Dominican Republic. Several back in Haiti hated him, for even though he sent back a good portion of his check to help them, they had demanded more and more of him until one day the graciousness of Sergei concluded when he realized that the funds he was giving to were not helping anyone but providing the monetary resources for a host of superficial do-gooders to parade around the island for its scenery instead of actual contribution to any meaningful change. Sergei despised the idea that the benefits of his toil were deemed entitled to others, and that these diversions of his wealth were paying for vacations for front-row artists from a church to say they had contributed to a great cause. He hated how faith was twisted and portrayed by these people.

It was also true that Guadalupe knew there were a few good people but as happens all too often with charity, the beneficiaries were no longer the people who truly needed it. Sergei Guadalupe was so much like Daniel, a man who tried to do the right thing, payed dearly for it, and found himself on this diamond trying to do the one thing that ever made sense to him. The two locked eyes, and even without talking they carried expressions that made the moment mean what it was. It was a second chance.

"Jugar a la pelota!"

Daniel knew far too little Spanish and far too much baseball to not know what was next. The ball dancing in his fingertips in the fashion he had tossed it since high school, Daniel looked behind the plate for a signal from his catcher. On the baseball diamond, the language barrier disappeared; a finger went down and pointed out calling for fastball away. Daniel reared back and delivered, causing the gun to read 93 miles per hour and Sergei to look back, wondering from what part of the bean-polish frame of Daniel such an admirable fastball came from. Sergei stood in the box awaiting strike two which flew by just as quickly, putting the count 0-2.

It was at this time Sergei started to feel the same rush Daniel had, that same stirring in his heart for his best, not because he now had awoken, but because he thought in that count of where he had come from and who he was. He thought of the little boy who spent several hours practicing this game and the conclusion of his education in the fifth grade. The way his friends all had to chop sugar cane to even keep food on the table, while he was afforded the opportunity to play baseball all day every day 365 days a year due to an innate talent afforded to him by the grace of God for finding the label on the baseball and sending the sweet spot of his bat into it. It may be true that it wasn't that eloquently stated in his mind while ten thousand fans gazed at the game of chess between him and Daniel, but those thoughts were there. Sergei wondered what he would do without baseball, and due to the fear of one day not being good enough and losing everything he had, he did what most of the young boys at the baseball academy in San Cristobal would; he took a deep breath to forget the past.

Pulling himself together, Sergei re-entered the batter's box. Daniel reached back for yet another fastball, but this time a mistake was made as the ball stood about belt high. Sergei thus strode forward with all his might and stared down the ball turning his hips into the small piece of leather and rocketing it out towards center field where it came back to earth somewhere on the second level. Sergei had slow-rolled the ball and flipped his bat in the most exuberant fashion, moving all limbs in a manner consistent with his adrenalized state. His dugout laughed heartily as the ball took its grand path out of the park and the crowd was interspersed with the sounds of booing and cheering. Guadalupe upon reaching home performed a cartwheel and went back to the dugout to pump fists with every member of his clubhouse.

Daniel hated it.

"That cocky bastard," he thought. "I'm going to show him."

In his rageful state, Daniel became a better pitcher. The following twenty-one outs came at no cost except two hits and the one surrendered home run.

"What the fuck is your issue?" asked Daniel as he walked off the field. Sergei ignored him.

"Hey mud, what is your problem?" asked Daniel again the next time he saw him in the on-deck circle, again ignored by Guadalupe.

The remainder of the game went much like this as Daniel tried to incite a response from Sergei, and he continued to act as if the pitcher didn't exist. All the while, the loosely held together team ignored the derogatory exchanges.

When the game was done, Sergei and Daniel met in a hallway both heading for the exit of the stadium, Sergei to his bus and Daniel to Sergei. In a dark column along the walk, Daniel found the despised man and grabbed him by the collar shoving his head into the concrete wall of a building as he asked him much the same question he did inside the stadium.

"One last time, what the fuck is your problem?" asked Daniel.

Sergei was terrified.

"Nothing man, why?" he asked in his panicked state.

"Then why the hell did you do that little fucking dance after bombing on me?"

Sergei in that alleyway flashed back to that moment, remembering how it felt as if he had just validated his being in professional baseball. How he threw his hands in the air and bat towards the infield for much the same reason the young boys across all the small island republics do, as an expression of thankfulness to the opportunities the game gave them, an expression of joy over moments like this that made playing this game worth it. Sergei didn't know that much English, and lacked the education to state much else besides,

"Because it feels goddamn good to be worth something."

Daniel looked at the young kid closely, his stare still menacing the boy. He thought about what those words meant to him. Few people besides Daniel and Sergei could ever comprehend the elation one feels when they discover their self-worth in whatever limited quantities they do, but Daniel understood. He thought of his teammates, who in their perfectly broken English explained to him the plight of coming from nothing and fighting for everything. How they had families they were going to try and raise on baseball and communities that they were going to try to reinvigorate with some financial influx like comes when a boy goes off to the United States to play professional baseball. In this way, Daniel could see much of himself in Sergei and his teammates. Daniel then realized that all the over the top celebration was not because people in the Dominican Republic had no sense of sportsmanship, but rather because they were thankful for the opportunity.

"I don't hate you man, I just love baseball," said Sergei who was trembling even more than when this interrogation started.

"Don't hurt me!" he whimpered in his trembling.

Daniel released Sergei and walked back to his apartment across the street from D'Aguila.

Chapter 75:

"All rise for the Honorable Judge Byron," said the bailiff.

David waited in his seat in anticipation. Anxiety reigned for in that bench he saw nothing anymore but a man in a long robe who would tear his family apart yet again. His home had been shattered so many times in his life that it seemed God probably didn't want him to have a family. Every time he found one, it was taken away like the Seminole wind blowing off to somewhere that wasn't here. David had yet to go to a courthouse for anything but having another thing taken from him. The trial had lasted a whole week as Jerry Tiner teamed with the Osceola county prosecutor to compile an extensive list of reasons as to why Jacob Clubber could not legally be the guardian of David.

"Because the defense cannot provide evidence that David Westboro was not brainwashed or had his mental capacity altered in any way which would inhibit an honest testimony to the conditions of his detainment, the court must penalize Mr. Clubber based on the Sec 20.03 of the Texas penal code which reads as follows: 'Sec. 20.03. KIDNAPPING. (a) A person commits an offense if he intentionally or knowingly abducts another person. (b) It is an affirmative defense to prosecution under this section that: (1) the abduction was not coupled with intent to use or to threaten to use deadly force; (2) the actor was a relative of the person abducted; and (3) the actor's sole intent was to assume lawful control of the victim.(c) An offense under this section is a felony of the third degree.' Of the defenses listed, Mr. Clubber is unable to prove any. The only verifiable thing in this entire trial is that David Westboro was a minor taken into custody by Mr. Clubber, and that such was done without consent of Mr. Westboro's father who maintained legal custody of Mr. Westboro at that time. Being that there is no outstanding agency that can substantiate the alleged abuse that the victim continues to present was the nature of his father in their relationship, It is the opinion of the prosecution that since the only verifiable parts of this case are those which present Mr. Westboro as an unlawfully detained minor, and Mr. Clubber as the executor of the offense, that the court has an obligation to the people of Texas to punish him per this great state's legal code.

 The defense will tell you that the charges cannot be pressed for there is no way to prove that Jacob Clubber did not use or threaten to use deadly force in his abduction of David Westboro. We have a court system which allocates punishment on the notion that all are innocent until proven guilty. I believe enough circumstantial evidence has been provided to show that Jacob Clubber is proven guilty, for there is no way to deny that Mr. Clubber took Mr. Westboro as a minor so many years ago. In contrast, the defense has yet to produce a single reason as to why Mr. Clubber is innocent beyond a list of hearsay evidence from the presumably brainwashed Mr. Westboro and a variety of character witnesses most likely acquiescing to a greater force of cronyism. Being that the argument of the defense is thereby invalid by all standards of law, and the practice thereof in this state, and the argument for the prosecution is built off of verifiable fact, I feel the jury will decide correctly and find Mr. Clubber to be guilty of kidnapping in the third degree. The prosecution rests its case," said Jerry Tiner as he went back to the prosecution table, feeling that the well-rehearsed closing arguments may have been enough to win over a jury.

 "Does the defense have any closing arguments?" Judge Byron asked.

"Yes, we do, Your Honor," responded Archibald Grieves.

"The defense believes that the matter of this case rests in intent. It comes down to a man driving in the middle of nowhere finding a boy who appeared lost, scared, and alone. In the matter of this case, there is nothing that the alleged victim said that the defendant did not corroborate, the road he was found on, the time of day, and the manner in which the meeting took place were exactly the same in both independent testimonies. Furthermore, multiple individuals came forth and said that Mr. Westboro displayed strange injuries over the year, and "surprisingly" none of them were ever documented in the LeHigh county court system. Something which I believe we can all attribute to the fact that his late father Robert was a police officer, and I doubt someone willing to take bribes, as he did with Jack Crawford, would be ethical enough to have his own sheriff's office honor any accusations against himself in cases of domestic abuse with any validity. There was such an inherent problem with the system, that I hardly believe we can trust the system to be the basis of our defense.

Yes, it is an argument that makes a lawyer like me cringe, the problem with law is law itself. The prosecution may be able to display the stacks of paper that speak contrary to the situation told by Mr. Westboro and Mr. Clubber, but why do we value the word of a piece of paper more than the word of a man when both are just as corruptible? How can documents that tell how great Robert was to his son matter more than the words of his own son? What makes it impossible to trust a man that lied for his family and would it be justice to do as the law books say and imprison Mr. Clubber for trying to help out a small neglected, lost, and abused kid on a country road? The best part of it all though," said Archibald while pausing and looking at the jury, "is that none of it matters."

An inquisitive look came from the jury.

"Per the United States Constitution, the supreme law of the land rests in the federal government. This means that Mr. Clubber is no longer subject to Texas state law, but to the matter of federal authority, if the federal prosecutor decides to press charges as is consistent with U.S. law code Chapter 55 § 1201, which if I am not mistaken occurred this morning. Because of this, I ask that the court take a recess so that jurisdiction of the case may be examined by you, Your Honor," said Archibald Grieves while Jerry Tiner busily raced through his law books and felt ashamed he hadn't arrived upon the same conclusions.

"Hmm... I will take the matter up with the feds. A half-hour recess, and then we shall return," said Judge Byron, still looking perplexed as to what had just happened.

When all parties of the case had returned from the recess Judge Byron presented a statement:

"After discussing with federal authorities in Dallas, it has been decided that this case no longer is in the jurisdiction of LeHigh County, but rather rests in the authority of the United States government. This court adjourns and dismisses all jury members as well as their verdicts. The case rests," said Judge Byron as he stood up from his chair and Archibald Grieves celebrated his legal maneuvering.

Jacob Clubber clutched at his throat slightly realizing he was now facing federal prosecution as he and David wondered what kind of lawyer they had retained. They wondered why he celebrated the movement for it seemed the only thing he did was move the location of the courtroom and make the stakes that much higher for Mr. Clubber.

It all became clear when three days later, fifth circuit federal prosecutor John Zachary dropped the charges on Jacob Clubber due to insubstantial evidence.

Mama Hart celebrated that day with David and Mr. Clubber, holding David in a loving embrace and graciously accepting the jersey from David with Hart on the back and all his teammate's signatures everywhere else on that fabric reserved for baseball royalty.

Samuel LaGrange released a statement on behalf of the LeHigh County law agencies that they were simply trying to do their job and they apologized for the inadequate handling of the David Westboro and Daniel Westboro trials. LaGrange offered to resign from his position as sheriff, but the city did not want to see the fixture that was Samuel and Anna leave for they were the only semblances of incorruptibility present in the law enforcement of LeHigh county. As for those who occupied offices for the past several years, they all lost their jobs.

Daniel's old teammates made their way to LeHigh to share a beer, a laugh, and a surreal moment of once again knowing that Daniel's little brother had made it. Although he had lost much of their trust, and a slight resentment emanated from some of Dan's old teammates when they saw his little brother, they still celebrated the long gone Westboro's return, for all knew that it meant the world to Daniel that his brother was alive. Coach Carlson, as feeble as he was in his old age, was also part of the reunion and grabbed David with all his might in a big bear hug as David said he was sorry to everyone who came down the line with mixed emotions of hatred, compassion, envy, relief, and contentment.

David went to the Cundiff River and watched the sun set all alone, wondering if he would ever see his brother again, which he believed was the last thing he deserved. He sent rocks skipping down the river much like the weight of having to be someone else, both moved by the relentless tide of time to somewhere behind him.

As for Jerry Tiner, he flew back to New York never to see anyone from his hometown ever again. Not even his father who died about a month later.

Chapter 76:

Daniel had a great showing in San Christobal that winter and was going to be home sometime after Christmas, but before New Years to the disappointment of Samantha Lawson. His passion for baseball reinvigorated, and proving himself a valuable pitching commodity, Daniel felt very good about the future while he crowd surfed the streets of Santo Domingo, his black and white striped uniform stained with champagne and multi-colored baby powder as the island country celebrated a Caribbean League championship with him. A band played, and an unplanned parade took place on the streets, the walking music of the Caribbean bouncing off the walls of all the buildings, and tourists from much colder places dancing to the celebration.

Daniel loved the feeling of being hoisted by these people, the way a whole city loved him for something so meaningless to the rest of the world. Westboro was not familiar with what these signs in his honor meant, the ones that said "Nos Encanta Daniel" or "Le victoria para los Leones", but they warmed his heart in much the same way the banners at Callahan Park did. For the first time in years, Daniel felt like the winner everyone used to tell him he was.

"You did it, Daniel, you fucking did it," said Pablo Escobedo in broken English. Pablo was a funny man who took a liking to Daniel, the man who taught Pablo the finer points of the English language such as the dirty joke, derogatory slur, and cussing.

How Pablo loved cussing when he learned about it. Although, Daniel still had to teach him the proper times and places to use such words. For example, when Daniel met Pablo's abuela and he introduced him as the "Best fucking pitcher he had ever goddamn seen."

Context. That was the lesson of the day for Pablo. Same thing with those jokes Daniel bestowed upon the much younger teammates in the clubhouse. One of the favorites of Pablo was one that Daniel learned from Coach Carlson.

"Hey, Pablo," Daniel said

"Yeah, Daniel?" asked Pablo

"How do you circumcise a guy from Haiti?"

"I don't know, how?"

"Kick his sister in the jaw."

Pablo tumbled over almost every time the joke was told or any derivative, but the antihaitianismo views shared by Escobedo and several of his Dominican teammates made this version the most popular.

Pablo was as good an influence on Daniel as Daniel was a poor influence on him. Pablo was a minority on this small Caribbean island, a black Dominican. Daniel used to hate people like that simply based on the fact they were colored. He never bothered to talk to them, thinking they were the embodiment of sloth, hatred, and greed; the epitome of all things that one resents within themselves as sin. He thought they smelled weird and talked funny, that they were beneath him. It wasn't until he was among them that he started to realize how alike they were, and how wrong his assumptions were.

Pablo told him about his father who used to slap him around with a cane switch when he was "acting devilish" and how after long baseball practices he went to work in the sugarcane fields with his friends. His father died with his mother in a mudslide while they were walking to town to sell some rugs his family made. He learned English from a priest at his church, but through life became unconvinced that God really was there, for there was no substantial way to prove anything happens beyond becoming dust among the dirt when the day of death comes. Pablo wanted reason and purpose, and all his pastor ever told him is that this God would explain it all when he was dead.

"What a convenient excuse," he'd think. A convenient excuse as to why the church wanted one tenth of everything he ever got, for they wanted him to buy his way to heaven. A contemporary Luther, Pablo didn't believe in going to the protestants either for they were equally guilty of using God to defend themselves and their sinful ways. He'd see the rich people who told of a wonderful God Who was good to anyone who worked hard, and then he'd watch them walk by the old shacks in town like the one where his little brother died in, not even pausing while he pleaded for money to feed his starving brother. The church was populated with people like that and because of such simply prayed he would heal, hoping God would provide a miracle for a little boy destined for the grave rather than pay for medical treatments. Pablo began to thin himself as he worked harder and harder to try and help his little brother until one day the Grim Reaper took hold of another soul.

Pablo was eight years old when he buried his six year old brother.

He put him under the tree Gabriel was learning how to climb because that is where his little brother seemed happiest and where he seemed closest to Heaven when he was alive. Pablo hoped for an afterlife where maybe he would find a happier life than this destitute land where so many came to view the beautiful face of a rapturous soil, but did not get his hopes up. Because of the death of Gabriel, Pablo decided he could no longer be a Catholic. Ever since his brother died he hadn't been to church. He liked to believe in a God above, but the thing he loved most was stolen from him, leading to a life of playing this game to hopefully run around the base pads fast enough to leave all memory of his brother behind him.

Daniel looked at Pablo when he learned about life from him and began to question himself and whether his struggle had any merit. At a minimum, he could look into the eyes of Pablo and as happens with troubled men, see the stains of time. Daniel and Pablo became friends because they were exactly like one another and just like Daniel hated all those "jigs," Pablo hated all those over-entitled white people and thought they all feigned morality in the same way as those missionaries who came and went much like the winds of El Nino. They were each integral in teaching the other that the color of one's skin does not define them.

"Hey man, you gotta see something," said Pablo.

"What is that Pab?" asked Daniel.

"The cleat-eaters, they've come! Time for you to party old man!" said Pablo, almost licking his lips in anticipation of the promiscuous women who rode with the victories of the Leones del Escogido.

Daniel responded with the same reaction as they began to fill the large room in which they were partying.

"Cual es tu nombre?" asked a black-haired woman. Her skin shined of that island complexion, her body curving as softly as the white sand beaches of the island, smelling of some enticing perfume, and with a voice that was equally provocative.

"Daniel," said Westboro who was becoming intoxicated by the way she moved to the reggae playing off a stereo.

"Quieres salir de aquí?" she asked running her fingers down the center of his chest.

"Que?"

Pablo saw the exchange going down and walked over grinning as he leaned toward Daniel and whispered in his ear, "Dude she wants you to hit some home runs," he said winking while proud of his ability to use the sexual euphemism.

Daniel was drunk and so he looked at her in a way that said yes as the two silently worked their way out the back of the crowd to a bedroom upstairs.

"So what do you like big boy?" she asked running her hands through his hair. Daniel was liking where it was going. She kissed him and moved in tighter holding him with an increasing grip making a face that asked him to get ever closer.

She was a fine woman, a total seductress. Damn, Daniel thought this was quite possibly the most feminine looking woman he had seen in his life with her buxom wares and guile begging for him to go further and further with her.

She grabbed his shirt and began to unbutton it before removing her own, it was clear the direction she had intended with these movements. Daniel was caught in the moment.

But then it hit him. He was a married man. He pushed her away as she was making efforts towards his belt leading her to ask,

"What's wrong?"

Daniel didn't know but did at the same time. He was married to Samantha Lawson. This was wrong. A real man didn't do this to his wife, and when he looked in the mirror he saw semblances of his father who unfortunately shared the same face.

"I have a wife," he said.

"I'm sorry, I can't"

"Why would she have to know?" she said flirtatiously, making a face that asked for things to return to the hot and heavy state.

"Come on, have a little fun, Champ."

Daniel was disappointed in himself as far as he had gone and said, "I'm sure you're a wonderful woman, whoever the hell you are, but I have a wife to take care of. I'm going home." He put his championship shirt back on and headed out the door.

Daniel left for home the next morning saying goodbye to all his teammates in Santo Domingo, for they were all to go home for a couple of months until the time they would play with the many major league organizations that were identified on the stat sheets as their "parents". Daniel saved his goodbye to Pablo for last.

"Have a good year, man. It's been a privilege playing with you."

"You think you're done seeing me?"

"Who do you play for?" Daniel asked.

"Play for Minnesota now, man, got signed yesterday." he said smiling at the accomplishment.

"I'm in the fucking major leagues!" he added with that enthusiasm typical of Pablo Escobedo.

"Damn, and I was hoping I was done putting up with your shitty fielding," he said to his second baseman.

"Don't worry, I'll drop everything when you're on the mound," he said to Daniel smiling widely.

"Wouldn't want it any other way," Daniel said putting a hand on his shoulder.

"See you there, Bitch," said Pablo as he walked away.

After Daniel's plane landed in Arizona to begin his slight break before the season started again, he made sure to take care of some promises. Daniel and Samantha went to Las Vegas.

Chapter 77:

It was a happy New Year for Samantha and Daniel as Daniel appeared to be on an upswing. He had not gambled very well in Vegas, losing somewhere close to 200 dollars, but the deficit of the excursion was not as important as the realization he had slowly made during the past few months since he met Samantha. When looking at Samantha in her red cocktail dress, he saw the full extent of her beauty, and more importantly in a retrospective self-examination he saw a woman who loved him.

He saw a girl who never doubted the notion of them even when he did. He saw a girl who stuck with a man at his lowest and was proud of him when he pursued a dream. For a while, Daniel tried to pretend that baseball wasn't the thing truest to his heart and that was a complete dishonesty to anyone who took the most superficial glance at his timeline, and Samantha was the one who called him on "his bullshit." That brought us to a moment in Vegas where Daniel said,

"Samantha, could I marry you for real?"

"What do you mean?" she asked looking up from the steak dinner Daniel had purchased her.

"I want to give you a real wedding, back at home with a preacher, and all our friends, and a big white dress. I'm sorry I didn't mean it before, but I really think that I love you, Sam," Daniel said.

Samantha's face made a countenance of glee as she stared downward.

"Sure," she said, "to quote a famous man."

So it was decided that the young couple would be the first ever to celebrate their honeymoon before their wedding, and that was just fine with both of them. Daniel's grandfather always told him that the key to a long happy life was:

"Find a woman who loves you and don't let her go, do something to make the world a little better each and every day, and," after checking around to make sure Daniel's liberal grandmother wasn't around to hear, "always vote Republican."

Well, Daniel had found that girl today, and he did drop a twenty for good measure in the Salvation Army bucket outside. Daniel then remembered he should probably register to vote one of these days.

They got married in February. It was decided they would hold the ceremony in Pine City at the Southern Free Baptist church. Before the marriage, the aging Pastor Thomas had some things to discuss with Daniel.

"Daniel, how can I join you with a wife in His name if you don't believe in Him," he asked as they strode slowly on the fine February day along the Cundiff River.

"Pastor, I'm a changed man, I swear," Daniel said.

"But Daniel, you outright refuted him last time I saw you. How can I believe that you truly love God with all your heart if you've walked away from Him before? Do you love God and want a holy marriage, or are you simply using me as a way to validate your attraction to this woman?" Pastor Thomas asked, as he lifted his foot over a root in the path. "Daniel, do you love her, or do you love what she looks like?"

Daniel paused for a moment putting his hands in his pockets and talking without looking at the good pastor.

"Pastor Thomas, I don't know if you truly know all the hell I went through to get to today. I watched my friend die, I was put behind bars for somethin' I didn't do, and I find myself havin' a hard time even imaginin' I liked the son of a bitch that almost got away with killin' June. I'd be a liar if I said I didn't think of June sometimes. The only damn thing I was ever sure of was being able to throw that curveball and sometimes I feel like I can't even do that anymore. I don't know why I love her or why I can be honest saying I love her when half my heart is still with June. I don't want it to make any sense, Pastor Thomas. I want to die with a woman who would do anything for me and could put up with me at my absolute worst because I know I'm an imperfect man. I'm not marryin' her because I want to get busy with her, Pastor. I want to marry her because it seems like she is the only thing that has happened to me for a good while that makes me happy. She was there when I struggled from the moment I met her and didn't doubt me, and she gave God back to me, because if God can give me that girl to lean on for the rest of my days, then none of that other shit matters because it all just led to today. Father, I promise you I ain't bullshittin' when I say any of that, either," said Daniel, still staring at the same sycamore tree with its leaves gently blowing in the wind.

Pastor Thomas said nothing else as they covered what little distance was left between the pickup truck and that place along the river.

Daniel was dropped off at the church and met Samantha out front, looking frazzled with his conversation with the good pastor, but at least moving in the right direction for what needed to be done to make this a holy marriage.

"I need to take you somewhere," said Daniel to Samantha grabbing her hand in a fashion that indicated this visit would not be optional.

Samantha hopped into the car in the passenger seat and Daniel drove down a meandering road for a short while, pointing out the old Tiner place which was adjacent to the field he was driving to. A simple plot of land, only an iron gate stood before it with its name intertwined in the wire, a small bit of fence around the edges with trees between the pathways. It was a delicate little place, the grass trimmed short with a soft feeling to it, unusual but not unheard of in these North Texas winters. Daniel stopped walking when he found what he was looking for.

"June," started Daniel. "I don't know where you are, but I want you to know that I'm doin' okay. In fact, I'm getting married in a couple of days," he said starting to choke up.

"I know that I bought the ring I'm giving away for you and that I wanted nothin' more in the world than to call you my wife, but I guess I don't get to decide how things happen. I always wanted the last thing I ever said to you to be 'I love you,' but I fucked that up too."

Daniel shook as he spoke tears flowing from his steeled eyes.

"I just want you to know I found a girl who loves me as much as you did and I hope that's good enough, June bug. She's goddamn beautiful, she talks as rough as I do, she's nothing like you, but is all the same. I hope heaven is wonderful and maybe someday we will all be together," he said collapsing to his knees in the cemetery.

"I love you, June. Always have, always will."

Samantha fell to hers too and held Daniel trying to the best of her ability to remove all the pain from this troubled man. Luke's headstone peered on the scene from atop a hill, looking from the hillside and wishing Daniel all the best.

Chapter 78:

The wedding was on Valentine's day, meaning of course that the church was dressed with a variety of paper cut-out hearts, and all the bridesmaids, who were some of Samantha's cousins, wore pink sun dresses, all the groomsmen what little amount of dressing up that you could convince an alliance of rednecks and baseball players to do, which essentially amounted to a collared shirt and some black pants for the majority of said populace.

"Didn't know they made suits for monkeys," said Andrew Thompson to Daniel as he punched the cold-footed man in the arm.

"I'm just hoping she shows up," said Daniel.

"You'll be fine, man, don't worry about it."

"Where's this motherfucker?" asked Pablo in his normal gregarious fashion as he walked into the same room Daniel and Andrew were in.

"He isn't one yet, Pab," said Andrew to his friend by association.

"Or are you?" asked Andrew with a grin as Daniel playfully shoved him with an equal countenance.

"It's a fair question. Figure the pastor has to know, too," added on Andrew digging himself deeper into that hole.

"See Pablo, you've gotta learn some damn English so you stop getting' me in trouble," said Daniel as Mama Hart walked in and gave him that terrifying stare only a mother could give to their child, or one that became her's by attrition like Daniel.

"Daniel Ellis Westboro, I better not have heard you swear. We're in church!"

"He's really fucking sorry," said Pablo with a straight face, not realizing entirely what he just said.

"Sorry, Ms. Hart, he doesn't know English too well," said Daniel.

"No, I don't know much English, Daniel is a good teacher," said Pablo as Ruth shook her head realizing that Daniel had taught him not much more than how to swear.

"Look, you're getting married in fifteen minutes and you haven't even run a comb through your hair, put on your tie, are those shoes untied..."

Mrs. Hart's voice sort of became part of the background as the gravity of the situation was falling upon Daniel.

"Holy shit, I'm getting married," he thought. Daniel always knew he wanted a day like this to come to start a family all his own, but nothing can prepare somebody for those moments before they decide to give part of themselves to someone else for the duration of forever. Daniel wasn't even capable of promising himself that his teeth would be brushed each morning, how could he vow to give feelings to a woman for the rest of time? What if things didn't work out? What if he wasn't as good for her as she thought he was? What if-

"Eh, fuck it," thought Daniel. It was like those days he walked onto the mound in front of all those thousands of people. Today, he was walking in front of his friends and swearing to the Lord Almighty he would do the best for Samantha Lawson, and who would doubt Daniel in giving his all?

I mean, it's the only thing he was ever good at.

Somehow, Ruth Hart managed to groom Daniel into something resemblant of a gentleman and somehow Daniel didn't fight at all during the process. He waited near the front at the altar with Pastor Thomas as Ms. Lawson was getting dressed the best she ever would as a Lawson and the first way she would be dressed as a Westboro. Per tradition, Daniel didn't get to see her in her gown until the last second of the wedding. Daniel was clearly nervous for being a man so renowned for his stoicism.

"You ever heard the one about the three priests?" asked Pastor Thomas.

"What?" asked Daniel.

"See these three priests are meeting at a convention and they decide to tell each other their secret sins. The first one says "I'm a gambler, and I go to the casino every Saturday before church". The second one says "I'm completely lazy, I copy and paste sermons I find online and deliver those every Sunday". The third one says "They say I love to gossip, but I think they're lying. By the way, do you know that guy gambles?""

The terrible joke at the altar was an act perfected over a number of years by the good pastor, timing it just perfectly so the thoroughly disappointing punchline arrived at about the same time that the bride did. Pachelbel's Canon in D emanated from the guitar of Christian Vier as his band played at the wedding, the ever-moving and so prolific melody cascading off the walls of the small church.

Samantha was beautiful with her veil and white dress. It would be a lie and a detriment to the story if one didn't point out the fact that Daniel's groomsmen were eyeing her up from the convenient angle with John Zachary reining in the baseball playing boys about him. Andrew Thompson looked at Daniel and back at Samantha making funny faces at him to indicate the depth of her attractiveness, and Daniel chuckled as his best man kept up the act until she stood at the altar with Daniel her hands in his, their faces smiling at one another.

Another telling of this story would include what Pastor Thomas said, but to be entirely frank, it didn't really matter. Everyone looking at the altar that day knew that what he was saying about living a life with Christ and holding vows was unnecessary as one partially kempt baseball player with his long hair held a pretty cowgirl that God chose for him already embodied the whole intent of the unnecessary sermon. Nobody said anything during the entire 'speak now or forever hold your piece' section of the service, except for Pablo's attempt at interjecting which was met quickly with a poke to the ribs by the cap of Andrew Thompson's elbow. There was no question of the I do's, and like that Daniel and

Samantha had become one flesh in the eyes of the Lord and legally wed in the eyes of the Great State of Texas. It may have been a repeat for Sam and Dan, but at least now they felt like God approved of them and that meant a lot.

"Good job, Old Man, you got yourself a babe," said Andrew in one of the brief moments the groom gets away from his new wife on his wedding day.

"Thanks," he said in passing much more concerned to take care of the overwhelming desire to take a leak than anything else in the world.

Daniel entered the latrine and felt watched while he relieved himself.

"Hi, Daniel," said a familiar voice from behind him. When he performed an about face he saw the last face he expected to see today. David Westboro.

"Congratulations," David said.

Daniel looked at him longer.

"So what, am I your brother when it is convenient for you then?" Daniel asked accusatively as a man tried to walk into the bathroom and Daniel hastily waved him away.

David took a moment to collect his thoughts before he said, "Daniel, you were always there for me, and I know I fucked up. I let you down. I let this whole place down. I should have stood up and told the world what kind of fucked up liar I was then, and I shouldn't have made you look like the batshit crazy asshole I did. I'm sorry. There's not much more I can say," said David looking remorseful.

"I went and did everything so I could be a little bit more like you, but I am not. I'm a fraud, I'm a phony, and I'm sure that God can find more than enough reason to send me to hell. I was mad at you for leaving me so many years ago, and I guess I didn't get over myself. And you know what? You're the one that paid for what I did wrong."

Daniel looked at him a little bit holding back all the negative energy in him from all the people that called him crazy, all the time he spent wondering if he was a lunatic, the very loss of his first true love in baseball. Then Daniel was quiet as the chords of a dreamy guitar gently swooned in the next room to the delight of the guests to the wedding who were moving to the ballad, but the joy of the song seemed to dissipate at the door.

"I forgive you, David. I'm mad at you, but I forgive you, because no matter what, no matter who gets in the way, no matter whenever the hell it happens to be, you're my brother and I will stand by you always," said Daniel as he walked over and hugged his little brother

"I love you little man and don't you ever forget that."

Chapter 79:

The following nine months or so for the Minnesota Twins were a compilation of yet another time the front office failed to deliver a product on the field to make September matter. Or the coaches. Maybe the players?

As often happens in sports, it was difficult to tell whose fault it really was, but in the end all that mattered to the owner, fans, and players was that they were losing and losing badly. With a deep rut and not much of a schedule left, the September call-ups were a method whereby a major league team could either build a larger roster to forge on into the playoffs or use as a rebuilding period to get younger and less experienced players some time at the major league level. It was a period like this that players like Daniel Westboro got excited about because of the impressive numbers he had put up in Rochester up to this point.

A 14-8 record in the Win-loss column had made Minnesota fans want to see the fabled Sheriff

West come guns a-blazing into the majors and spark some sort of pitching in the arm-starved bullpen of the Twins. Rumors spread around the league of the way that old man Dan seemed to throw curveballs that started behind the batter and ended up in the dirt on the other side, leading to many a young boy swinging futily at the killer pitch and putting another K in the box score for the elder Westboro. The radar gun read 93 miles an hour when the fastball came tumbling out of his long fingers and cracked the leather of Andrew Thompson's glove up until sometime around August when he was called up to replace the injured starter Aiden Beloit, being that he was doing something not even the injured Beloit was great at and that was catching the curveball of the heavy finesse staff that had been put in place. Daniel couldn't wait for this day of September the first, for there was an off chance he might get the opportunity to pitch to Andrew in a major league uniform.

Time. That was the main enemy to Daniel's major league dream and its biggest aid all the same. Time spent poorly by the fielders who lazily flopped their glove for grounders and outfielders who wasted time tiptoeing underneath towering fly balls were the reason the professional organization was in the shape it was. But time also made Daniel 34 years old.

The average major league pitcher retires when they are about 38 years old usually because the structures of the arms so thoroughly abused by the major league pitcher finally cease to work as they once did around then. This leads to careers ending either in tear-filled press conferences where mighty stallions thank a few good men for a great many opportunities, or the natural process of the ever-changing major league roster does it for them.

Either way, Daniel was not a fresh face and because of that, he was not afforded the same opportunity as a younger man to make mistakes and develop, for there was less time to profit off of him than a younger fellow no matter how well he played in the minors. No, if he were to make an appearance and stay at a higher level he had to reach and maintain a higher level of performance than ever before.

Time. That is what was on Daniel's mind.

To many, the reading of the September call-ups was a moment to be anxious for. In a world with so many great ballplayers, some couldn't help but get to a point where simply wanting a chance to prove themselves was enough. Sure, there is the heart of the athlete that commands they convince themselves they are as capable of being the best as the next guy, but the reality was that grown men are just little boys with deeper voices. A championship season and riding off to the sunset with a team of the world's best may have been the dream that got sensationalized in all the movies, books, and television programs, but merely getting a chance to stand in a major league ballpark and hear your number called would make anybody's heart light up. Every member of Rochester who waited patiently by their phone that morning was not doing it because they were going to make any meaningful impact on the organization, but because they wanted that opportunity to carry out a dream, to validate a body of work and a system of struggle because at the end of the day all anyone really wants out of Herculean effort is to know it as worth it. Or at least that is what Daniel wanted.

Daniel remembered telling Coach Carlson so many years ago about how he would fight for that little kid in himself. He remembered Luke Hart and how much he wanted out of life, and he remembered how much he and June and Coach all believed in him. For them, he needed to do this. There was no option, or maybe, Daniel was going to play major league baseball and if he couldn't be called up in

September for some meaningless games to end out a horrendous season, then he would have to wonder himself just what he was doing playing for some state where the people all talk funny and words like "lefse" and "lutefisk" are commonplace terms. The phone rang and Daniel lifted it.

"Daniel, this is Trent, remember me?" asked Trent Anderson.

"How could I forget you? What's good?" asked Daniel, feigning confidence in what the call was about.

"I don't need to tell you what this call is about, but I will anyways. Your contract has been purchased by the Minnesota Twins and you will be reporting to Texas in two days. Congratulations, Daniel. Welcome to big leagues," said Trent in that general manager kind of voice where they avoid any impartation of emotion behind any decision they make.

"I'll be there," said Daniel shaking his feet and dancing while projecting a voice that attempted to remain as dry as Trent's.

"Check your email, plane ticket and all that is there. Alright, bye," said the GM before hanging up the phone prior to Daniel being afforded the same opportunity to say goodbye.

Nothing could take the wind out of his sails at that time. Daniel had done what he had set out to do, and Sheriff West was going to get his chance to draw his pistols with the best duelists of the era. Daniel was happy, that rare kind of happy where one feels literally nothing can bother them, for all that is good in the world is visible and all that is wrong is dissolved.

That is, until the phone rang a second time.

"Daniel?" said Mama Hart.

"Yes Mrs. Hart?"

"Daniel, did you hear the news?"

"Yes, Mrs. Hart, I made it to the majors! I'm going to be there in two days! Make sure to tell everyone!" said Daniel, excitation bursting from his voice as the flood of dopamine could almost be tasted in the tonality his voice chose.

"Daniel," said Ruth in a manner which made him aware this was not cheerful news. "It's John."

"Which John? What happened?" Daniel was thinking. He knew a lot of Johns, a John Zachary, a John Gibbons, a John Terowoltz, a John...

"Carlson," he recounted. "What's wrong with coach?" asked Daniel with concern in his voice.

"You did know he had lung cancer, right, Dan?"

"Lung cancer?" thought Daniel. He knew last time he saw him he was looking worse for wear and talking about death, but old men are prone to do that even when they aren't on the doorstep of death.

"Daniel, he's got three days to live they're saying. I know how much he meant to you. I think you need to come home," said Mama Hart.

Daniel looked silently at the carpet of the hotel he was in.

"Daniel?"

"I'll be there, Mrs. Hart," said Daniel.

Daniel put his head in his hands and had a look of anguish and confusion on his face which emanated from the inner part of his soul. Such tends to happen when one is watching their dad die.

Chapter 80:

The walls were blank, the floor with strange tessellations of red and white tiling, begging for a variety of games to be played by children who walked in and observed such an enticing pattern to identify as lava. From these floors the characteristic odor of iodoform rose and entered the nostrils. The sights and sounds of the hospital waiting room were repetitive and in some ways scary. Periodically the coffee pot on the counter would go empty and somebody waiting in the lobby would go over to the machine and go through the cyclical process of replacing coffee grounds and brewing more of that fine nepenthe. Coffee, that fine beverage that held the eyes staunchly open while sleep tried so hard to intern the affected souls. Sleep was something that didn't happen often in this room unless at the desperate ends of one's soul, for this room was built to house people waiting on God to make a verdict of life or death for their loved ones.

Daniel looked around the room. He saw a young mother holding her small child waiting for the equally young father who got in a fight with the wrong types of fellows to hopefully break from the coma he had been in the past week. He saw a family holding hands and praying in Hebrew that a young boy involved in a car accident may recover from the atrocious injuries. Daniel looked at himself, Ruth, and Samantha as they sat waiting for a doctor to allow them to say goodbye to John Carlson for what was presumably the last time. Nobody in this room ever wanted to come here, but they had to.

That is the pain of family and love. Wonderful as they both sound, one must also remember that an accompanying sadness at the end of either is inherent with both institutions. People end up like Daniel, wondering about all the time they didn't spend with their coach after all he had done for them and questioned their own validity as a righteous soul. They thought about what Anne Frank once said about flowers and how hardly anybody brings flowers to someone while they live, but shower them with them when they die. It's a mystery how the human species works, but one must be able to see that it is more strongly affected by the forces of regret than those of compassion.

"It'll be okay," said Mrs. Westboro as she rubbed his back.

"Don't worry, Dan. God's got a plan for him."

God's plan. Daniel often questioned it. I guess the sign of true belief is that through all the questioning someone still manages to find faith in what they believe. Just because his faith said that this process was right, it didn't mean he had to like it.

"Mr. Westboro, you can see him now," said a nurse, clearly overworked and exhausted. Holding a clipboard, she guided Daniel and Samantha to the room, yawning into the back of her hand as they walked through the door she pointed at.

"Coach," said Daniel.

"West," said Coach Carlson as he rolled over, a smile trying so hard to work its way out from behind an oxygen mask which now served the purpose his compromised lungs once did.

"Coach, I made it," said Daniel, tears now forming in his eyes.

"I'm in the major leagues, Coach," said Daniel as he showed him a photograph of himself in his uniform, and unzipped his jacket to show the jersey which read "Twins" in elegant cursive upon the torso.

"I did everything you ever told me, and it all worked out, Coach. I thought you needed to hear that," said Daniel, trying very hard to stay strong.

"I'm proud of you Daniel," said Coach Carlson as he smiled tenderly at him. "I always knew you could do it."

All Daniel ever wanted out of his life was to hear someone tell him that. All he ever wanted was to show Coach Carlson that he could outwork everyone, and make a man out of himself. Daniel knew his time was limited before he had to report to the stadium for the game that night and told Carlson the rest of what he wanted to say.

"Coach, I'm having a kid with my wife. We were wondering if we could name him after you."

Coach Carlson blinked and took in another breath of the hospital oxygen from the tank attached to his facemask.

"She's beautiful, Daniel," Carlson said as he looked at Samantha, currently two months pregnant. "I'd like that a lot. Just not his first name," said Coach. "You deserve to give him the first one yourself, and you better bet I'll haunt you from the grave if you try and give him mine," said Carlson who tried to chuckle but then sputtered. The cancer was making it very difficult to breathe let alone laugh.

"Coach, I have a game tonight. They said it'll be on the TV and all that, but coach said I could stay here and watch the boys with you."

"Don't you dare try," Coach Carlson said.

"Daniel, I just want you to put your head down, work hard, and at the end we both can laugh our asses off at the scoreboard," said John.

"Coach, I don't think I can do it."

"Daniel, if there's anyone that can do it it would be you. Make an old man proud and go and beat my Rangers," said Coach with a warm smile on his face. "I'm a dying man, Daniel, you should do what I ask of you."

Daniel acknowledged him. "I love you, Coach," said Daniel in a sob.

"I love you, too, Daniel. Go and make LeHigh proud," said Carlson as he hugged Daniel.

With that Daniel and Samantha left the hospital for Arlington Stadium, so Daniel could warm up.

Chapter 81:

In Arlington Stadium, Daniel Westboro warmed up in the outfield throwing back and forth with Pablo Escobedo. It truly was a meaningless game, neither Texas nor Minnesota could improve their position in the league no matter what they did at this point. The difference lay in the fact that Texas had won so frequently that they were guaranteed a one seed and Minnesota had lost so frequently that the only thing they could improve is moving from dead last to second to last place if they were to win out the remainder of their games. It was hardly worth even commenting on the game, except that the bandwagon fans had branded themselves with the culture of winning in the Texas Rangers clubhouse. Minnesota was so far out of it that all the starters were triple-A players a mere week ago on this day, sans Andrew Thompson who still got to play credited to his young age and commendable performance. Partially to light a fire in the bellies of the alleged starters, partially to give game experience to players not exposed to this environment, and partially to protect the aged veterans from more wear and tear than they needed to suffer were the reasons why the lineup was as such. Regardless, the lights were on and Daniel was playing catch to prepare to pitch against his former team, and that is all that was important to him at this time.

It was decided when he was called up that he would be in the rotation and join as the fourth man, meaning that he was not supposed to make an appearance for two days. Nonetheless, he was to toss to keep his arm loose and if a blowout were to occur he was predictably the first to take over long relief duties in the Minnesota bullpen.

"Major leagues man! Playing under the lights," said Pablo. His face clearly showed all the joy that flooded him in getting the privilege to take the field with the world's best after a lifetime of preparation. It may not have the same impact as the World Series, but any rookie who has been called off the bench for his opportunity to play under those lights can remember what it felt like the first time he saw his name on the lineup card.

"I know," said Daniel, in a manner about as vocal as he was going to get prior to the start of a game. A variety of warm-up exercises took place prior to the calling of captains by the umpire, and after that, all players went to the dugout if they were unused position men or the dugout in left-center if they were pitchers like Daniel.

The game took a completely unexpected course over the next eight innings, as Minnesota pounded in ten runs and allowed only two. The commentators questioned just what sort of miracle was taking place, for the last thing anyone watching this ever expected was for Minnesota to be so triumphant. They had not put up ten runs in the prior ten games combined. This led Minnesota's young team to start acting very cocky and to talk about what sort of post-game celebrations would occur after the game.

Daniel looked on from the dugout thinking about Coach Carlson and how proud he would be to see a team Daniel was on dominating so wholly, a thought which brought a smile to the face of the 34-year-old strike specialist.

"Daniel, get loose," said Coach Tenenbaum.

"What?"

"You're going in, get loose," repeated the coach,

"C'mon, we're almost back in the field."

Daniel took his orders and made way to the bullpen to start playing catch with Red Woogley, some kid from Alabama with a bit too much braun and a bit too little brain.

"Go and fuck them up, Daniel!" said Red as he patted Daniel on the butt while he exited the outfield bullpen and jogged to the mound to take the ball and close out the stomping.

When Daniel's foot hit the mound, he looked all around and felt he was the smallest man in the world being observed under some grossly assembled microscope.

"WEST! WEST! WEST!" shouted the seats in right field occupied by what seemed the whole of LeHigh County. It wasn't far from all of that little north Texas county that bought tickets to this series on the off chance they got to see their hero play. Daniel tried to seal out the noise, but clearly was unprepared for all the cameras and screams when he was on the mound.

"Time!" yelled Thompson as he ran out to the mound.

"Hey man, let's just win this one and go home. They love you," said Thompson. "Stare at my glove and don't you dare think about a damn thing. We got this."

Andrew Thompson ran back behind the plate and crouched. Daniel nodded at Andrew. Andrew nodded back, a look of seriousness on his face. Signaling for an inside fastball, Daniel delivered, hitting the corner and blowing past the batsman. Strike one. The next two strikes came just as easily as the nine spot went back to the bench and the leadoff man walked up. The next batter was retired just as quickly, for he had not expected Daniel to climb the ladder so easily and finish him with the high changeup.

Two strikeouts down, Daniel was on the cusp of a franchise record in being the first Twins pitcher to get three strikeouts on nine pitches, as the announcers on the millions of television screens back home were saying. Andrew Thompson called time again.

"We're changing nothing, just stare at my glove and throw that shit, we're almost there, man," said Thompson going back behind the plate again.

Thompson needed to discuss the batter with Daniel, for Kent Grover was a big-swingman from the plains of Iowa. He seemed to resemble Luke Hart in stature and rotund composition, but he was somehow larger, his muscles bulging in the arms and wrists from many hours spent on his farm practicing that mighty cut of his. Daniel had flashbacks to his friend and playing baseball with him.

At that moment, he remembered something about that swing of Luke Hart's, and because of it he waved off the call for an inside fastball from Thompson. He threw a large sweeping curve down and away that Grover swung mightily at but watched tumble out of reach. It seemed everybody in the stadium was surprised by the movement of Daniel's curveball signified by a collective gasp from the crowd as the usually sure-swinging Grover was made to look a fool on the first pitch. He followed it up with a second invitation in the same spot, again watching Grover flail at the ball and miss.

An 0-2 count, and one pitch away from a Twins franchise record, Daniel used what he set up and threw his fastball eyeball high to see if he could get the same amount of over-ambition from this hitter as he once did from his power-hitting friend. A 34-inch long bat waved at a column of air after the ball was already concealed in Andrew Thompson's glove. The game ended with Daniel getting three strikeouts in his first major league appearance.

The crowd went wild and soon enough not only were the fans in right field shouting "West!", but the entire stadium removed their hats and tipped them to the man that became baseball on that September day, including Simon Juarez who gave a single nod from the stands to Daniel as he reentered the dugout. One couldn't help but appreciate how much Daniel worked for this moment and love the story of a man who had a dream he never quit on, finally getting a victory against the team he always envisioned playing for. The number 21 took the entire country by firestorm the ensuing months as all the commentators discussed a late-bloomer with a tricky curveball and players around the league spoke highly of what watching Sheriff West get his chance at the majors meant to them.

Meanwhile, that night in the hospital, Coach Carlson watched the most meaningful meaningless game of all time and died laughing his ass off at the lopsided scoreboard.

Chapter 93:

Eleven years later with a ring on my finger, I stopped writing this book to go and play catch with Eli John Westboro.

About The Author:

Grant "Stick" Udstrand is an author from Champlin, Minnesota blessed with way too many good friends and a loving family. He will be graduating from Champlin Park High School before going to the University of Minnesota to study Biomedical Engineering, but he isn't quite sure yet either if that's what he'll do with his life. Grant has always been an avid sports fan and thus, like most any American boy, grew up playing football, baseball, and archery, between playing with his bands "Spilt Coffee" and "The Good For Nothings". His main hope in life is to lead by an example set by his grandfather to live life to the fullest and hope maybe a couple people follow him just the same.